SANCTUARY

THE CHOSEN TRILOGY

CHEYENNE NIKOLE,
ELISABETH FOWLER

For all the believers who love the Most High and his son,

Christ.

We hope you enjoy reading this book just as much as we

enjoyed writing it.

PROLOGUE

"It is said that fear is the opposite of faith. That fear is only 'false evidence appearing real'. Now, these words are not found in the Bible, however, the concept is. Whenever we are overcome with fear, it's because we have accepted what we see, what we hear or feel, to be true, and it leaves us feeling hopeless and afraid..."

-Dad

ONE

BOREDOM BEGAN TO CREEP up on me.

I sat near the back of the vast tent, leaning in my lawn chair, watching the food being circled by a gang of flies.

I watched them bounce haphazardly, up and down over the dishes, hopelessly looking for a way in.

It was all covered tightly with aluminum foil and Cling-Wrap. My mom and the other ladies made sure no one, not even the flies, would be eating before my dad's sermon was over.

My dad's enamoring voice gradually drew me back into the lesson. I shifted from my fly-watching expedition and flipped my Bible page to the following scripture to be read.

We were positioned on the front lawn of our newly acquired land, all huddled together under the large, sun-bleached white tent, which flapped noisily when the wind blew too hard.

It was getting old...that tent.

We had it for nearly ten years. It was a weathered yet comforting reminder to me. Whenever it was pulled out, I immediately recalled its original purpose of bringing like-minded people together under its flimsy canopy.

We picked it out from the sporting goods store when I was seven.

My brother, Juda, pointed it out as the obvious choice because it was the most spacious.

"For all the new people," he had said, smiling.

He was ten years old at the time, and he understood then what I had not about the significance of his statement.

I get it now.

I daydreamed as my dad preached and Brother Elijah read the scriptures beside him.

I picked at the lint on my green and white cotton dress as I thought about our life before he became a "man of the Most High[1] ".

On Sundays, we went to a mega church in Atlanta where the pastor was an ancient white man who spat a

---

1. the Most High- God

little when he got into his message. His fiery sermons were usually surrounding tithes[2].

I rolled my eyes subconsciously, reminiscing about that.

Now, we kept service on Saturday, the Sabbath[3], and no one ever spoke about tithes in the way the pastor did.

There was no collection plate, no ministry-of-this-fund, or charity-of-that-fund... blah, blah, blah.

We just had what we needed when we needed it. The congregation moved like the church in Acts[4]. Everyone did what they could, and the Most High continuously increased it.

Before I realized it, it was time to pray out. Service was over, and everyone was discreetly moving to their ideal areas of enjoyment.

My mom and some of the other women got out serving spoons from a covered picnic basket so they could fix plates. They were swatting at the abundant amount of flies with their free hands.

---

2. monetary offerings to churches

3. usually kept sundown Friday to sundown Saturday

4. Acts 2: 42-47

The remaining women occupied themselves in conversation on the other side of the tent, cackling about this or the other.

The men were still under the tent, lording over the now empty lawn chairs, discussing the scriptures and what other precepts[5] edified the last.

Some had washcloths tucked in their hands and dabbed at their sweaty foreheads as they talked and listened, in turn.

Some of us older children moved towards the pond to entertain the babies and younger children by the water and to keep them occupied so they wouldn't whine about being hungry too soon.

It was a peaceful day, even with the sweltering heat.

There was nothing to warn us of the convoy of military trucks racing down the dirt road, kicking up pebbles and dust. They couldn't have been passing through, as the road only led to our property and dead-ended.

They were headed straight for us and could have only come for one purpose.

---

5. scriptures

We had known about the influx of attacks toward people of color by the police and the racist comments, calling people who believed like us a 'hate group'.

It was all in the media.

Who didn't know about it?

Politicians were calling for a complete eradication of all terrorist groups, international and domestic. They only stopped short of calling every minority race a hate group on all the major news channels.

That had nothing to do with us, though.

The convoy pulled up quickly as if rushing to get the whole interaction over with. About twenty soldiers emerged from the back of the covered trucks clutching semi-automatic guns.

All their weapons were pointing at us, but we didn't know why.

What have we done?

My dad and a few of the other men started to cautiously walk toward the lead truck.

A towering, hostile-looking man, in an all-black suit, emerged from its interior. He had dark blond hair that was receding on the sides. There was sweat building up on his jagged hairline and in the creases of his thick neck. His eyes were shielded by his dark shades, but I could sense from his body language that he was vexed to be there.

He glared at our people scattered out on the lawn who were staring curiously back at him. He lowered his gaze deliberately to the phone in his hand then continued to loiter on our lawn as if he owned the place and we were invading his space.

When he made no effort to formally address us, my dad stopped walking and stretched both arms slowly in the air, as if to show we meant no threat.

He then asked, "Can we help you?"

As soon as the last words came out of my dad's mouth, the immediate response from the intruders was an ear-splitting shrill, then a more succinct buzzing. It sounded like a bunch of supersonic bees whizzing by.

But it wasn't bees...it was bullets.

Then the screaming erupted.

It was a chorus of screams, not in unison, but in their respective tenor, alto, and soprano scales.

People were shrieking in long bursts of notes...then everyone started running, trying to outrun the buzzing.

Two

Raya. Raya.
RAYA!!!

I COULD HEAR MY name being called but it sounded as if I was underwater, being pulled down under the depths of murkiness. Whoever was calling me was far beyond the surface, their voice distant and gargled.

Am I drowning?

I couldn't have been but my brain felt waterlogged.

The pond wasn't even that deep and I could swim better than any fish in the ocean. At least, that's what Mama always told me.

I was overwhelmingly tired and heavy. Like an elephant was sitting on my chest. My body was rigid and I couldn't move my limbs, but I could feel my head and shoulders being violently shaken.

I wanted it to stop but my mouth was watering and I couldn't form the words. I didn't have the energy to make whoever was shaking me to get off.

Thoughts and images were pinging back and forth in my mind and there was a loud buzzing sound flooding my ear canals.

What is that noise?

It was so familiar but I couldn't grasp the right thought for it. My brain couldn't make the connection no matter how hard I tried.

My eyelids fluttered open and I was slowly able to make eye contact with my brother. Juda was about as close to my face as a pair of cheap sunglasses. His eyes were wide open and wild. He looked completely deranged with anguish.

His extremely distressed expression filled me with immediate panic.

He promptly stopped shaking me, giving me instant relief, but then he was clutching me close to him, cradling me a bit too hard for a brother, rocking me back and forth, sobbing breathlessly in my ear.

It was as if I was his long, lost baby that he finally reunited with.

It was weird.

"Get off me, Juda! What's wrong with you?" I finally breathed, my arms still limply by my sides, not strong enough to fully resist.

He moved back only slightly and that's when I fully saw his face.

There was blood spattered on his shirt collar and some of it had partially dried within his hairline. It didn't seem to be his blood, which was a direct relief, in some twisted way.

There was dust caked up on his grimy cheeks. It was streaked by fresh tears, mingling with the soot.

There was something else on his face that distorted him considerably.

It was fear.

No, not fear, it was something different, something beyond fear...it was dread.

My nineteen-year-old brother, who never cried for anything, was terrified by something now.

I was imagining horrible, life-altering events.

Why was Juda bloodied and crying? What was he so afraid of? Whose blood was that?

"What happened? Where are we?" I finally asked, still in shock and disbelief.

Before he could answer, I scanned the room.

It was not a place I had ever been in or seen.

The entire room was constructed from a muted chrome metal. I could see stairs farther down towards the back of the deep room that led up and down into darkness, both ways. There were sporadically placed chairs near the metallic walls, mostly occupied by some of the younger church members, holding children and other people's babies.

Everyone had the same look as Juda on their faces. The look of dread and despair.

"They're gone, Raya!" my brother whispered harshly. "They're all GONE!"

"Who's all gone?" I asked in alarm. "Where are we?"

He pushed away from me as he wept in his hands. He tried to turn himself away from the other faces watching us but everyone knew he was sobbing.

I could hear some of the children weeping softly to themselves, too, calling out for their absent mamas.

"Mom. Dad. All the grown-ups. Shiri. The whole church...they're all gone," he continued to explain.

Juda couldn't bring himself to look back at me.

Instead, he stared at the floor so I could no longer see the depths of sorrow and confusion in his deep brown eyes.

"Where did they go, Juda?"

"They're dead, Raya, okay? They're all dead. Is that what you needed to hear?"

Now he sounded more like himself.

Indignant.

Maybe it was the shock still gripping me tightly, but what he said didn't enter any depths of my understanding. It just bounced around on the top of my head as a distant idea that made no sense. Like watching a cartoon where a character falls off a cliff but is unharmed in the next scene.

Of course, our parents couldn't possibly be dead.

No one had died recently in our church either.

What is he even saying?

I stood up slowly, stumbling, and grasping for a nearby chair. I sat down once my hand connected with the seat of the chair. I was so confused and didn't understand any of this.

Why don't I remember how we got here?

"What is this place?" I mumbled to my brother while visually exploring the room.

He looked up at me from where he sat on the floor.

"This is the Sanctuary," he said as if I was supposed to immediately understand.

He cut his eyes at me, irritated by my simplistic, yet never-ending, questioning.

I just blankly stared at him, waiting for more of an explanation.

"Dad, Solo, and I built this place over the past two years. Every time we took those long fishing trips, the hunting trips, the men's only trips...we came here instead. Dad said we could never say anything about it until the time came for us to use it."

Solo!

Oh my gosh, where is my cousin?

Even though Solo was my cousin, he was also the closest thing to a male best friend that I had ever had in the whole world.

It kind of hurt to hear that he was involved in this secret space being built and he never so much as hinted at anything called 'the Sanctuary'.

I thought we told each other everything. I would have to harass him about this later.

Solo's dad was my father's younger brother but he never actually lived with my uncle. His mom and my uncle never officially married.

Solo's real name was Solomon.

We started calling him Solo because he generally kept to himself but eventually the nickname gave him this larger-than-life persona that he quite enjoyed. Like he was too cool and too righteous to be involved with regular people. But in all honesty, Solo was the coolest person I knew.

He was a tech genius and a math prodigy. He could engineer just about anything you could imagine.

He didn't go outside much and always acted like the sun was too much for his precious praline-colored skin but we all knew it was because there were no video games outside.

Solo just turned eighteen and was part of our church, too. His mom had agreed to let him live with us temporarily back when he was fifteen because he was withdrawing within himself to a point that was very concerning and toxic to her. He even told her that he didn't believe in God and he didn't think God was a real "thing".

He said no one in his school was into the whole higher power thing and it was YOLO[1] for him, too. Even his teachers discouraged such beliefs, saying that science overruled any faith-based arguments and would often, instead, encourage students to explore forms of self-idolatry. This

---

1. "You Only Live Once"

pushed most of them to believe that their wants, desires, and happiness were king to all else.

His mom didn't understand what path he was being led down and thought my dad...being a pastor, could help guide him, spiritually. She had tried everything else but Solo just wasn't complying or responding positively to any of her efforts. Living with us for a while was the absolute last resort.

She didn't fully understand our beliefs or our ways either but she was desperate for her son to have faith in something.

Originally, it was only supposed to be for a summer, but when he went home, he was completely changed, just not in the way his mom intended.

Not only did he believe in God, but he wanted to follow the Bible to the fullest...page by page. He had a righteous zeal about his faith and wouldn't back down, even to his mom.

She was so shocked to find him altered like that and thought he was going from one extreme to the next.

She just wanted her son to have a little more faith and discipline but didn't expect him to want to be home-schooled and stop doing certain things that they used to enjoy together.

They started bumping heads over holidays, activities, and even meals.

Auntie Mei was Filipino... holidays and pork were her two favorite love interests.

Solo wanted no part of either, so finally with her frustrated blessing, he joined our household permanently and we've been close ever since.

I looked frantically around the room but couldn't find his face peppered amongst the worn-down-looking group.

As if summoned silently by my frazzled thoughts of his well-being, Solo appeared walking up the dark stairs in the farthest part of this so-called sanctuary, his usually fresh-looking cornrows now full of sticks, twigs, and frizz.

"The solar-powered generators will hold. And we have enough of the emergency food supply to last at least six years, if not more," Solo said, sounding drained of all energy.

He dragged himself towards our side of the massive metallic room, looking for a chair to plop down into. He noticed a folded lawn chair leaning against the wall, quickly grabbed it, and pulled it open carefully. He sank into whatever material the chair was made out of. It looked like some kind of thick canvas but faker.

His statement was directed towards my brother but I wasn't sure if Juda was even coherent at this point.

He was still wallowing on the floor, staring into his lap. Much like Solo, he also had woodsy debris in his tapered, short free-form locs.

But he was no longer crying.

He was now just staring into some deep abyss of sadness. He looked as if he was peering into a mirror and the only thing he would ever see reflecting back would be complete and utter darkness.

I knew I couldn't reach him when he got like that.

No one would be able to.

He had to come back to himself on his own, with the Most High's help.

I had only seen him like that once before when his best friend, Eitan, was shot and killed over some shoes. That was about a year ago, exactly.

The police were responding to a burglary at a cheap shoe store and saw Eitan running down the street, away from the store. They automatically assumed, as he was a light-skinned black boy with locs, that he was the perp and shot him point blank in the back.

In truth, Eitan was trying to get home quickly because he had just remembered his mom told him to take some chicken out the freezer to thaw out for dinner. He just happened to be in the wrong place at the wrong time.

No one was ever charged in Eitan's murder, with the police stating it was an accidental discharge.

My brother was infuriated and ready to march in the streets for justice.

My dad practically manhandled Juda into his SUV that night and sped off with him and Solo on an impromptu men's retreat to get him away from all the craziness and chaos at the time.

Now, I was sure that they had come here to work on this place.

Solo looked at me briefly then looked away just as quickly. His shoulders were drooping and shame was etched into his face, but I didn't understand why.

What has he got to be ashamed of?

I blinked at Solo and turned my gaze back down to Juda.

My brother's skin tone was a rich, dark bronze and he was a full six inches taller than me, but at that moment, he seemed trivial and pale.

Without warning, he suddenly stood up, elevating himself to his full stature.

He faced Jerusalem[2], lifted his hands, palms upwards, and began to pray.

---

2. Psalms 138: 2

THREE

— · —

As Juda prayed out loud, everyone who understood what was happening, raised up and bowed their heads in worship.

I found myself gravitating towards him, desperately needing my brother to feel that I was beside him...that I was with him no matter the trial.

I grabbed his hand and silently prayed for his strength and endurance, for understanding, peace, and guidance.

When he had ceased praying, everyone was crying again, but there was a sense of driving purpose to it as if their tears were washing them clean of whatever extreme trauma they had just experienced.

I didn't remember any details and did not understand the burden of what everyone else was carrying.

Was that a gift or a curse?

Juda had said everyone was dead but I was still grasping at the 'how' and the 'why'.

He stood tall and faced everyone before I had a chance to ask him any more pressing questions.

He no longer looked insignificant and washed out, but captivating and magnetic.

"I know you all are scared and confused. Most of our parents were...taken...today. We will get through this together and in some kind of way, the Most High will get the glory from it. He saved us for a reason, for a purpose, and it's our duty to follow it through. Whatever His will is, let it be done!" Juda boomed.

There was a reverent silence in the room for several moments.

Then came a slight cough from somewhere in the room, followed by a smallish voice speaking out.

It was Adina.

She was new to our fellowship, with her mom and little sister, Zara.

Zara was tucked behind Adina's skirt, making Adina look like a makeshift mother to her little sister, who was five years old. Adina was seventeen and very quiet. She never really spoke openly to the other girls in our age group, unless she was asked a direct question.

She mostly only focused on looking after her sister, making sure that Zara ate her food properly and no one picked on her for the way she looked.

Zara was born with a cleft palate that had to be repaired when she was just a baby and it was somewhat noticeable to the other children. They were ruthlessly direct about it and asked questions, like "What's that line on your upper lip?" and "Why is your nose so flat?"

Adina was very sensitive about her sister's feelings and tried to shield her from criticism as much as possible.

"Is there somewhere I can go to clean off all this dirt from my sister's face?" she asked curtly.

Her voice was so muted, that it almost seemed like a bird had chirped in the room, then flapped silently away in the wind.

"Yeah. There are bathrooms down those stairs," my brother responded, pointing to his right.

"We can all take turns getting cleaned up but be mindful of how much water you use. We need to ration for now. I'm not sure how long we will be down here," Solo followed up when he figured Juda was not going to explain anything further.

I turned to my cousin and asked him quietly, "Where are we exactly? Are we near the house?"

He looked quizzically at me for a few seconds, as if deciding something.

Then he spoke, "Right now, we are about three miles from the pond. There are two openings to this sanctuary. One is about a quarter mile from the pond, which is where we came in at, and the other comes out by the woods near the main interstate."

I scratched the back of my head in confusion.

I was still trying to grasp the concept of this place and what did he mean by 'this' sanctuary?

One question at a time though.

"Why did y'all spend years building it?" I asked.

"You'll have to ask Uncle Zeke—" He quickly stopped talking and looked at the ground again. "—I'm sorry."

I was numb.

I didn't feel the gravity of his words and didn't accept them as an offense or a finality.

"It's okay. I will ask him when I get the chance," I answered, briskly.

His head whipped back towards me, staring at me like I had an alien invasion on my forehead.

He stared at me like I was delusional.

"Your dad died today, Raya. I saw it happen. We all saw it happen."

"Y'all keep saying that, but it's not true. At least, I don't believe it's true. I can't explain it but I'm not scared. I know everyone is okay, including him."

He turned and mumbled something about checking the radio and the security defenses before walking towards the dark staircase that led up.

"Wait a sec, Solo!" I scream-whispered at his back.

He stopped but didn't turn around again, his head slightly downcast.

"How big is this place?"

All I heard him say was "big" before he disappeared up the stairs.

I decided to look around for myself.

I got up and went to the back stairs to the right. I figured I would go to the so-called bathrooms and have a look at myself if there were any mirrors down there.

There were about fourteen of us in this whole space.

As far as I could tell, only five were under the age of six years old, including a toddler and a ten-month-old baby.

Everyone else was either a teenager or a young adult.

The ten-month-old was with his young mother, Drea. She was twenty-two and had gotten married two years ago to Brother Isaiah. I recall Isaiah being kind-hearted and always smiling. They were forever laughing and smiling quietly to themselves after church service and holy day celebrations[1] and they were both so excited when they found out she was pregnant.

Now, instead of calling him Brother Isaiah, we all called him Big Isaiah and the baby, Little Isaiah.

Today I couldn't see any more hints of happiness on Drea's face. There was only tired defeat marked under her dirty headwrap.

I passed Drea on the stairs and she had her son hitched up on her right hip. He was fast asleep but she didn't look like she had any intentions of putting him down. She went silently towards a chair in the main room and sank in it, looking like sleep would overtake her at any moment.

"Should I find a blanket or a bed for you?" I asked her, trying to be as sensitive as possible to her needs.

"No, thank you. I just need to sit here for a while. I'll be okay," Drea said, giving me a small, slightly strained smile.

I returned the smile and then kept going down.

Up close, the stairs weren't as dark as they looked from across the large metal room.

I descended about six steps, getting a chill as the air became cooler the further I went.

---

1. biblical feast days/holidays

I located the bathrooms right off the stairway.

When I walked closer, I noticed the actual room was set into the neutrally painted drywall. It was like the outline of a rectangular shipping container that was transformed into something more useful.

I didn't feel confined or cramped at all in this space. The entire area was surprisingly roomy and welcoming.

I wondered just how many containers were set up down here.

This container room held two sets of bathrooms, like separate stalls, lining each wall. There was a divide immediately when you stepped into the room. You could either go left or right into the stalls. The bathrooms on the left were painted a softer purple. The ones on the right were painted a darker teal.

It looked like something my mom would have designed. She loved bold, contrasting colors. That made me wonder if I was the only person that didn't know about this place.

I didn't recall my mother ever putting up much of an argument whenever my dad announced one of his 'trips'.

Maybe she knew, too.

I went to the left, to the purple stalls.

For an underground bunker, these bathrooms were surprisingly better than I had anticipated.

I was expecting a bucket with cat litter in it, a hose pipe nearby, or just small bottles of water, and maybe, if I was lucky, a small hand mirror.

These had actual toilets that flushed and stand-up showers in each stall. A mirror was mounted above a small sink, as well. I didn't even see any of the piping.

My dad must have designed this place with all things in mind.

It was very nice, considering the circumstances.

I started to wash my hands and looked up into the mirror as the water ran. My headwrap was hanging to the back of my head, showing peaks of my short cropped coils. I usually brushed and gelled it down but I guess sweat or some kind of moisture curled it back up in the process of getting here.

I hated my hair.

For the life of me, it would not grow more than an inch. After that, it would commence to breaking off. I finally let go of the idea of long-flowing curls when I hit puberty.

I figured this was just what it was meant to be.

Most High's will be done in all things.

I splashed my face with water and washed my hands one more time before turning it off and shaking the excess moisture from my hands.

I didn't see any towels in the bathroom, but beggars can't be choosers.

I looked again in the mirror, readjusted my headwrap until I was satisfied with its position, and then stepped out of the stall.

As I was leaving, I noticed another container room directly behind that level of stairs. The color combination of it was hunter green and sky gray. It was another set of bathrooms but for the males.

I was thoroughly impressed at this point.

The main hallway continued down to other 'rooms' and spidered out to more hallways. I continued down the main hallway and peeked inside one of the openings in the wall.

It was like a room or pod.

I continued walking and peeking into rooms.

Each pod had two or three sets of bunk beds, a small writing table, and a few click-clack mini sofas that could double as more bedding. Each bunk had blankets and toiletry kits on them; the same care packages we gave out to the homeless every month. They contained unisex socks, toothbrushes, toothpaste, Band-Aids, a small aluminum-free deodorant, Shea butter, and 2 sets of underwear. There was also a small pile of plain-colored scarves, neatly folded on the writing desk.

After I had satisfied my curiosity with the rooms, I went back up to the main floor which was all metal, and took full inventory of that room, too.

Besides the open random chairs, there were long, hard plastic tables lining every wall, with more chairs leaning against the walls.

This had to be the community room or dining hall.

I walked deeper into the huge room and something out of place caught my eye. It was located on the inner-most wall.

It was a door knob but it appeared to be randomly placed in the middle of the wall. There were no creases or openings in the wall that indicated an actual door.

I kept walking towards it until I finally reached it.

I put my hand on the knob, twisted it, and pulled it towards myself.

Nothing happened.

I looked at the knob again then decided to twist and push it instead.

I half expected nothing to happen again...maybe the door knob was a fluke, but metallic flakes started tumbling down around me from fine creases in the wall overhead. Creases that I had not seen at first glance.

The looming metal door, that was camouflaged into the wall, opened inward to reveal a cavernous inner room.

When I peered inside the room, it looked like a grocery store with a commercial kitchen attached to it.

When I stepped fully inside, the lights automatically came on.

Pantry shelves lined every wall.

They were placed in strategic rows from the top all the way down to the bottom of each wall.

The shelves were full of canned goods, bags of beef and deer jerky, jars of spices, jugs of water, dish towels, and plenty more.

Every wall was filled to the brim with items I thought could never be found in an underground bunker.

In the middle of all this, was an oversized island that could easily double as a culinary food prep table. There were a few hot plates stacked in their respective boxes on top of the island. Not that they were needed, because I noticed two daunting commercial stoves/ovens wedged in between shelving on the inner wall of that room.

Maybe the hot plates were for backup.

In the far right corner of the room, near the stoves, were a few manual washing machines. The kind you had to crank with your hand.

After my brief observation of the kitchen/pantry, I walked out and closed the door.

Who could even begin to think of food at a moment like this?

Just as I was letting go of the doorknob, Juda walked over slowly, as if he had a secret to tell and wasn't sure who to trust.

He looked around and saw that only Drea and the baby remained in the room and she was nodding off, far away from us.

He turned to me and said quietly, "A group of us need to go back up and assess...the situation."

I nodded my head in naïve agreement, not fully comprehending what exactly needed to be assessed or why we had to be so hush, hush about it.

"...and we need to bury all of our parents," he squeaked out.

He sounded just like he did when his voice changed at fourteen. It was high-pitched, then deep in the same sentence.

He was choking on his words.

"We do need to find out what's going on...but our parents aren't dead, Juda. If anyone is dead, we do owe them a burial, though. The shovels should still be in the shed by the house. Do you think it's safe to go tonight?" I asked, as muted as I could.

"I don't know, but Solo has a police scanner and he is listening to the chatter. If he says it's safe, we will go tonight," Juda answered.

As he was saying this, Solo emerged from the top of the stairs.

It was like he had Spidey senses or something, always showing up when his name was mentioned or when he was thought of.

If the situation hadn't been what it was, this would have made me peel over in laughter.

Solo looked between us both and said, "It's not safe tonight. Those government people are still looking for us. They've put out a BOLO[2] to all police precincts and divisions in middle and South Georgia."

"Great..." Juda responded, narrowing his eyes, impatient to leave the bunker.

---

2. "Be On The Look Out"

"Okay, we will need one or two other people to go with us when we do go up. Let's get some sleep and figure out a team tomorrow," he concluded.

Me and Solo nodded in unison.

I walked over to Drea and gently woke her up.

"Drea, please come with me. It's time to get some real rest."

She got up sleepily, still cradling her baby to her hip, and followed me down the short set of stairs.

I showed her to one of the bedroom pods and her eyes got wide in amazement.

Clearly, she didn't have any interest in exploring past the bathrooms earlier.

"I'll let you get settled in. Good night."

I tried to sound as calm as possible so she would be reassured but she seemed much more fragile now than I ever recalled.

I walked to the opposing pod and peered in. It was occupied by the small children, along with Adina.

Most of the little kids were already in bed, being tucked in by Adina, or waiting patiently to be picked up and loved on.

She looked at me with weary eyes and said something about her taking charge of the younger children for as long as we needed.

I breathed a 'thank you' to her and she nodded, turning back to the babies and Zara.

I walked to another adjacent pod because I just wanted to be alone.

I laid down to try and detangle today's events in my mind. Sleep nested behind my eyes before I even had time to realize that I was absolutely exhausted.

FOUR

"So, how do we overcome the temptation to give in to fear? First off, let's be totally honest with ourselves. Sometimes the things that we fear are very real and we can't just ignore them and act as though they are not real, but the fear doesn't have to be. God Most High can and will give us the strength to overcome..."

MY DAD IS STILL speaking...Brother Elijah is standing right next to him with his Bible open, waiting to read the next precept.

"Get Psalm 46:1-11."

Brother Elijah's deep booming voice carries in the wind, *"PSALM 46 STARTING AT VERSE 1...'God is our refuge and strength, a very present help in trouble'..."*

I blink toward the bright sunlight then there is only my parents before me.

The lesson is over.

I turn to see some of my church friends are over by the pond and the sun is dancing orange shimmers on the crystal blue water.

I feel the soft, green grass brush against my ankles as I walk towards them and I smile while taking in the full view of beautiful woods that form a deep semicircle around the pond.

Juda is dancing to the praise music blasting from the nearby speakers. The children are laughing at his offbeat dance moves. I laugh at him, too.

I look back and see Mama in her beautiful, pale blue dress and matching headscarf, handing Dad a plate full of salad. He pauses his conversation with the brothers and gives her a peck on the check in return and she gives him a soft, radiant smile before retreating back to the side of the tent with the rest of the sisters.

I turn my attention back to the water and admire how the sun makes it sparkle and shine.

"Thank you, Lord, for another Shabbat," I whisper in the gentle rustling of a much-needed breeze.

The sound of footsteps approaches me from behind and it's not long before I can see my brother's reflection in the water. He and Solo plop down onto the grassy spot beside me along with my best friend, Shiri.

"So, basically, we got shoo-ed away for asking for food," Shiri says, dipping her bare feet into the water.

I only laugh slightly, because, of course, they did.

The sisters usually serve their husbands first and then the small kids. We normally fix our plates after them.

Solo sighs and throws a stick into the water.

"I'm so hungry, bro," he balks.

Just then, I get a deathly sick feeling in my stomach.

I turn and look towards the road.

I can only see dust and darkness.

I hear buzzing, buzzing, buzzing...then screams.

I'm drowning in darkness.

⎯⎯◆⎯⎯

I woke up shaking and disturbed while lying in slightly damp sheets. For a brief moment, I couldn't recognize where I was.

I looked around at the bunk beds and breathed a quick sigh of relief.

That dream was so real.

Was it a dream or a memory?

I yawned wide and reached down to grab the toiletry bag from the floor. I had probably kicked it there in my sleep.

I walked down to the bathroom and chose the same purple stall as before.

I brushed my teeth and washed my face. I thought maybe I should wait to take a shower. I didn't have anything to change into.

Maybe I could grab some clothes from the house, but what about everyone else?

I needed to bring this up to Juda.

After I put the toiletry bag back in my room, I took two steps at a time until I reached the community/dining room.

Some of the large, sturdy tables had been unfolded and the children were sitting at one of them. They were eating cereal and milk.

The older teenagers were lounging at a table closer to the pantry/kitchen. They sat with bottles of water and protein bars, talking in hushed, dejected voices.

"Where did you find milk?" I asked Adina before I realized my mouth was moving.

"There was a huge sack of powdered milk in the pantry. I hope that's ok," she almost whispered.

"Yeah, I'm just surprised we had milk, that's all."

"Solo and your brother told me to tell you to meet them upstairs when you woke up," she said quickly as if this was too much conversation for her and she was ready for it to end.

I looked towards the stairs and then back at her.

"Cool, thanks."

I grabbed a protein bar from the pantry and made my way up the short stairs.

The stairs led up to an arched tunnel that made up the top shape of a 'T'. Once I made it to the tunnel, I could only go left or right; not further up or straight.

I looked both ways down the long, empty-looking tunnel.

I was trying to decide which way was the right way when Solo poked his head out of an opening about ten paces away, down the left side of the tunnel.

"I heard your big feet on the steps. This way," he said.

I followed him down the left corridor and into a side-pocketed room.

"What's this place?" I asked curiously, touching some of the electronic devices.

"It's my own design," Solo said, beaming and full of himself. "I call it 'The Lookout'. I have everything we need to track what's going on topside. Police scanners, laptops, a drone...I've even hacked into some of the town's CCTV cameras."

Solo was definitely in his element here.

Juda just sat there in a foldout chair, rubbing his temples. Gone was his laughing, joking attitude.

He was all serious and brooding.

"So here is the plan, Raya. We will go back up tonight and find out what's what at the house...and bury our dead. I've asked James and Naomi to come with us," my brother blurted out. "They both have strong stomachs and can keep a secret."

"Okay..." I hesitantly responded.

"What? What's wrong with that plan?"

"Nothing. I just needed to add some things to it," I said.

"Like?"

"Like, everyone needs clothes to change into eventually, and I didn't see any diapers for Little Isaiah, and..."

They both looked at me like I was making this more difficult by the second or like I was speaking on irrelevant things.

"And...we need to find out if there are others under attack. Others, like us, that may need help. There is plenty of room down here. We could help a lot of people."

There was a brief silence then Juda cleared his throat.

"I don't know, sis. Can we even trust people we don't know like that? What if they tell the wrong people and we all get caught or murdered? It's too risky."

"Thoughts, Solo?" I asked, ignoring Juda.

Solo looked like he was caught by the neck in some chicken wire. He fumbled to his chair by the laptops and pretended to be occupied with some pop-up on one of his screens before speaking.

"Well, I'm just the tech guy, right, not a referee," Solo paused and waved wildly for us to come over. "—Listen! Listen to this."

We leaned in and heard a PSA on his pseudo-social media page.

This is a Public Service Announcement...

All minority race members found without an approved, chipped passport will be arrested on-site and without question. Please report to your local sheriff's office for processing and approval of chipped passports ONLY. To gain approval, you must first be considered crucial or essential personnel. Terrorists will not be tolerated. We, the great nation of the US of A, will not tolerate race wars!

"Race wars? What are they talking about? This can't be serious," Juda said. "This must be some hoax."

"Nah. I heard a lot of chatter on the police scanner last night. All police personnel are authorized to pick up anyone of a minority race, mixed people included. All you have to do is look 'other'. And get this...they aren't taking them to jail, neither."

"What do you mean? Where do they take them?" I asked hurriedly.

"To some facility somewhere here in the Southeast. I don't know exactly where, but they kept calling it the TRP. Not sure what that stands for," Solo responded.

"Yeah, well, I'm still not convinced this isn't a hoax. I don't know if Dad wanted strangers down here either way. It was supposed to be for the congregation in case something happened," Juda protested.

I wanted to shake some sense into my brother.

What is wrong with him?

"Dad would have wanted us to do our part and help anyone that needed help!" I heard myself almost yelling.

"Juda, we have to. Could you live with yourself knowing you could have prevented even one person from going into the TRP?"

My voice was calm but stern, seeing his obvious distress.

"This sanctuary is for our body," he tried to reason.

"Exactly! For the WHOLE body of Christ...like Dad always says! We don't have time to be camp-checking people, Juda. We never have! That's not of the Most High!"

My words were rapid fire but I couldn't tell if the target was struck or dodging.

Juda looked like he was, in fact, battling a war, but in his mind.

"How would we even get to people anyways?" he retorted.

"Oh, that wouldn't be a problem at all," Solo finally interjected.

He smiled mischievously and pulled out a whole rack of keys from behind the drone.

Juda and I looked at each other as if saying 'Of course he has keys'.

This new inside joke between me and my brother temporarily broke the tension.

"I need to think it over, Raya. Let's not do anything or say anything about it until we figure out what's happening outside," Juda concluded.

"Fine."

What else could I do but agree right now?

"What time are we leaving tonight?" I asked, instead.

Solo went on and on about the best time to go would always be around dusk, so 7:30 PM was finally decided.

I went back down the stairs into the community room, leaving Juda and Solo in the tunnel to work out some more of the details about tonight's undertaking.

Adina was sitting at a table, telling the little kids a story about scared bears living in the woods. They were all laughing at how the scaredy bears hid from pretend monsters.

Everyone else was just sitting around, bored, waiting for whatever was next.

I didn't see Drea or Little Isaiah, though.

"Anybody seen Drea?" I asked the older group.

"I think she is still down in her sleeping pod," Naomi responded. "Do you want me to go check on her? I haven't seen her come up here at all."

"That's ok. I'll do it," I responded.

I went down to the sleeping pods, not sure what I would find.

Drea was still lying on the bottom bunk near the back of the room. Little Isaiah was pulling up on the metal frame, practicing, getting ready to walk any day now.

His diaper was disgustingly full. No doubt it was the same one from yesterday.

"Knock-knock. Can I get you anything?" I asked at the opening, where a door honestly should have been.

She didn't answer right away, but eventually, she leaned forward, propping her head up with her elbow.

"Can you tell Big Isaiah to bring down the diaper bag? Baby needs his butt changed," she said dreamily.

What she said rattled me temporarily. I could only respond with a weak 'sure'.

I turned on my heels and booked it back up the stairs without saying another word.

By the time I made it up the stairs, Juda and Solo were already in the community room, raiding the pantry for bottled water and jerky.

I power walked over to them and told them about my interaction with Drea.

"What should we do?" I asked desperately.

It was hard for the others not to overhear our conversation. It wasn't like there were rugs or curtains in the metal room to absorb any loose sounds.

Naomi walked over and hissed, "She's the oldest out of all of us. She, of all people, has to stay in her right mind or none of this is gonna work."

Naomi was the same age as Juda and had been a part of the church for three years now.

Her parents were eating under the tent when all the commotion started and everyone just assumed that they were deceased as well.

Everyone assumed that anybody not in the sanctuary with us was dead.

"I'll go talk to her and pray with her. She just needs to be reminded that this is our current reality and we are in a safe place. Naomi, will you come with me?" I heard Juda ask.

"Of course."

Naomi looked like she was so honored to be singled out.

But honestly, who else, besides me or Adina, could he ask?

I knew he didn't want to go without a female chaperone to Drea's bedroom to chat.

Dad always taught us that it's best to have a witness or two when dealing with the opposite sex.

I rolled my eyes to myself.

I often caught Naomi staring at my brother during service. She did not hide it well, either. I didn't think they would make a very good match, though.

She had a churlish quality to her like she would make a great gang leader in prison. She could be bossy and domineering when she wanted to be, especially towards anyone younger than her, including me.

She usually hid this quality extremely well around others, but I had been on the receiving end of her attitude on more than one occasion and knew full well what lurked beneath her character.

She was very outwardly pretty, though.

Her skin was a flawless caramel cream color and she had light brown, long locs that reached the middle of her back. She didn't have any acne scars like a lot of girls our age and she had a very good sense of style. She always looked well put together and modest.

That wasn't really what my brother needed.

He didn't need to be focused on any girl before or after yesterday's events.

He was still a bit on the immature side and could stand a few more years of manly guidance from Dad and the other brothers.

But I kind of understood why he gravitated towards Naomi. She reminded him a lot of Mama, at least outwardly.

Mama was beautiful and it didn't matter what she wore or how she styled her hair, it was as if there was an effortless, underlying allure to her.

Her smile was genuinely infectious and she hardly ever raised her voice, even to us. She was one of those people that before you realized it, you were two weeks into being old friends with, whether you meant to or not.

She wasn't a particularly small woman but she wasn't overly big either. She was...just right.

She and Dad had married right out of high school and they've been inseparable ever since.

She had Juda when she was twenty years old, then me when she was twenty-three, so there was always this fluid youthful energy surrounding her, too.

It had only been one day, but there was this gaping black hole left where she had once stood.

It was like running through a maze and knowing she was just around the next corner but she never materialized no matter where I turned. I could only see the hem of her blue dress moving further each time I rounded another bend.

I said a silent prayer for her to remain strong and to endure, wherever she was.

I had a few hours before it was time to go back up to the house. I figured I should make a list of everything we needed to accomplish topside.

I went back to my pod and sat at the writing desk.

I could faintly hear Juda's voice nearby.

There was a small drawer in the desk and it contained a meager amount of paper and pens. There was a small Bible tucked into the corner of the drawer, as well, like they used to do at some hotels.

I took out a sheet of loose paper and a cheap-looking black pen and started to write:

-clothes for everyone

-burials

-diapers

-books & toys for the kids

-find others

I sat there for a long time, trying to figure out what else to write and trying hard not to eavesdrop on Juda's conversation with Drea and Naomi.

I laid my head down on top of the paper and stared at the bunk beds to my left.

Even though Drea's pod was close to mine, I couldn't make out all the words anyway...

Not coming...we love you...need...survive.

I stopped focusing on their words and my scrap of paper. I stared over at the bunk bed, unblinking, unmoving.

The next thing I saw was a distant light.

It was soft and comforting and I felt safe to close my eyes.

FIVE

—·—

"The very first thing that we must do in moments of fear is pray! When fear is present it usually means that we feel we have no control over the situation, but always remember that the Most High does have full control, and so let us pray to Him...Get 1 PETER 5: 7," Dad says.

*E*LIJAH READS, *"FIRST PETER...CHAPTER 5...VERSE 7...'Casting all your care upon him; for he careth for you'."*

Odd. I've been here before...

I am back by the pond, sitting next to Shiri.

The lesson is over.

"I thought the food was done," I offer, "and I saw my mom fix a plate for my dad."

"And that means... what? You know 'pastor' always eats first," one of the older kids retorts nearby.

I just roll my eyes subconsciously at the nickname and I know Juda is somewhere behind me doing the same thing. We never see our dad as anything other than just Dad.

"Well, anyway, the food is ready, but your mom told us to come over here and wait for our names to be called, because SOMEBODY kept pestering the women about a plate," Shiri says, emphasizing the 'somebody'.

I glare at Solomon jokingly, assuming that he is the 'somebody' that Shiri is referring to.

"Why you looking at me?" he screeches.

"Actually, it was the little ones," Juda says, jumping into the conversation. "The ladies just wanted us to keep an eye on 'em - Hey! Jeremiah, get out of that water!"

He runs toward the small group of children who are dangerously close to the pond's edge and that's when we hear Shiri's name being called from the tent. I guess it's her turn to fix her plate.

She gets up and half jogs toward the tent. Solo watches her go as if he just couldn't wait for her to leave and that's so like him.

"So, enjoying your Shabbat, cuz?" I ask.

Solo just gives a half-crooked smile. So that means no. I know he doesn't like the sun...or nature, for that matter. I open my mouth to tease him about it but then stop short when I hear an unfamiliar sound somewhere in the distance. Solo hears it too because he turns toward the dirt road where the sound is coming from.

"Were we expecting more people?" he asks.

"What people?"

It's a rhetorical question, but I don't have to explain that to my cousin.

Suddenly the sound turns visual as big military trucks come thundering up the dirt road. Solo and I both stand at the same time and I'm sure we are both thinking the same thing.

What in the world is going on?

Juda is beside me suddenly, the same question plastered on his face but there is also something else...like 'oh no' in his expression.

"Solo, get the kids and take them into the woods. NOW!" he rushedly said. "Raya, go with him."

"What? Why? What's happening?" I ask nervously.

My anxiety spikes when I don't get a response and Juda takes off at a brisk pace towards Dad, who is already making his way to the trucks with a few other brothers at his side.

"Raya."

Solo takes hold of my arm and drags me away from the pond.

"We should do what your brother says."

I hesitate.

"Come on, Raya!"

He turns back and tells all the older kids to carry the smaller ones quickly up the rounded hill that leads back into the dense woods.

Then there's a distinct gunshot.

I spin around, my heart hammering in my chest, my ears ringing from the horrible buzzing sound.

"JUDA!" I hear myself yelling for my brother.

Just as I begin to sprint toward the commotion, I feel myself being dragged backward by Solo's strong grip on my dress.

"Raya, NO!" Solomon's eyes are wild with fear and confusion. "NO." he whisper-yells again.

"MY FAMILY IS OVER THERE!"

I snatch away and take off.

Gunshot fires through the air and I fall to the ground on instinct, panting. Women are screaming up ahead and all I can think is...Mama.

More gunshots. All in quick succession. White men in navy blue camouflage surround the camp swiftly, shooting at whatever and whoever moves.

I can only watch and scream as my church family, one by one, hit the ground, encircled in rings of their own blood.

A short man in blue camo marches up to the tent and drops something small next to one of the poles. Suddenly the whole thing goes up in flames.

Nooooooo!

I force myself up then, tears rolling down my cheeks, something like the ocean roaring in my ears, making the screaming sound muffled.

Then I see her...

I see her pale blue dress turning red as she sits crouched over a lifeless form in the bloodstained grass. She is shrieking hoarsely like a wounded animal that knows it's about to die.

No no no no no...

I don't realize that I'm running until I'm suddenly knocked to the ground by some invisible force. Juda is somehow next to me but pain shoots up the back of my right shoulder keeping me from getting back up. There is blood spatter on Juda's face.

I try to crawl but Juda is pulling me back towards the woods.

"MAMA!" I scream, my voice inaudible to my ears.

I see her breathlessly look up, turning frantically, searching to find the direction of my voice, only to be yanked up from the ground by her now uncovered hair. The man in the black suit and dark shades had grabbed her and she was being drug away through the smoke, kicking and screaming.

The body she was crying over is also being dragged through the bloody grass and I see finally, clearly, who it is.

My heart sinks into an abyss as I picture my father, full of life and laughter, only moments before, now lying there, unresistant; his favorite white fringed shirt shot through the chest and stained heavily with blood.

Bile snakes its way up into my throat and I couldn't help but vomit in the dirt.

My sight is wavering. Little specks of darkness dance across my vision.

Just before everything goes completely black, I can almost feel myself being lifted from the ground, carried away from the carnage.

I opened my eyes and blinked slowly.

I must have fallen asleep.

What time is it?

I lifted my head from the desk and the paper was partially stuck to my face. It fell away as I sat upright. I rubbed the side of my neck, which was beyond stiff.

I remember everything.

Tears involuntarily filled my eyes and I had to keep blinking them down.

The image of my dad lying face up in the grass kept playing in my mind like a glitchy movie.

I felt myself getting physically sick. My stomach was lurching and rolling, its contents threatening to spew up at any moment.

There was only one thing I could think to do to make the sickness cease and subdue my heightened emotions.

I closed my eyes tightly and began to pray rapidly, under my breath.

Father...Abba[1] , gracious and holy is Your name. I humbly come before You giving You all thanks, praise, and honor. Glory be to Your loving kindness, Your grace, and Your mercy. Father, please forgive me if I have caused any offense against myself or to others, and help me forgive those who have done evil against me. Please, Abba, remove all

---

1. Aramaic word for Father

sickness, hurt, harm, and danger from me. Lead me and guide me in the way that I should go. Comfort us all, Father, with Your peace that surpasses all understanding. Protect us as we go forth into unknown paths and give us the strength to endure the trials and tribulations that You desire us to get the victory from. In all these things, I pray, through your beloved son and our savior, Yeshua Hamashiach[2], Amen.

I opened my eyes again and breathed deeply, pulling on all my faith to surface, so I could overcome the intensity of emotions flowing through me.

Just then, I heard Juda's clumsy feet shuffling into my pod. I knew that lazy gait from anywhere.

Without getting up from the chair, I turned towards him and he gave me a nod as if to say 'It's time'.

"It's 6:30 PM. We need to get going. It's a three-mile trek through the tunnels to get to the entrance and we need to move quickly if we are gonna get there by dusk," Juda said matter-of-factly.

"Ok. I wish I had some better shoes though. All I got are these flats. That's a hike," I responded.

---

2. one Hebraic variation of the name for Jesus the Messiah or Jesus Christ

"Come on. I'll show you the storage room. It's on the lowest level. There's clothes and shoes and stuff down there. You can get some tennis shoes."

"Storage room? I thought I saw everything yesterday. I walked this whole place."

Juda chuckled to himself for a second, then answered, "No, you didn't. This place is bigger than you think. It's a whole vibe down here. Dad made sure of that."

Our dad was not only the leader of our church but he was an architect by trade. He went to college then grad school and was now considered a master at his craft.

He designed urban and suburban communities for a living and sold his plans to major builders. He was especially gifted at drafting blueprints for tiny home communities.

I shouldn't have been remotely surprised he designed such a place as the 'Sanctuary'.

Juda led me to the very last level and stepped into what looked like any other sleeping pod. It looked just like the others, except instead of having to walk down a hallway to get to it, the room was right at the end of the stairs.

Juda stood by one of the bunks, nearest the right wall, and just gawked at me for a long pause.

I just stood there waiting for the *ta-da* moment.

Sensing my anticipation had turned into impatience, he huffed and pushed slightly on the bunk's middle railing, then pulled on it after we heard a faint *click.* He continued pulling on the metal rail like it was a wide door.

After a few seconds, I realized that's exactly what it was.

After opening the bunk bed door, Juda stepped inside, activating the lights overhead and a strip of lights on the floor. When the whole room became illuminated, I couldn't believe my eyes.

This 'room' was as big as a mid-sized grocery store.

I stepped through the entryway and Juda pointed down the first long corridor. "Shoes are that way. Hurry up though...we don't have much time."

I was speechless.

There were shoes, clothes, books, diapers, toys, more food and water, everything, absolutely everything, even...*weapons.*

I would have to come back later and do a full inventory and pull out the things on my list.

Juda should have said something earlier when I mentioned needing clothes and diapers, but I guessed he had other stuff on his mind.

I grabbed some tennis shoes and some loose-fitting lounge pants and pulled them on under my dress. I found a

T-shirt and slipped into it quickly, as well. After discarding my flats and the dress, I quickly laced the tennis shoes.

As I passed the diapers, I grabbed a pack for Little Isaiah that I hoped was the right size.

While hurrying back towards the doorway, I noticed Juda grabbing a few rifles and a hunting knife from an encased armory.

I wasn't going to protest even though I hated guns in general. My dad had taught both Juda and me how to hunt and safely use guns but the kickback on them always freaked me out more than I was willing to admit.

I much preferred hand-to-hand combat.

Some of my earliest memories were sparring at the boxing gym.

Apparently, I liked to fight the other kids in daycare and would get reprimanded often. My mom thought it would be good for me to redirect that energy into a controlled environment so my parents agreed to let me try boxing and karate. Juda was forced to go, as well, so I wouldn't be all by myself.

I excelled at both and trained three times a week since I was six years old.

Although I hadn't fought professionally in any tournaments, I knew I could hold my own, if need be.

Everyone was always so surprised when they found out I could fight because I didn't have a typical boxer's build and appeared very feminine, which, of course, I was to my very core.

I loved sewing, crafting, and cooking, among other things.

I never understood why people had such deep-rooted stereotypes about how a fighter should look or carry themselves.

"You ready?" Juda asked, handing me the sheathed hunting knife.

I nodded my head affirmatively while strapping the knife to my waist.

When we exited the storage room, the lights automatically cut off. Juda closed the bunk bed door behind us.

This place was truly amazing, just like my dad's mind.

On our way up to the tunnel, I thought about my list last minute.

I decided to run down to my pod to grab it and the pen, just in case:

-~~clothes for everyone~~
-burials
-~~diapers~~
-~~books & toys for the kids~~
-find others

Six

After leaving the diapers with Adina, we finally bounded up the stairs and into the tunnel.

Solo, James, and Naomi were waiting for us off to the right.

When Naomi saw us come up, she abruptly paused her conversation with James and gave a look of indecisiveness towards my pants.

I wasn't sure if she wanted a pair or if she was genuinely disgusted by my choice of clothing.

I really didn't have time to care, either way, and she didn't make any comment.

We just stood there for a few awkward seconds in silence.

Juda passed Solo a rifle and asked James if he knew how to use one. He shook his head in the negative. Juda hesitated a second then asked Naomi if she knew how to use one.

She nodded and said, "Of course. I've been to the shooting range with my uncles, like a thousand times."

He looked at her blankly but handed her the rifle anyway.

"Ok, so that makes you the lookout," he said to James. James looked a bit disappointed but nodded in agreement.

"Where is the safety on this thing? I'm used to a .22," asked Naomi, as we started at a quick pace through the tunnels.

"It's on the tang,[1] " I responded before Solo or Juda could reply.

She looked a little sheepish for a second then asked, "So this red dot?"

I smirked a little but responded, "Well yeah, that means the safety is engaged. Do you need some help?"

"Um, yeah, but just with that. I got the rest."

I slowed my pace to meet hers and showed her the small lever to push and told her when she couldn't see the red dot anymore, that meant she was ready to fire. I wasn't sure if I imagined it, but she looked a bit disappointed that it was

---

1. an extension of a firearm that attaches the barrel to the stock

me and not Juda who volunteered to help her. She kept glancing at him while I gave her the tutorial.

"Keep up," Juda pointedly said to us both.

He was already ahead of us by quite a few yards.

We initially walked at a swift stride but within a few minutes of us progressing at that pace, we all naturally started to jog.

Three miles was a good distance and we had a long way to go.

We were all remarkably silent, not wanting to break concentration or wear ourselves out too fast by the extra exertion that talking required.

To pass the time, I started to examine the tunnel while we made our progress.

The tunnel was constructed purely of rough concrete and the dry walls arched like a perfectly gray rainbow into the ceiling, which was approximately eight feet high. It was about six feet wide; just enough space for two people to be side by side comfortably.

Every eight feet or so hung a suspended light fixture that radiated a soft yellow glow. It was just bright enough for us to make it to the next illuminated section without being completely overtaken in shadowy darkness.

Even though there was enough space to comfortably make it through, it had just a hint of claustrophobia clinging to it.

I could see myself giving into a panic attack down here under any other circumstance. I was more than relieved that I had never been forced to come down here before.

I could only imagine how Juda or Solo must have felt coming here so many times to make this place a reality with Dad.

After almost an hour of jogging, with only our thoughts and the rhythmic pounding of shoes on the pavement to keep us company, Solo came to a complete standstill at the end of the tunnel.

We all gratefully stopped behind him.

Everyone was catching their breath and fanning themselves from the warmness we had worked up.

The air in the tunnel was extremely stifling, too. I could almost smell our collective breath in the loose circle we had formed.

Solo laid his rifle on the ground and slid his backpack off. He dug through it and then suddenly pulled out a device a little larger than a cell phone but no bigger than a tablet.

He caught me focusing on it and explained calculatedly to all of us, "It's one of my inventions. It's like a cell-phone—" He was trying to catch his breath in between words. "—I can 'communicate' with cell towers incogni-to...and pick up any electronic activity...within a 50-mile radius...I call it a...phablet."

He grinned through his labored breaths, amused at himself.

"So...what does it...say?" wheezed James.

He looked like he needed to sit down from being over-run.

James was my age but he wasn't in the greatest of shape and had a doughy body build. Like Solo, he didn't like to go outside much, but unlike Solo, no one ever really made him, either. He was a nice guy and knew his scriptures from front to back, but he was no soldier type.

In my mind, I concluded it was a good thing he was elected to be the lookout.

Solo was starting to recover from exertion and answered, "There is some sporadic activity about 10 miles out but it looks like regular data use, maybe from neighbors on their phones or computers. I do see one strong signal coming from, I'm guessing, the house, but maybe somebody for-got to turn off the computer. Maybe that was me."

Solo was known for not turning off his electronics when he wasn't using them or picking up behind himself, in general, so there was a strong possibility that he was the culprit.

"Should we be worried?" Juda asked.

Solo started to explain that it was likely nothing at all and the reasons why, when Juda waved him off, impatient to leave.

Solo looked a little hurt by this but stopped talking and gathered his rifle and backpack casually.

"Ok, Naomi, you go with Solo. Raya, you're with me. James, when we make it to the house, I need you to stand guard on the hill by the pond. It has the best vantage point and if something pops off, you can make it back to the tunnel and warn the others without being noticed. If you see ANYTHING, do a bird call or something."

"What kind of bird?" James asked seriously.

"A White-breasted Nuthatch...BRUH...it doesn't matter! Just any bird. No birds are out at this time of day. We'll know it's you," Juda said anxiously.

"Um...I think I should go with you and Raya should go with Solo. Don't you think?" Naomi quipped. "I mean, she doesn't have a gun, so she can help him hold his equipment and stuff, right? Doesn't that make more sense?"

Solo shrugged as if he really could care less.

Juda thought about it for a second.

"Fine. Whatever. Come on. Let's just get this over with."

He started to climb up the ladder that looked like nothing more than metal pipes rounded into the base of the wall.

A few seconds later he was typing a code into a tiny keypad near the top. Before he turned the handle to the hatch, something beeped and groaned, signaling him to proceed.

The hatch opened with little resistance and he hoisted himself over the edge. He was now free of the tunnel, with its stale air and suppressing grip.

The rest of us scrambled to get to the top after him, craving that same taste of freedom.

Once we all made it over the edge of the hatch opening, we could see that we had made good timing. The sun wasn't completely set and there were majestic strokes of orange and red in the evening sky. We would have just enough light to make our way out of the woods with considerable ease.

Before moving out, I was curious as to how the entrance looked to the outside world and how well-concealed it actually was.

I also wanted to make sure I could find it again if we had to split up.

The hatch swiveled flatly when Juda closed it and growing from the top of it was the most majestic Franklin tree I had ever seen. Even though the tree was native to Georgia, it was so rare that I had only ever seen one once before today. The first and only time I glimpsed a Franklin was at a botanical research center on a school field trip. I distinctly remembered it because they kept calling it a tree but it looked more like an overgrown Camellia bush and the fragrant white flowers, growing in clusters, contrasted deeply against its dark green foliage. I was glad I had paid attention on that field trip, notwithstanding the pop quiz that was guaranteed afterward.

I would be able to recognize the entrance with no issue, but I had no clue how to make it open again.

Before I could ask, Juda instructed, "If anyone needs to get into the tunnel before we all make it back, this is how you open it."

He pulled on a white flower that was growing alone in the middle of the tree/bush. If I hadn't known any better, the single flower wouldn't have been significant to me but these flowers only grow in clusters and now that he showed us, the single flower did appear out of place.

Something beeped and groaned again and he was able to reach underneath the tree and swivel the hatch open again.

"I saw you type in a code. Isn't there a code or something to get in, too?" asked Naomi.

"Not to get in...only to get out," Solo volunteered.

Silence.

Neither Solo nor Juda volunteered the code.

After what seemed like an eternity of pause, Juda said, "Ok. Let's move out."

"When we get there, me and you will move to the left of the yard," he said while facing Naomi.

"Solo, y'all flank us to the right. James...you know what to do. If there is anything at all...bird call."

We all nodded unanimously and moved out cautiously in a wide horizontal grouping.

Solo and Juda had their rifles poised and began scanning the path every few moments for activity.

We moved as one through the woods, walking north and then slightly turning west. There was an outcropping of huge boulders to our left that I had never seen before.

Interesting.

If I hadn't known any better, I would have guessed that the boulders were staged.

We continued like this for a quarter mile, then finally the wood line broke and the tan paneled house became visible. It was situated down a familiar grassy sloped hill.

All the terrible memories came flooding back.

I felt sick again but quickly swallowed it down. Now was not the time.

I wondered what would greet us by the burnt-out tent and how many graves we would have to dig tonight.

By now, the sun had fully set and only faint darkness welcomed us.

Solo gestured for us all to stop for a second.

He rummaged through his backpack again and pulled out some thick-looking goggles.

"Night vision," he explained without being pressed.

He put the goggles on and took his time scanning the scene.

"It's clear."

Juda and Naomi veered off to the left towards the house, while Solo and I maneuvered to the right towards what was left of the tent.

I was almost relieved that there was only obscure moonlight to highlight against the dark gloomy view.

I didn't want to easily see the suspended details of terror on the faces of my church family which would be forever recorded in death.

And even though deep down in my heart, I believed my dad had not perished, I was afraid to flirt with the truth. I had seen him lying there, unnaturally still and limp.

As we got closer to the burnt-out shell of a tent, we started to realize that we weren't bumping into any bodies. There was just flattened grass every so often; the only indication that any type of disturbance had even occurred.

As much as I was not looking forward to finding bodies and having to bury so many loved ones, not finding anyone was equally disturbing.

The hairs stood up on the back of my neck.

Everyone was gone.

Juda had been right all along.

"Are you seeing this?" I asked Solo.

"Yeah. This is wild bro. Where are all the bodies?" he whispered, pulling his night vision goggles up onto the top of his head.

Before I could even speculate, we both heard a quick, then muffled, scream coming from the house.

It sounded like Naomi.

We both took off for the house as fast as our tired legs could take us. The door was wide open but the lights were still off.

As soon as we burst into the foyer, I could make out Juda's outline as well as Naomi's. They were deeper into the living room, but a larger person was standing incredibly close behind Naomi. I could make out his arm by her head.

I assumed he was covering her mouth to keep her from screaming again.

"Put the guns down—" a menacingly deep voice rumbled behind Naomi.

That voice seemed vaguely familiar but I couldn't quite place it. I didn't trust my racing thoughts and I wasn't about to take any chances by assuming I had any connection with whoever this was.

As Juda and Solo slowly lowered their rifles, I made a rash decision to pull out the hunting knife and go for the stranger's throat. I couldn't fully see him but I saw the outline of his head.

It was only anatomy from there.

I was so rapid in my movements that within three seconds, I was at my target, ready to slice.

He was so startled by my agility that he let go of Naomi and tripped backward. He didn't fully avoid my swing; however, and my knife made direct contact with skin and muscle.

I had wounded him but I wasn't sure what part of him.

Just then, Juda flipped the light switch on for the living room.

Elijah!

Every ounce of trepidation instantly left my body at the sight of Brother Elijah breathing heavily on the floor, bleeding steadily from his forearm.

As the light came on, I could see he was fully prepared to defend himself in return, but when my face surfaced in front of him, he also instantly let down his guard.

I fell into his arms, hugging him with tears welling up in my eyes. We always called him Uncle Elijah but he was more than family to us, if that's even possible.

"You tried to kill me, girl," he said incredulously.

I laughed softly through my tears and said a silent *thank you* to the Father that he tripped and I missed.

As I began to put my knife back into its sheath, I heard a faint but unnatural noise coming from outside.

"Did y'all hear that? Shhhh...listen," Solo said, still standing in the foyer.

CAW CAW. CAW CAW. HOOTIE WHOOOOOO. TWEET TWEET TWEET...

SEVEN

— • —

"**W**E GOTTA GO," JUDA shrieked.

"Wait...where did y'all come from?" Elijah asked.

"No time to explain. We gotta move NOW!" Juda almost yelled.

"Boy, who you raising your voice at—" Elijah was trying to reply, but we were already at the door, headed back into the night.

He took the hint and quickly started for the door right behind us, clutching his bloodied arm. The cut was decidedly deep.

It was very apparent that I was aiming to cause fatal damage.

We all looked towards the road when we made it back out into the yard and saw headlights cautiously approaching. It looked to be just one vehicle but it was still suspicious. It was a dark-looking SUV and it reminded all of us of the military convoy that pulled up and wretched havoc just the other day.

They must have still been searching for the ones that got away that day.

Searching for us.

I wondered if they saw the same signal being emitted from the house and were coming to investigate.

Cautiously, we climbed up the grassy hill and disappeared into the thick woods.

As we began to run, I could faintly hear a male's voice saying, "That lead panned out. Someone was definitely here. Looks like a scuffle happened in the house and the lights are on. Can you follow the tracks? I see fresh blood drops, too."

My senses became super heightened at his comment and I reached down and ripped the hem of my shirt, tearing the bottom of the fabric all the way around. I clumsily reached over to Elijah's dripping arm and tied it off with the loose piece of fabric as best I could.

Hopefully, that would stop the bleeding and the trail.

James was nowhere to be seen.

He must have taken off after his poor excuse of a warning call. I couldn't say that I blamed him, but I hoped he didn't get lost out here in the dark woods or worse, caught.

Juda said he could keep a secret but I wasn't so sure how long he could hold out from giving up our location if he had to endure any kind of torture or deprivation. He didn't strike me as the fasting-often type. They could probably starve the information right out of him.

I prayed he would find his way back to the tunnel safely, not just for his sake but for ours.

Solo pushed his night vision goggles back down over the bridge of his nose and barely audibly said, *"This way."*

Everyone fell into a quick stride behind him, in a uniform line. Even though we moved as a stealthy unit, we still made some faint noises as we progressed, crackling against leaves and snapping small twigs underfoot.

Somewhat behind and off to the right of us, we could see beams of flashlights diligently hunting for traces of disturbance throughout the tree line.

I could hear Juda whispering a prayer to himself and I began to do the same. After a few seconds, I detected everyone saying their own separate prayer requests.

After a few minutes of futile searching, the gleaming flashlights began confidently trailing us. They must have finally locked onto our position after finding our not-so-hidden clues in the troubled landscape.

I could hear that same male's voice calling out, "THIS WAY!"

We mustered all of our remaining strength and began sprinting wildly through the brush, barely able to make out more than three feet in front of our faces.

Without Solo's night vision goggles to help avoid the trees and larger thickets of bramble bushes, we would have been caught before we even really got started.

Everyone's apprehension started to come to a head, knowing we would all be inevitably captured and then only the Lord knew what else was in store for us.

As if the Most High, in that instant, answered our pleas for help, a strong wind picked up all around us and behind us, blowing everything.

Leaves, dirt, and twigs swirled to the east, no doubt removing any and all trace of our present course. Even the howling of the sudden windstorm masked the sounds of our footfall incredibly.

Thank you, Abba. Bless Your holy name. Bless You!

This gave us a renewed sense of hope and we continued running until we got to the oddly situated boulders, now positioned to our right. Only then did we begin to slow down to a resigned trot.

As we passed the outcropping, we heard footsteps moving toward us from behind the boulders and everyone abruptly stopped.

We were all on immediate guard.

Solo and Juda rapidly raised their rifles toward the sound, while Naomi nervously handed hers over to Elijah. Without much effort or thought, she stepped behind the sizeable man for protection. I pulled my knife out from its sheath. It was still slightly sticky from Elijah's blood.

If they wanted a fight, we were more than ready to give them one.

James stumbled out from behind the boulders with both his arms raised high in the air. We could clearly see him in the moonlight, now that our eyes were fully adjusted to the darkness.

"Whoa, whoa, whoa! It's just me! Don't shoot," he cried out.

"What in the world is going on now?" Elijah asked frustratedly, being the only one still mentally in the dark.

"I got scared...I thought I could make it to the tunnel...but I forgot the way. When I saw the rocks...I went to hide...then I heard y'all coming. Brother Elijah! Whoa." James blurted out.

Juda was still on edge.

He looked back and forth, checking for more activity. We all could hear the men still searching, although their sounds were, thankfully, moving away from us.

Juda completely ignored what James had said.

"Let's move," he commanded.

No one said a word in response. We just followed him and Solo in silence, not wanting to give away our location again.

The people following us must have forked to the west because their sounds were getting fainter until we could only hear our own breathing and our own steps.

When we eventually made it back to the Franklin tree unscathed, Juda pulled the single flower in the middle of the tree/bush without hesitation.

We heard the faint groaning and beeping noise of the entrance unlocking. Juda then reached under the base of the tree, swiveling the hatch door open.

I had never been so happy to climb down into a pit of darkness in my entire life.

EIGHT

E LIJAH'S FACE WAS COMPLETELY emotionless.

I guessed, at this point, he couldn't be shocked by anything we did anymore. He just robotically followed us down the dark hole into the tunnel without any protest or questioning.

Solo descended last, maneuvering the hatch door back into its locked position after doing a final scan around the area.

The loud *click* was a comforting sound, signaling safety in my mind.

We made it...

I felt like I had been holding my breath the entire journey back.

Being held captive in a continual fight-or-flight loop had taken its toll on my mental state. I finally exhaled deeply, content to be back in the stifling tunnel, moving back towards the Sanctuary.

At first, we were all impulsively quiet as we began the long trek back to the living quarters. We were moving at a slower pace than we were during the initial journey, and I'm sure we were all thankful for it.

My legs, in particular, felt like a pudding popsicle that was beginning to melt in the summer heat.

We were still covering good ground, though.

Then Elijah finally broke the silence.

"Anyone plan on telling me what in the world is going on? And start from the beginning. I'm tired and I don't think I can handle having to think up any more questions."

Juda looked at me as if to say 'You want me to tell him or you?'

I nodded at him to go ahead.

He might as well be the one to do it since he was conscious the whole time, remembered everything more clearly than me, and was in the know from the beginning about this place.

Juda began to explain to Elijah how this bunker came to be in the first place and how they constructed it with very little outside help.

This part interested me the most because I hadn't gotten the chance to ask all my own questions about it yet.

Juda told him how our dad could replicate his tiny home blueprints into underground communities and how he had shared his vision from the Most High to start building them. He even explained what some of the rooms were and where they were located.

I had no clue we even had a hydroponics[1] room to grow organic fruits, vegetables, and herbs. Apparently, it was near Solo's Lookout.

I had not ventured past Solo's electronics room and truly thought only the exit was that way.

I needed to do some more exploring.

Then he told Elijah of all the events that led up to us finding him.

Now it was Elijah's turn to explain how he came to be in the house.

"Well, that's an interesting story, actually," he laughingly said. "The Most High must have caused it to be."

He said this and gave a dramatic pause for theatrical effect. It worked and he had our full and undivided attention, as we walked purposefully through the core of the tunnel.

---

1. growing crops without soil

"After eating the plate Sister Sandra had piled high with potato salad and coleslaw and such...I had to heed the call of nature...if you know what I mean."

We all snickered at this like little children do when someone says the word 'poop'.

He continued, "I went to the guest bathroom just inside the garage entrance to the house. You know, the little one...and I was handling my business when I heard the gunshots going off. I heard screaming, too, but I couldn't exactly get up right at that second—" another pause, but this one was more so for comical relief, "—then the gunshots stopped just as quickly as they had started. I heard soldiers buss up in the house. I knew it was soldiers on account of the sound of their boots on the ground. They were clearing the house for more people, I guess."

"How come you didn't get caught?" cut in James, enraptured by Elijah's story.

"Well, that's where I'm sure the Most High came in and saved me. See, that little bathroom is right behind the garage entrance door and when they came in through that way, the garage door must have blocked my door from view when they opened it inwards. They walked right past me! If I had gone into any other bathroom in the house...I would have been done."

"Seriously?!" Solo exclaimed. "That's crazy, yo! I mean sir...that's crazy, sir."

I smiled to myself.

Leave it to Solo to be the comedian in a time like this.

Elijah went on to explain, not at all amused by Solo's interruption, "I waited a long time to come out, not sure if they were still there, but finally when I came out...there was nothing and no one left. I went outside and everyone was gone. I saw blood on the ground and the tent was smoldering, but that was it. I didn't know if I should leave or stay or what, but I decided to stay in case this was happening all over the state. At least, at the house, I knew they likely wouldn't come back. When I couldn't take it anymore, I turned on my cell phone and got on social media to see what other people were experiencing, then you showed up. Then those men showed up."

"So YOU were the signal I saw coming from the house," declared Solo. "If I saw you, I know they saw you, too."

"Saw me what, exactly?" asked Elijah, confused.

Solo explained all the technical details of how his cell phone and social media apps were pinging from the communication towers.

Elijah, all of a sudden, stopped dead in his tracks and blurted out, "I still got my cell phone and it's on."

My heart skipped a beat when he said that. I'm sure everyone else's did, too.

Solo chuckled slightly and replied, "Don't worry. I have a signal scrambler activated down here. Your phone doesn't work. It's just an expensive brick now. You can throw it as a weapon if you need, but that's pretty much all it's good for down here. Only my special phablet and laptops work down here because I've designed a unique incognito coding for them. Not even the government would be able to detect us."

Elijah looked down at his phone relieved and saddened at the same time.

"I know how you feel...but you'll get used to it," Naomi empathetically said to him.

She had been like a crackhead with her phone before; constantly needing to update her feeds and craving to see what everyone else was posting at any given moment.

With all this discussion masking our progress, we made it to the stairs leading down to the community room before anyone realized the distance we covered.

"Do you want to settle down into one of the sleeping pods first or get something to eat?" I asked Uncle Elijah.

"Actually, I think I may need some stitches," he said, a little bit more seriously than I had anticipated.

He did look a bit pale from blood loss. That is if a surly, dark-skinned black man could look pale.

"I can do it," a small but sure voice said, coming from the front of the kitchen/pantry.

It was Adina.

She swiftly went back into the pantry and pulled out a first aid kit, housed in a large red bag with a white cross on the front.

She opened it and quickly scanned for all the items she would need to give Elijah the proper care. She pulled out a stitch kit that contained suture thread, some forceps, scissors, and a curved needle.

Elijah plopped down at one of the hard tables and unwrapped the flimsy fabric from his arm.

His wound now looked angry and inflamed.

Adina grabbed a bottle of saline solution and began rinsing it. After delicately dabbing at his sliced skin, she sprayed the surrounding area with a numbing solution. She then threaded the needle with the assistance of the forceps and made quick work of sewing the layers of his wound closed. She knotted the end of the thread and cut it loose from the needle. Finally, with the expertise of a skilled nurse, she gently wrapped his arm with gauze, covering it completely to make sure it would not be exposed to any infection. She had finished all of that within fifteen minutes or less.

"Where did you learn to do that?" I asked, astonished at her level of skill.

"Before my dad passed away, he enjoyed teaching me everything he knew about healing and the holistic practice of herbalism. Part of that training included administering basic first aid and CPR. My dad was a naturopathic[2] doctor," Adina replied shyly.

"I'm sorry about your dad. He must have been a great doctor," I sympathetically said.

She gave a reserved smile, appearing to reflect on him, "Oh, he was...and the best father."

She then looked withdrawn and sad suddenly but continued, "He died last year in a car accident."

No wonder she took such good care of her sister. She was a natural caregiver and had a gravitating sense of empathy about her.

I decided, right then and there, that we would be the best of friends. Her countenance was the perfect example of peacefulness, protection, and humility.

---

2. alternative medicinal approach that uses natural medicines and herbs

James and Naomi had gone to the hydroponics room to get some leafy greens to make Elijah a big salad. Adina told them it was good for him to eat iron-rich foods after so much blood loss. Juda went into the kitchen/pantry and pulled out some beef jerky sticks for him, as well.

"Why were you in here so late anyway?" Naomi questioned Adina after she was done preparing the salad for Elijah.

"It looks like everyone has gone to bed," Naomi added.

"I put all the little ones to bed but then I couldn't sleep, so I came up here to have a look around. I wanted to see if there were any powdered eggs in the pantry for breakfast tomorrow."

"Maybe I can help you fix breakfast in the morning? I can bake some bread and we can have toast to go with the eggs," I volunteered.

She smiled at me and looked pleasantly surprised that I knew how to bake.

I hoped that she wanted to get to know more about me just as much as I wanted to learn more about her.

She agreed, and then we all went down to the sleeping pods. Elijah picked out a pod closest to the men's bathroom and we all mentally chuckled.

I needed a shower and stat.

I took the quiet opportunity to revisit the storage room, grabbing towels and pulling out a bag of clothes and shoes I thought most of us would be able to fit.

For myself, I chose a long brown linen skirt and a roomy white cotton pullover that had a functional hood. I then made my way to my sleeping pod.

I put down the bag of garments. I pulled the toiletry bag that contained the undergarments and soap from off the top of the bed and then left the pod again.

Once I made it to the bathrooms, I checked to see if anyone was in there. I saw that I was all alone and gave a sigh of relief.

I desperately needed some privacy to reflect on what today's events meant.

The shower was a bit narrow but tolerable to move around in. After disrobing, I turned the tap on and got in.

The water was deliciously hot and had a decent pressure. I could feel all of the stress melt from my body and I just stood there for a few minutes, letting the water wash away the tension.

After I began my bathing routine, I noticed a small amount of blood going down the drain as I washed. After checking myself over thoroughly, I glimpsed old blood being rinsed away from the edges of a small round hole on the back of my right shoulder.

It almost looked like I had been...*shot.*

Nine

"Juda. Juda...wake up," I whispered.

I could tell Juda was in a deep sleep but I couldn't keep myself from waking him.

I needed to know.

"Juda...get up," I repeated.

He groaned softly and turned over in his bed.

"Whaaaat?" he replied, half awake.

I pulled my hoodie down over my right shoulder and revealed the small wound to him.

"Look at this," I gently demanded.

He rubbed his face with the back of his hands and I could tell his vision hadn't fully recovered from being woken prematurely. He stared at it but couldn't fully see the small hole.

"Cut the light on," he groggily said.

I moved away from his bed and rotated the circular dimmer switch too hastily. The immediate flood of harsh light was an attack on both our eyes. We both winced and grimaced at it for a few seconds before I thought to turn it back down so our eyes could easily adjust.

I walked back over to him and sat on the edge of his bed so he could get a better look.

"What's this on my shoulder? What's it look like to you?" I repeated.

"You really don't remember much do you?" he responded, looking as if he pitied me, or maybe it was envy I was detecting.

I couldn't decide.

"I remember a lot now but this...I have no clue what this is," I said.

"You were shot, Raya," he began. "It's why you passed out in the first place. At the time, I really thought you were dying but I couldn't just leave you there."

"What do you mean?" I asked, cluelessly.

"They were dragging people away. I couldn't lose you...too." Juda's words tapered off, filled with emotion.

He took a second to compose himself before continuing.

"I carried you the whole way down here, hoping it wasn't too late. When you woke up, I really couldn't believe it. It was a miracle. It was like you hadn't been shot at all."

I looked into his face and recalled the moments after I came to. He looked so relieved, so overjoyed, but deeply terrified at the same time.

I couldn't fully appreciate what he must have gone through internally, until just now.

I would have done the exact same thing.

Even if I had to drag him, I wouldn't have ever left my brother behind.

"It's not deep and it doesn't hurt. It's so weird...that couldn't have been a regular bullet. It didn't pass through either so it should still be there. I tried to feel around as best I could but I couldn't find it. You think I should ask Adina to check it out?" I blurted out, trying to move on from his emotionally charged recollections.

"Yeah, but wait until the morning. Don't wake nobody else up," he teasingly said.

I nodded in agreement and dimmed his light all the way off, before leaving the room.

"Good night," I finally said, as I exited his pod.

"Night," he vaguely responded.

As I made my way back to my pod, I passed by Drea's room. She was lying down on her side but was rocking slightly as if she were stuck in a nightmare. I wasn't sure if I should wake her or leave her be.

I made the quick decision to not disturb her.

I couldn't remember if it was bad to wake someone up suddenly while they were dreaming or having a nightmare or not.

I made a mental note to check in with her tomorrow.

I continued to my pod and laid down without hesitation. Sleep consumed me instantly and for the first time in days, it was a dreamless night.

⸻◄O►⸻

The next morning, I was stirred out of my sleep by the sounds of screaming and shouting. It seemed to be coming from Drea's room.

I bolted up in a panic and quickly made it over to her pod to see what could possibly be happening.

She was screaming and shouting at Adina, who was standing in front of her.

Drea was accusing her of trying to steal her baby.

Adina had both hands extended out with her palms facing Drea, trying to get her to calm down.

"SHE TRIED TO STEAL MY SON!!! WHAT'S WRONG WITH YOU?!" Drea continued to scream.

Adina's eyes darted over to me and Elijah, who just appeared out of thin air behind me.

She looked like a trapped bird, searching for the nearest exit to fly out.

"I...I didn't mean any harm. I thought maybe Little Isaiah would like some breakfast and Drea could use a break. She hasn't left this room since we got down here. I...I'm sorry. I wasn't trying to steal anything or anyone," she pleaded, more to us than to Drea.

"It's ok, baby girl," reassured Elijah. "You didn't do anything wrong. You were just trying to help Sister Drea, right?"

She nodded slowly not wanting to trigger Drea further.

"She's a liar!" Drea spat out.

She had Little Isaiah on her hip and was jerking him around uncontrollably. He began to cry loudly in distress. It was apparent that he might have been beyond hungry and he needed his diaper changed, too.

"Can I take him for you for a little while?" I questioned, hoping we could diffuse the heated situation before it escalated any further.

She was more familiar with me than Adina.

"I'll keep him with me the whole time."

She looked at all of us, in turn, before answering.

I could tell she was starting to ease down off her mental breakdown ledge before confirming, "Yeah...but YOU...only you."

Everyone agreed to her terms and she handed me her son so roughly, that it almost seemed to signal that she could care less about him or his needs.

I didn't understand, seeing how she needlessly attacked Adina in his defense but threw him off on me like a sack of dirty laundry.

Still...I breathed a sigh of relief that the unprovoked ordeal was finally over.

Drea moved on quickly and in her next breath asked for some breakfast to be brought to her.

"Of course," I wearily replied.

—◦—

After breakfast was finished and everything was cleaned up, I took the liberty of bathing Little Isaiah, then changed his diaper and clothes before I brought him back to his mother.

I found a diaper bag, as well, in the storage room, and filled it with supplies that Drea would need to change him and to occupy his time with toys while in the room alone.

When I gave it to her, she peeked inside and asked where the tablet was so he could watch cartoons.

I had to explain a few times to her that this wasn't her original bag and that whatever tablet she had was long gone. She did not seem very receptive to that and irritatedly dismissed me in a huff.

I was happy to oblige.

I meant to talk to Adina about my gunshot wound but there was no time during breakfast. I figured she may still be in the dining/community room so I went to approach her about it.

She was rearranging some items in the large pantry when I found her.

"Adina, do you have a sec? I could use some honest medical advice about something," I approached.

"Sure. What's up?" she quickly responded.

I looked around to make sure no one else was watching before I pulled down my hoodie to show her my shoulder.

Adina laughed at me knowingly and explained that everyone had gone to the training room with Juda and James to get some exercise.

We were all alone.

Even the small ones wanted to go because Juda said there was an indoor playground across from the training room.

After I was inwardly satisfied that no one was around to see, I showed her my bullet hole.

Adina looked at my wound closely and felt around the edges of it. She asked if she could press into it to try and find the bullet. I agreed and she methodically began pushing deeper into the hole.

It was slightly uncomfortable but the pain was still tolerable.

After she found nothing, she concluded, "I don't think it was a bullet that hit you."

"What do you mean? Juda said he witnessed the shot and he thought I was going to die from it," I replied.

"The wound suggests that it was like a bullet, but there is no abrasion ring, and whatever it was, it was fired with a high-powered weapon, but the slug was blunt when it made contact with your skin. It penetrated from the velocity of the weapon but then kinda...exploded at and into the entrance site," she explained.

"English, please," I retorted, not knowing what in the world most of that meant.

She sighed to herself, then started over, "It means that how it went in...does not match how a typical bullet would enter. Whatever this was...was meant to inject you with something or weaken you somehow."

"Like a tranquilizer?"

"Exactly!" she replied, a little bit too excited at the correlation.

She took a long pause as if calculating something in her head. Then her face scrunched up at whatever her conclusion was.

"But it couldn't have been just a tranquilizer. My mom...she was...I saw her. There was too much blood," she trailed off and looked away from me.

"I'm sorry, Adina, I didn't mean to—" I tried to get out.

"It's fine. Anyways...I don't know what this is but it doesn't make a lot of medical sense," she said, cutting me off, abruptly.

I looked at her and I could tell the anguish was ready to breach the surface. She had been trying so hard to mask it since we came down here.

I wanted to give her hope by sharing my testimony.

I wanted to let her know that I had faith that everyone, including her mom, would be found alive and well. Yet there was some nagging discernment within me that stopped me from articulating it. Deep down, I knew it wouldn't have been well received, so I held my peace.

That would be a conversation for another day.

Just then, Solo came bounding down the stairs and burst into the community room.

"It's happening again. Another raid is about to go down," he blurted out.

"Go get Juda," I automatically responded.

TEN

—·—

"I'M NOT FEELING IT," Juda said. "It's too risky what y'all are trying to do."

"We should at least go warn these people," Solo tried to reason.

"No…the least we should do is bring them back here so they will be safe," I countered. "Uncle Elijah, what do you think?"

I had called a quick private meeting in Solo's lookout room to discuss this upcoming raid on another camp of believers. Only Juda, Elijah, Solo, Naomi, and I were present.

We were running out of time to do something if we were going to do anything at all.

Solo explained that from what he gleaned off the police scanners, they were about to raid a black Hebrew wedding. They were projecting at least fifty people in attendance and it was going to go down at around five o'clock today.

We only had about three or four hours to decide if we were doing this, formulate a plan, and then execute it if we were.

According to Solo, the wedding was happening about ten miles away from our tunnel exit to the west. We would have to stay close to the interstate in order to find the wedding venue and then figure out a way to avoid being seen by the government soldiers on the way back.

"I think all of y'all are right. We need to be very careful about who all knows about this place and we don't know these people…but at the same time we do want to operate in the spirit of the Good Samaritan[1] parable," Elijah finally weighed in.

I smiled to myself.

I knew if anyone understood this, it would be him. No one wants to be left out or left behind.

We had to at least warn these people that trouble was headed their way.

Juda was deep in thought, then he finally spoke up.

"It's not that I don't want to help. I do. I want to help everyone and I wish there was a safe way to do that. I

---

1. Luke 10: 25-37

just…we can't do this right now. What if we lose one of our own?"

He looked so forlorn and broken in that moment, empathetic tears filled the back of my eyes and threatened to uncover my own feelings.

I reached out and grabbed his hand.

"We aren't going to lose anyone, Juda. The Most High will protect us and keep us always. His will must be done in all things. Let's all think and pray on this for a bit and revisit it in an hour. Then we can decide?"

"Fine, but I'm not going to change my mind, Raya," Juda retorted, briskly.

I didn't say anything else, just let go of his hand and walked out, reflecting on his words.

I needed to go to my pod and pray about everything.

I had a strong desire to do something other than wait around for more of our people to be taken unsuspectedly. They didn't deserve that, just like we didn't deserve it.

When I made it to my room, Naomi was surprisingly behind me.

I never even heard her footsteps.

"Raya, I'm gonna go warn those people no matter what. I won't be able to stand before the Most High with a clean conscience if I don't go," she spat out.

"Let's pray on it together," I replied.

She nodded in agreement, but before we could begin, Solo burst through the doorway.

"We have to go warn those people y'all. What if that was us and somebody knew it was about to happen and didn't say anything to us?" he said, resolved.

I admired them both.

Maybe this was my confirmation.

"Solo, we need to pray about it. Will you?" I responded.

He nodded and began to pray with us.

After our prayer, all three of us were resolute in spirit.

We had to go warn the wedding party.

"We need a plan," I said, thinking out loud.

We were all quietly scheming the best way to leave without being noticed, get to the wedding site, and return safely.

Then Solo snapped his fingers and exclaimed, "I got it! Raya, you go get some handguns, put them in a backpack, and then meet us in my lookout room. Get there as fast as you can. I'll handle the rest."

I nodded in agreement and watched the two of them disappear up the metal stairs. After they left, I peeked outside of my pod to make sure no one was coming.

The coast was clear, so I swiftly made my way down to the pod that held the storage room.

After opening the bunk bed door, I went over to the armory and pulled out three G38s, grabbed a small crossover bag, and placed them carefully inside, making sure all the safeties were engaged.

Satisfied that I had stored them properly in the bag, I put it across my left shoulder and walked out.

I tried to close the bunk bed door as softly as I could manage, but it kept getting jammed about an inch or two from the catch. I tried a few more times but with no luck. I prayed that no one would come down here and notice. I had no choice but to leave it partially ajar.

I wasn't sure what else to do about it at the moment.

I held onto the bag as if precious jewels were inside and I stowed away up the stairs toward Solo's Lookout.

I was sure no one had seen me by the time I got there.

I kept the bag on and approached Naomi.

She was engrossed by whatever Solo was explaining to her. I only caught the tail end of their conversation.

"—this is going to be the best route but we will have to stay off the highway. Just stay close to the tree line. I'll hook up the wagons just in case," Solo was explaining to Naomi.

"I got the weapons," I interjected.

They both turned around and waved me forward to come look at the map Solo had put up on one of his screens. He used a stylus to mark out a ten-mile path from here to the wedding venue, which headed west off of I-82. We would have to pass a few exits on the way.

He had circled an outcropping of rocks about fifty paces from the 'X' he marked for the exit of the tunnel. It was a little bit out of the way from his lined route so I asked, "What's that?" —and pointed to the rocks.

"That's our ride."

I looked again at the map.

We wouldn't have any problems hiking there but I was still curious about what 'ride' we were talking about.

He must have seen the skepticism on my face because he continued, "We have a few ATVs hidden there. That's what the keys are for...that I showed you and Juda the other day. I have a few hiding spots for them."

Still baffled, I asked, "What ATVs?"

He huffed, annoyed with the follow-up question.

"You'll see," he quipped.

He turned back to the map and studied it before pulling out his phablet from his backpack.

He checked to see if it was charged and after confirming that it was, placed it back in the bag, satisfied.

He grabbed three sets of keys, all color-coded, and threw those inside as well.

We huddled in a circle and Solo began, "Ok...so I downloaded the map to my phablet. I'll lead...Raya, you bring up the rear. Whatever you do, stay off the road. No matter what, DO NOT get on the road. Once we make it to the ATVs, Naomi will help me hook up the wagons...Raya, you will stand guard until we are done. And please no more bird calls. If you see anything...shoot it."

I snickered slightly and so did Naomi.

"Now...since that's understood, once we get there, we warn the people and get the heck out of Dodge[2]. Capeesh?[3]"

We both nodded in unison.

"Let's move," he finished.

We each had a bag of sorts, although I had no clue what Naomi thought to bring with her.

"Wait. The guns," I remembered.

I unzipped my crossover bag, pulled one out, and handed it to Solo. He placed it into his bag.

He looked like he was more than ready to leave.

---

2. to leave a place in a hasty manner

3. Understood

Then I pulled the other one out for Naomi.

"You good with this one right?" I asked her, jokingly.

She smiled sarcastically, understanding my joke.

"Yes, I'm good," she coolly replied.

"Okay...nowww let's go," Solo moaned.

We headed left from his security room and passed the hydroponics room, the training room, and what looked to be a park or playground on the right.

That must have been where all the little kids ran off to earlier.

It was as pretty as a picture.

There were medium-sized potted trees sporadically placed throughout and green modular raised garden beds filled to the brim with wild, colorful perennials. Hanging from exposed wooden beams overhead, delicate vines of white jasmine gave off the most deliciously floral scent I had ever experienced. In between the potted trees and raised beds, was a swing set and slide. There were also some oversized tic-tac-toe rugs and chips in a basket off to the far right-hand corner. There was a dart board hanging from the wall but it was covered in Velcro with smallish green and red balls stuck to it.

I couldn't believe my eyes.

I felt like I was experiencing outside, at the park.

"Raya...this way," Solo nudged, impatiently.

My feet and brain were not on one accord.

My feet began walking slowly toward Solo and Naomi, but my mind wanted to take in more of the scenery.

My feet eventually overruled my brain and I fell in line with their steps, breaking my wonderment with the beautiful playground.

As we continued to march, I looked at Solo inquisitively and asked, "How does it look so much like outside?"

He answered, "It's because of the high-tech grow lights...same as in the hydroponics room."

I wasn't sure if I could be more impressed with this place.

I could see myself sitting on the bench in the playground room, reading various books for hours in complete tranquility.

But there were more pressing matters at hand and we needed to hike a little less than a mile this time to get out of the tunnel. We rounded a bend and were then completely out of sight.

I looked back once more, halfway expecting Juda to run around the corner to stop us, but we continued walking for a good twenty minutes and he never showed.

Once we reached the end of the tunnel, I was surprised to see that there was no keypad at the end of the piped railings of the ladder leading out.

"This is the exit. Anyone can leave," Solo spontaneously answered my thoughts. "There is a keypad to enter this way. It's on the base of the Franklin tree planted on top of this hatch."

"Good to know," I responded.

He climbed up first, swiveled the hatch open with little effort, and disappeared over the rim. Naomi went up next with no issue but when it was my turn, my right foot slipped on the final railing and I felt myself slipping backwards to inevitably hit my head on the ground. Naomi caught my hoodie by the drawstrings at the last minute.

This saved me from falling back but choked me slightly in the process.

"My bad," Naomi said flatly.

As I attempted to catch my breath while coughing, I shook my head and waved my arms as if to say 'Don't worry about it'.

Solo closed the hatch door behind us, swishing the Franklin tree slightly. It was such a uniquely beautiful tree. I could spend a good deal of time just staring at it but we had to move on.

I focused my gaze ahead now as we jogged through the tree line, following closely behind Solo.

After about twenty minutes of walking northwest, we finally approached the boulders.

They looked strangely familiar.

If I hadn't known any better, I would say these were the same large patches of rock we passed leaving the house to get to the tunnel entrance.

"Anytime you see rocks like this out here...they aren't rocks. They're storage units. Some house vehicles, others, weapons, but mostly vehicles," Solo explained. "Okay, stick to the plan."

I nodded and moved about ten feet away while they continued to the rock storage.

I took out my G38 and disengaged the safety, cocked it, and was ready to fire. I left it pointing at an angle towards the ground, while I looked in all directions. I never saw anything move though.

We were good to go so far.

I heard some faint beeping noises and glanced back towards the boulders. Obviously, there was a keypad somewhere to unlock the strange storage units, too.

I went back to my job of scanning the woods.

When I looked again, the boulders were flipped open like a cracked egg.

Inside, revealed four ATVs and two ATV trailers. The trailers were full-sized and looked like they could each carry a large horse or a bull.

They hooked them up to two of the ATVs within ten minutes.

"Okay, we're good. Y'all ready for an adventure?" Solo excitedly said.

No one replied.

Solo sulked and acted like he was so affronted.

I laughed at him.

Naomi got on one of the ATVs with the trailer and Solo got on the other one.

I was left with the stand-alone ATV.

"Oh, I forgot...keys," Solo said.

He got off and walked over to Naomi, handed her a purple key and she stuck it into the purple coded ignition.

Once she started the ATV, I wondered if it was broken. There was no roaring of the engine. She looked just as bewildered as me and looked around the ATV to see if there was anything wrong with it.

Solo began laughing a little too loudly and we stared at him questioning.

"It's on. These are special," he smiled while explaining.

"I rebuilt them with a solar-powered, electrical exhaust so they are silent. The wheels are lightly padded with leather to make as little traction as possible and that acts as noise cancelation, too. We are riding in stealth mode, ladies."

"So basically, you put moccasins on the wheels?" Naomi asked sarcastically.

Solo looked very pleased at that analogy and grinned big.

"They've been under these boulder thingies for a long time, Solo. How do we know they are charged if they are solar-powered?" I asked, very interested in his mechanics, as always.

"Simple. The boulders have camouflaged solar capsules embedded all over and the ATVs do as well...on all the exposed panels, that is. Trust me...they are good to go. Won't be no problems getting there and back and then some."

Solo handed me a green key to match my green ignition while his color coordinated with his red key.

We started our four-wheelers but also heard nothing.

It was truly amazing what Solo could think up in theory and then put to application.

He pulled out in front of us to lead the way, attaching his phablet to a hands-free mount on his ATV.

I looked down at the front end of my ATV and saw that I also had a phone/tablet mount, but I had no device for it. I must have lost my phone at the pond Saturday.

I put my gun back into my crossover bag and slung it gently over my back and left shoulder. My long flowy skirt was hiked up badly while straddling the large four-wheeler. It wasn't uncomfortable but I was glad Naomi and I usually wore leggings underneath our clothes or it would have been a highly inappropriate ride.

Naomi moved slowly into place, trying to get a handle on the accelerator button's pressure. She pushed it with her thumb a little too hard at first and almost ran into the rear of Solo's trailer.

She managed to swerve to the left and avoid it by mere inches. She slowly moved back into the correct position and I fell in line behind her effortlessly.

Four-wheeling was a fun pastime for me and my family and getting back on one was like riding a bicycle.

We moved like that for a few minutes towards the highway, slightly veering away from it when it came into sight.

Then we continued west, passing several exits when the coast was clear.

We rode in complete silence, each enjoying the wind as it smacked us in the face and brought involuntary tears to the corners of our eyes.

No one had thought to bring helmets or goggles.

I continued to act as the lookout from the rear, my head on a constant swivel. I didn't see or hear anything outside of a random passing car here and there.

In this area, traffic was always really light, even on a Monday afternoon.

Solo started to slow down, then made a complete stop after we had traveled the ten miles.

Naomi pulled up next to him and I pulled up slightly behind but in between them, like an ATV triangle.

"We are going to have to cross the road here. The venue is on the backside of that building over there," he said, pointing to a very large whitewashed banquet hall. The sign to the banquet hall read 'The Swan House'.

We looked both ways simultaneously and after about ten minutes of waiting for cars to pass, traffic dissipated completely and we were clear to leave the tree line and cross.

We punched the gas to get across the two lanes of paved asphalt as quickly as possible, holding our breaths the entire way.

It would have been devastating to come all this way, just to get caught at the last minute.

When we finally made it to the back side of the venue, everyone exhaled in relief.

We made it.

Further down the grassy ridge, we noticed the wedding procession happening by a brook no wider than one of the ATVs. Everyone was dressed in all white with variations of blue ribbons and fringes[4]. The bride had on a white silk headwrap and a shimmering beaded caftan that had a flowing white cape attached. She wore a simple golden headpiece that had a small pendant that dipped between her perfectly manicured eyebrows. She looked very regal, like a queen next to a king.

By all accounts, it was a very moving thing to behold.

We parked our ATVs next to the banquet hall on the side that was not facing the street and got down on foot to approach the wedding party.

We were not dressed to fit in, that was for sure, but hopefully, decorum could be overlooked this once.

---

4. Num 15: 38

As we approached, people began to notice our presence and started to look back at us and whisper amongst themselves.

At the same moment we made it just within a few feet of the back of the gathering, the brother presiding over the ceremony asked the crowd if there were any objections to the union.

"I OBJECT!" yelled Solo.

Eleven

NAOMI AND I CUT our eyes at Solo in utter disbelief.

I shook my head at him trying to somehow dispel his words from reality.

"What? I've always wanted to do that," he explained to us, in a more muted tone.

We kept walking closer to the front while everyone leered at us in hushed whispers. We were in the aisle now, approaching the bride, groom, and officiant.

"Stop right there!" bellowed the groom.

His skin was a mocha chocolate color and he easily towered over Solo, who was a good five-foot-eleven. His beard was perfectly rounded and thick. His locs were twisted neatly and circled his head in a most interesting design. He appeared to be in his mid-thirties.

There was an aggressive scowl on his face and he looked ready to fight.

He was agitated at the unnecessary interruption on what was supposed to be a joyous occasion and rightfully so.

We held our hands up to show we had no immediate weapons and did not come with malicious intent.

We knew better than to continue walking towards them and stayed rooted halfway down the aisle.

"I'm sorry. My cousin had a 'TV' moment. We didn't come to start any trouble, sir...and ma'am. You look amazing, by the way," I said, sidetracked by her dress.

She, however, did not crack so much as an appreciative smile in my direction.

"We came to warn you."

"About?" the officiant asked, concerned.

"We picked up on police chatter this morning that your party would be raided by the government soldiers who arrest and take away minority groups. They are shooting our people and dragging them off to some facility to do God knows what," Solo responded quickly.

The groom scoffed and responded sarcastically, "Those are just rumors. Nothing like that is happening here. I heard it was all a hoax."

"No! No, it's not. It happened to us just a few days ago while we were having sabbath service," Naomi said, raising her voice so that everyone could hear. "They killed our parents and dragged others away. Only a handful of us barely escaped."

By this time, Naomi had tears in her eyes and her voice began to break while she spoke, "You have to listen! This is real. No games...no jokes...this is real. Please...you have to leave NOW."

People were deliberating and still whispering in quietened groupings.

There seemed to be some panic rising amongst them but it was still too delayed.

"Y'all gotta leave now. They said they would be here by five o' clo—" I tried to get out when black SUVs and large dark trucks could be seen approaching from the roadway.

"Oh my God. It's too late," Naomi choked out.

She then cuffed her mouth with her hands.

People were staring at the vehicles as if they were trivial things; nothing to bat an eye at. The vehicles made no turn-offs and headed straight for the ridge we all occupied.

Dread immediately entered my heart but I shook it loose just as quickly. The Most High had protected us thus far. I didn't believe He would want us to react in fear now.

I impulsively reached around to my bag and pulled out my Glock and cocked it.

I was determined that things would go differently. I was no helpless little girl this time. I knew I had an expected end, but this was not it.

The vehicles came to a swift halt near the brook, riding all the way down the grassy knoll.

Then soldiers in that same nauseatingly blue camo flooded forth from the trucks and SUVs. Every one of them was armed.

They predictably raised their high-powered weapons and began shooting, without so much as a verbal warning.

I hear buzzing, buzzing, buzzing...then screams.

I looked over at Solo and he was already ducked down, moving with his gun in hand, towards the back of a white resin folding chair. He folded it up in one swift move and held the headrest like a makeshift shield.

Me and Naomi followed suit.

People were running in all directions in a frenzied panic and it was hard to dodge being trampled.

I was trying to maneuver towards the bride.

My goal was to get to her before a bullet did.

She was just standing there in utter disbelief with her mouth gaping. She was frozen to the spot she stood upon; a clear, open target.

A millisecond before I could make it to her and offer what little protection I could, a bullet whizzed by me and struck her square in the stomach.

It was a violent strike and blood instantly spattered out, splotching my chair-shield like it was a contemporary art project. Some small droplets met the right side of my face, as well.

I winced at its warm contact with my skin.

I was too late.

Her perfectly white dress was marred with crimson, like the scene of a mutilating crime. She fell back at once, hitting the back of her head on the grassy earth. Her head covering fell off as soon as she made contact with the ground, revealing her intricate braids.

I looked up and followed the angle from where the bullet originated.

I caught the eye of the soldier who still had his rifle lifted, with a tinge of smoke wafting from the freshly fired muzzle.

His face wasn't covered up like some of them.

He looked too young to be there and he appeared to be in a daze. No, not a daze...it was more like the beginning of a panic attack. He looked disgusted with himself as if he couldn't believe that he had pulled his own trigger.

As I stared at him for that split second, he looked directly back at me.

In the next instant, we both raised our guns at one another, but there was some invisible force that kept either one of us from firing.

We just locked eyes and dared not to move.

A loud POP sounded to my left, distracting me from my standoff with the too-young soldier. His attention must have been broken, too, because when I glanced back in the next second, he was gone.

I looked back to my left and the popping noise was coming from Solo and Naomi's handguns. They were firing back at the soldiers, methodically.

Solo caught one of the soldiers in the leg, then another in the shoulder. Naomi didn't seem to be making any contact with bodies but the effort was still appreciated.

There were outlines of white clothing and blue fringes attached to bodies scattered throughout the area, now marked in pervasively red patches.

We were outnumbered and outgunned.

There was no chance we were going to make it back to the tunnel unscathed, or at all, for that matter.

Everything turned into slow motion before me.

I could hear myself breathing and my heart pounding through my chest. I ducked at the sound of a bullet buzzing by and turned to my cousin.

Solo looked resolved to his fate but continued striking targets to disable them.

I knew his goal was not to kill anyone, as was mine.

Naomi's face was scrunched up in concentration while firing and trying to keep the chair shield near the trunk of her body in self-defense.

I turned to the other side and saw the groom heaving white folding chairs towards the soldiers.

They were the only weapons he could get his hands on but he seemed more than determined to do his part.

He was wailing loudly and chucking the chairs like he was a discus Olympian.

I had never seen anything like it.

His strength was almost barbaric.

The scene put me in mind of the story of Samson knocking down the pillars of the temple[1] .

---

1. Judges 16: 25-30

In my mind, everything sped back up, and I was again present and ready to do my part.

Like Solo, I was resolved to not going down without a fight.

I raised my gun again, pointing at the closest soldier to me. Just as I had his right thigh in my sight, he was blasted in the torso and fell to the ground...but I hadn't pulled the trigger.

I looked towards the person doing the shooting.

It was a close-range shot from the soldier to his left.

Surprisingly, the culprit was the young white boy soldier with dark auburn hair. The one that had just shot the bride moments ago.

He locked eyes with me briefly then lifted his rifle again and blasted towards the other soldiers, picking off the ones that Solo and the groom had not struck down.

I was now the one in utter disbelief.

Was he actually...*helping* us?

He had a feverish look in his eyes. He never blinked nor backed down from his fellow team, turned targets. He didn't stop pulling his trigger until all of them were lying on the ground amongst the wedding party.

I didn't have time to fully process this but praised the Most High all the same.

When everything was said and done, there were only about nine people who had attended the wedding and remained unharmed during the fray.

The groom slumped over to his bride, picking her up gingerly, and howled something incoherent.

He was in an emotional frenzy and no one could blame him for it. His wife was just splayed out, unconsciously hanging from his arms.

"We got to go!" yelled Solo. "More of them could be on the way."

I looked at the nine remaining and hesitated.

"Come with us," I rushed out.

Neither Solo nor Naomi voiced any objections. They just continued in a quick jog towards the ATVs.

"My name is Raya, and we can take you somewhere safe, but once you go in, it's best that you stay. Please decide quickly."

Everyone looked at each other and nodded in agreement.

By the time everyone got their bearings and were on their feet, Solo and Naomi had made it down the ridge with the trailers.

Besides the groom, the remaining eight got in the back of them listlessly. They sat down, all the while crying silently to themselves.

The groom brought his limp bride to Naomi's trailer and effortlessly got in while still clutching her splayed-out body.

I started walking up the grassy knoll to get my ATV when the auburn-haired soldier stepped towards me with his rifle half-aimed.

I didn't flinch nor did I stop walking. He fell in line with my steps without saying a word.

"What are you doing, crazy?" I hissed.

He looked scared to reply more than anything.

Finally, he spoke up in a shockingly deep voice.

"Can I come with you, too?"

I looked him up and down, sizing him up, trying to figure out what was his actual problem.

"You really have lost your mind. No. Absolutely not."

"Please. They will kill me when they find out what I did. I saved you," he implied as if that was an automatic 'in'.

"You shot us! That's what you did. Look!" I said with a raised voice, pointing to the limp bride in the back of Naomi's wagon.

"She will be alright," he indignantly responded.

My eyes got big in disbelief.

Surely, I was having a hard time hearing from all the gunfire and screaming.

"Please. You said your name was...Raya? You said you were going somewhere safe. I heard you....and...and...I can help you! I know things about this whole operation. Valuable things!"

"Yeah? Like what...how to double cross your own side?" I sneered.

He looked dejected, but still very much determined to come along.

"Like...those bullets. They are meant to disable and disorient the victim. They aren't mostly meant to kill...just look like it," he said matter-of-factly.

I looked at him again, but this time with more curiosity.

What did he mean by 'mostly'?

We had made it up to my ATV now and I needed to make a split-second decision.

I took a short pause to think, then sighed in surrender.

"Get on."

I started the four-wheeler and drove up behind Naomi and Solo, with the boy-soldier sitting behind me. He was holding the back bar tightly to steady himself as if he had never been on an ATV in his life.

Solo and Naomi both gave me a 'Are you serious' look, but I ignored them both.

"Lead the way, Solo," I said, confidently.

He shrugged his shoulders, turned around, and pressed his accelerator.

Naomi fell in line behind him, then I brought up the rear again.

The boy-soldier rode in silence behind me, but from what I could hear, he seemed to be fighting a bit of motion sickness from all the bumps we were hitting on the way.

We didn't have time to slow down for him, though.

My mind went towards the people down in the Sanctuary.

One thing was for certain, Juda was not gonna like this...not one bit.

Twelve

ONCE WE SUCCESSFULLY MADE it to the Franklin tree exit, everyone climbed out of the trailers, still riling from the horrific event they had just undertaken.

The boy-soldier slid off my ATV like a dead fish and looked as if he were ready to kiss the ground.

I didn't think the ride was that bad.

"We'll be right back," Solo announced to everyone else, while motioning to me and Naomi to walk a little bit away from the group but still remain within view of them.

Solo seemed nervous about potential runners, especially the soldier.

"Raya, you'll need to take them down, while me and Naomi take the four-wheelers and trailers back to storage. I can load your ATV onto my trailer," he said.

I didn't want to be the one to take them all down and have to face Juda by myself.

My nerves were completely on edge at having to explain our actions to my brother and Uncle Elijah.

Since it couldn't be helped, I just nodded in agreement.

I was resigned to my fate.

They looked like they were about to walk off when I remembered I didn't know the code to get in.

"Wait, Solo! I need the code," I quickly blurted out.

He smirked and said, "Try your birthday."

Interesting.

They quickly maneuvered through the small group, got my ATV loaded onto Solo's trailer, and sped away.

Everyone turned their attention to me.

"Okay, so let me explain. Please don't be afraid because there is nothing to fear. We're going underground where it's safe and no one can find you unless you want to be found. Please stick together and wait for me," I said, like a school field trip tour guide.

I turned towards the tree base and felt for the keypad. Once I located it, I typed in my birthday, all while holding my breath.

Solo sometimes liked to pull pranks on me and Juda. I wasn't sure if this was one of those times. If it was, embarrassment would have overtaken me.

3712

I heard the mechanical beep and saw a green light flash on the keypad.

I exhaled in relief.

I pulled the tunnel's hatch door latch and it groaned against the pressure but swiveled open effortlessly.

I peered down into the tunnel and saw that it was still lit.

I motioned for everyone to climb in.

After everyone had made it down, only the groom was left, still sitting on the ground clutching his bride.

He couldn't take his eyes off her, so he just sat there, rocking in anguish.

"Can I help you get her down?" I asked, meekly.

"I...just...no. I can do it," he said, heartbrokenly.

He folded her over his shoulder like she weighed nothing more than a baby doll would, then silently climbed down the metal railings.

After checking my surroundings once more and being satisfied that no one had followed us, I climbed down and swiveled the hatch shut, until I heard the reassuring *click*.

I moved past the group, shuffling against the wall to get in front of them.

I then asked everyone to walk with me deeper into the passageway. I explained that it would be about a quarter-mile trek to get to the heart of the bunker. I heard some groaning at that comment but chose to ignore them.

The auburn-haired boy-soldier stuck to the back of the group, holding his head down the entire time.

Maybe he was deep in thought or deeply ashamed, I couldn't speculate. I just knew that if anything negative came from him being down here, it would be all my fault.

I said a quick prayer that I had made the wise choice.

We walked on for the twenty-five minutes it took to shuffle to the inner workings of the Sanctuary.

When we passed the playground/park and the hydroponics room, I heard some 'ohs and ahs'. Solo's Lookout was locked and it just looked like any other closed storage door.

Then we reached the stairs.

I took a deep breath and asked everyone to come down the stairs and have a seat at any of the many tables.

We all entered the community room and to my surprise, no one was waiting for us.

Everyone took a seat, gratefully, and talked quietly amongst themselves.

I walked over to Groom and asked him for his name.

"David, but my friends call me Big Man," he responded in his macho voice.

"This is my wife, Chava."

"Do you want to lay her on one of the tables? I will go get some help... someone to check her over," I offered.

"Please," he responded, with a hint of despair.

I told everyone that I would be right back and walked down the stairs to the pods.

Adina was sitting on the floor of her room, reading a book to the little children in a silly voice, making them laugh in return.

"Excuse me, Adina. Have you seen my brother?"

She turned and looked up at me. "Oh, um...Elijah said he got stuck in a storage room. He went to find some tools or something to help get him out, I think. Everything okay? I haven't seen you around for a few hours."

I must have looked amazed at her statement because she stared back at me, puzzled.

"Is something going on?" she asked skeptically.

"Actually...yes....and I need your help. Can you come with me real quick?"

"Sure, let me just ask Gabriel if he can watch the kids for a second," she responded.

She went down the walkway and returned in under a minute with Gabriel.

He was kind of on the short side for a fifteen-year-old, but very mild-mannered and quiet. I always liked his company at gatherings. He didn't say much but knew exactly when to add a good joke.

He smiled up at me since I was a few inches taller than him, then went into Adina's pod to finish the book she had been reading to them.

She followed me up the stairs into the community room and her eyes immediately got wide in surprise.

"What—" she started before I cut her off.

"It's a long story. I have an injured sister named Chava, that could really use some medical attention if you don't mind."

She nodded and ran to the pantry to get the first aid kit. When she came back out, she walked over to Chava, who was now laid out on one of the hard plastic tables.

Chava was still unconscious and her stomach wound looked very serious, even through her clothes.

Adina took out some scissors and began to carefully cut away the dress at the wound site. Once it was fully displayed, she gently pressed down around the area, checking for tenderness, internal bleeding, and the bullet, itself.

She looked at me all of a sudden and said, "This wound is exactly like yours. There is no bullet."

"Yes...so she will live, correct?" I asked.

"I believe she will make a full recovery, Most High willing. I will stitch up the wound and dress it. I'm not sure when she will come to though."

Big Man looked extremely relieved to hear it.

As Adina began her work, Solo and Naomi appeared down the stairs.

After spotting me, they walked over in my direction.

"How did Juda take it? Where is he anyways?" Solo asked.

I looked at him amused.

"You won't believe this but Juda is stuck in the storage room. He doesn't even know we left in the first place."

Solo had a look of bewilderment on his face.

"Really?"

I nodded.

Just then, Elijah appeared, holding a hammer.

He looked at us, then to all the newcomers, and his eyes widened in surprise.

"What in the name of Christ and all his disciples is going on here?" he asked us.

"Well, we went to warn that wedding party...you know...the one we were discussing earlier? Well, we got attacked...BUT...we managed to get these few out. They agreed to come with us and here we are," Naomi spoke up, shrugging her shoulders like it was no big deal.

Elijah didn't immediately respond.

He looked to be calculating something in his head while scanning the new group.

"Okay. Well, let me go introduce myself and lay down some house rules. By the way, Juda will be up in just a second. Prepare yourselves."

"Oh...what happened to him? Adina said something about him being locked in the storage room or something like that," I asked.

Elijah chuckled and said, "I guess the Most High needed him out the way for a few hours, huh? I was able to get him out just now. The door was jammed and I couldn't figure it out for the longest but all of a sudden it just loosened and he was free...and here we are."

He went forward into the room and made his rounds introducing himself to the nine conscious people.

There were eight adults, if including Chava, and two kids who looked to be around nine or ten years old.

Elijah walked up to Big Man last, not wanting to disturb him while his wife was getting medical attention.

Adina looked up at Elijah and told him she was just about done. She was taping gauze to the wound and then pulled the cut pieces of her dress back over her stomach before walking away.

"I'm gonna go get cleaned up and get back to the kids," she said, excusing herself.

I could hear Juda's lazy gait shuffling up the stairs and anxiety immediately gripped my chest.

When he made it to the top of the stairs, the first thing he saw was a woman laid out on display on one of the tables with blood defacing her dress.

He looked at Solo and me, then back towards the scene in the community room.

"Look...we went to the wedding—" I began when he cut me off.

"I can see that, Raya," Juda said, tight-lipped. "Let's all discuss this upstairs, shall we?"

Solo, Naomi, and I dragged ourselves up the stairs slowly, like schoolchildren about to be reprimanded.

"Are y'all crazy? Have you literally lost your everlasting minds?" he continued, as soon as we stepped into the tunnel.

"Bro...we saved those people down there. It was our duty to warn them whether you liked it or not," Solo replied, quickly and loudly.

Juda pinched the bridge of his nose with his fingers and shut his eyes in disbelief.

"How is that keeping US safe? Anything could have happened to y'all. ANYTHING!"

"But we are fine. The Most High protected us. You won't believe how—" Naomi started to say, before Juda cut her off, too.

"This is not the time, Naomi!" he said harshly.

She appeared to physically shrink at his words and didn't say anything further.

"That's not fair, Juda! Don't talk to her like that. The Most High led us and He DID protect us. It's not for you to speak against it!" I finally said, then stormed back down the stairs before he could interject.

As I walked away, I heard Solo say something to Juda but it just sounded like garbled noise to me.

I was beyond upset with him and his overreaction. I didn't even understand why though.

His response was expected. I just had naively hoped he would have been proud of us instead.

I was sorely mistaken.

I stomped past the community room and went all the way down to my pod. I threw myself on the bed, screaming into my pillow so it would be muffled. Tears began to fall from my eyes like water from a leaky faucet.

After my sobs subsided, I wiped my face with the sleeve of my hoodie and just laid there, unmoving.

Sleep overtook me before I could finish processing my feelings.

Thirteen

The situation may not change immediately, but what the Most High will grant us is peace and strength to endure:

PHILIPPIANS 4:7 And the peace of God, which passeth all understanding, shall keep your hearts and minds through Christ.

We may not fully understand our sufferings in the moment but as we move further along, eventually we'll understand why.

1 PETER 5:10 But the God of all grace, who hath called us unto his eternal glory by Christ, after that ye have suffered a while, make you perfect, stablish, strengthen, settle you.

I WOKE UP AT peace and was comforted by the words I heard Dad speaking in my dream.

It wasn't even a full week yet since he and Mama were taken, but I still felt their words and teachings sticking to me like the clothes I wore.

I missed my parents.

Adina poked her head into my pod, then continued walking in.

"Good. You are awake. Come get some breakfast. We are all about to sit down and go over some things as a group. Elijah told me to come wake you, but looks like no need," she said rapidly.

"Mmmmmm....okay," I yawned. "Let me run to the bathroom real quick and I will be up there in a sec."

She nodded then walked away.

I did my normal bunker bathroom routine, prayed, changed my clothes, then headed up the stairs.

There were twenty-five of us now.

Even with more bodies in the room, it still looked relatively empty.

We only took up, maybe, ten percent or less of the space.

I sat down in an empty chair between Naomi and Adina.

Adina handed me a warm cheese Danish.

I was shocked to see Drea's face peppered in amongst the group but at the same time, I was glad she finally decided to leave her room.

An older lady sitting next to her, donning a medium-sized afro, was holding Little Isaiah on her lap.

After how Drea snapped on Adina the other day, I didn't think she would ever allow anyone else to hold her son. Maybe she was truly feeling like her old self, again.

I prayed so.

Juda and Elijah were standing near the kitchen/pantry. Everyone was talking quietly to themselves when Elijah's heavy voice ricocheted throughout the metallic room.

"Shalawam[1] everyone! Welcome, welcome. We just wanted to give the opportunity to get to know one another

---

1. Hebraic greeting meaning peace

and set some order in place now that we will be living amongst each other for the foreseeable future."

One lady raised her hand, immediately.

After Elijah acknowledged her, she asked in a heavily southern accent, "How long will we be down here exactly? Why were we attacked in the first place?"

Juda stepped forward with his back straight and his hands clasped diplomatically behind him.

"We aren't exactly sure how long we will need to be down here but be assured we have enough supplies to last a very, very long time, if needed. From what we know...which is very little currently...believers within minority races are being attacked all over the country and taken to some kind of facility, but we aren't exactly sure why."

"I know why," a voice resonated from the back of the room, nearest the stairs.

It was the boy-soldier we brought down.

He stood up, making a loud dramatic screeching sound when his chair pushed back against the metal floor.

"My name is Ryan...and believe it or not...I'm one of you."

There were some whispers and sarcastic 'hmms' floating around the room.

"Listen. Please. I know it sounds weird and unbelievable but I was forced to become a soldier!" He continued, "A week ago, those same people took down MY congregation. My mom, stepdad, stepsisters, and little brother were taken. My stepdad's name is Abraham Yasharahla[2]. He met my mom before he found his faith. He already had two daughters from his previous marriage...his first wife died from breast cancer. They had my baby brother six years ago and he is mixed."

He said all this as if reading from a worn-out script. Like he had to repeat it much too often.

Looking at him, I'm sure it was somewhat strange to see him and his mother at one of our gatherings. Although it was rare, it wasn't prohibited or looked down upon. All of mankind was welcomed to join the faith if they diligently sought after the Most High and strove to keep His laws, statutes, and commandments.

"After they took my family, they put me and my mom in a separate vehicle and we went to some other facility where they tried to brainwash us. After we completed their program, we were given uniforms and orders to do the same thing to other minority groups of believers. That's

---

2. word signifying people of Israelite descent

why I was there yesterday at your wedding," Ryan nodded his head towards Big Man. "—I'm not sure where they sent my mom."

He looked at the floor for a second, then faced us again.

"My mind was…I can't explain it really…it felt stretched out of place. I wasn't myself but after…certain events…I came to. I realized what I was doing was wrong. Now I'm here…and I want to help."

"But that doesn't quite answer my question," the original lady responded, "Why is this happening, young man?"

"Because the government is afraid that too many people are waking up to the truth. There are more believers in the United States than the entire army combined, so it's an imminent threat to their control. They think certain believers in Christ will rise against them and try to overrun the government."

Everyone exclaimed and questioned loudly why the government would contemplate that.

No one group of believers wanted to take over the country in that manner.

That was not how the Bible told us to operate.

"There are some fringe extremist groups out there that want to do just that. The government will not take any chances trying to distinguish who's who. Everyone is a threat, in their eyes, and will be dealt with accordingly," Ryan continued to explain.

"Thank you for that," Juda responded, vexed.

Everyone turned back in his direction to listen. Ryan sat back down, submitting to Juda's takeover.

"Now...everyone...let's settle back down. Y'all are safe here regardless of what is happening on the surface. Please calm down."

Elijah took over the announcements again.

"Like we were saying, we have some house rules, if you please. Our resources here are precious. Be mindful of what you truly need and don't get more than that. That's regarding food, clothes, toiletries, whatever. If you don't NEED it, don't take it. Next, DO NOT LEAVE, if at all possible. But if you do need to leave, notify one of us—" he said this while pointing between himself and Juda, "—so proper arrangements can be made to make sure you are safe and we are safe. No one can know about this place or we will all be in danger."

"And NO WEAPONS...if you have any on you right now, please see me so I can properly store them during your stay," interjected Juda.

"Now that that's out of the way, if you are comfortable with introducing yourselves, please do so at this time," Elijah concluded but remained standing next to Juda.

The nine newcomers looked back and forth at each other to see who would be brave enough to go first.

Big Man stood up from his chair.

"My name is David...but my friends call me Big Man. I hope to consider all of you 'friends' but you can call me whichever you like. It was my wedding day yesterday to my wife, Chava. Please pray for her...she hasn't woken up yet." He looked down, genuinely grieved, but continued, "As some of you know, I'm a personal fitness trainer and I run a construction company...or ran a construction company, I should say. I would like to help wherever and however y'all see fit."

He sat back down again.

A few seconds passed, and then the older woman, who was still holding Little Isaiah, stood up with him in her arms.

"My name is Deborah. I'm a retired second grade teacher and I'm the aunt of Chava...the bride. I also would like to help wherever y'all see fit. I love babies, by the way..." She pinched Little Isaiah's cheek meat and showed a wide, toothy grin at him.

Deborah sat down then a man stood up that appeared to be in his late forties.

"My name is John. This is my wife, Lynn, and my sons, Anthony and Malik."

He pointed down to the nine and ten-year-old boys.

"We own a farm about fifty miles north of here. Big Man is my cousin. We don't necessarily share the same religious beliefs but anyone that would risk their lives on our behalf is alright with me."

Lynn was the woman who had asked all the questions.

A young woman stood up next.

"My name is Shoshanna and these are my sisters, Stalana and Saraiah. We are triplets, as you can probably tell. We attend Big Man and Chava's church."

She looked over in my direction.

"Bless you for saving us yesterday."

"Most High's will be done in all things, sis," I responded and smiled at her.

Elijah thanked everyone for their time and consideration, then asked if there was anyone who would like a proper tour of the place.

Just about all of the newcomers gladly accepted his offer and they exited up the stairs toward the tunnel.

I saw Juda cross over the room to Ryan before he could disappear with the crowd. After exchanging some words, he clutched Ryan's left arm forcefully, then they moved up the stairs towards Solo's Lookout.

I wondered what that was all about, but I didn't follow them.

Big Man remained rooted to his chair and looked at the table with no particular interest, so I moved over to his table and sat down across from him.

"I will pray for your wife. I know she will be okay though. God will keep her and heal her," I comforted, in a soft voice.

He looked up at me quizzically, then said, "How do you know? Why is your faith so strong, little one?"

I smiled to myself, thinking of the best way to explain.

"I know because I have a testimony. So many things have happened to me in the past few days but the Most High has given me peace that surpasses all understanding. He has saved me every time the situation seemed hopeless. I get it now," I confidently replied. "I was shot just like Chava, with one of those special bullets they're using. I was out for a few hours and couldn't remember what had happened at first. They got me in the shoulder. I would imagine with

Chava taking a direct hit to her organs, it may take a bit more time for her to come around...but she will."

He nodded, then abruptly said, "You know...you remind me of my own sister, Anedra."

He looked sullen and hurt all of a sudden.

"She was there, too, at my wedding, you know. I hadn't seen her in years, but she was so proud of me...that I had finally found the right woman to settle down with. She told me that she wouldn't miss it for the world."

He smiled big, briefly showing his perfectly straight teeth.

"She had a real zeal for the Most High that was almost contagious...just like you. I left her there. I thought she was dead...I didn't know."

Unrequited tears started to stream down his face.

"I didn't know..." he repeated.

"You will see her again, Most High willing. This isn't the end," I said matter-of-factly.

He looked at me through his unashamed tears, searching my face for answers.

"What I mean is I plan on going back out there and finding more people. You never know...we may find Anedra," I explained.

"Well, like I said before, I will help however I'm needed. If it's all the same to you...count me in."

With that, he wiped his face with his hands and got up to leave.

He went down towards his pod...towards his wife.

FOURTEEN

— ◆ —

As I got closer to Solo's Lookout, I heard his voice briefly. Then that Ryan kid responded.

Again, his voice was unexpectedly deep.

I wasn't sure if I would ever get used to it.

He must not look his true age.

I guessed he was about Juda's age, maybe a little older. I was anxious to confirm my guess.

I stood at Solo's door, not wanting to interrupt, but curious about what intel this kid had.

"—It's biological tech. These bullets are designed to incapacitate the victim and temporarily confuse them once they wake up. Like a temporary amnesia. But…it's deeper than that. Whatever chemical is inside…it has the capability of killing, too," Ryan was explaining.

I watched him as he pulled out an ammo magazine from one of his side pockets and popped out the top bullet with his thumb. He held it up to the light. It looked like a normal slug to me but the tip of it was not as rounded or pointed.

"They drilled it into us to shoot everyone, no matter what, but to leave those that didn't match the blue code."

"What's the blue code?" Juda asked, intensely.

I hadn't seen him standing in the corner, with his back to me. I wanted to make sure he didn't see me either so I took a step back, just in case.

I was still very angry and disappointed in him. I wasn't ready to finish our discussion from yesterday, either.

"They gave us these handheld scanners. Here."

He pulled a device out of the back pocket of his blue camo cargo pants.

So many pockets.

It was the size of a handheld calculator. Solo took it, turning it over and over in his hands, mentally checking out its schematics.

"They said to scan every body with this thing before removal. If it flashed blue, they went on the truck for relocation. If it flashed red, we had to leave them there for another truck meant for burial," he continued to explain. "I was assigned to the extraction truck."

He paused to give Solo a moment to process before further explaining, "These bullets will destroy anyone already dealing with a major disease or who is old and feeble. Their immune systems can't handle the chemicals. They also told us to be careful where we aim...to not strike the head or heart because that can kill even a healthy person."

"I don't get it...how can it be so precise like that?" Solo puzzled out loud.

He may have been a tech genius, but he was no master in biology or chemistry.

I didn't hear or process Ryan's full response to Solo's question.

It was something about people giving their DNA away to find out their ancestry and the government doing testing on specific strands of DNA belonging to minority groups from that.

My mind; however, was fully occupied with the memory of my dad being shot.

He was hit directly in the chest.

From what little I could remember, it must have struck him in the heart.

I clasped my mouth with my hands and let out an involuntary whelp.

Solo, Juda, and Ryan turned around startled.

"Does that mean Dad might really be dead, Juda?" I cried out to my brother.

He fixed his gaze down at his shoes. He couldn't bring himself to look me in the eyes.

Solo ran up to me and buried my face into his shirt while wrapping his arms around my shoulders and neck.

I began to sob uncontrollably.

Had I been wrong all along?

I felt my faith wavering and it gave me a queasy feeling in the pit of my stomach.

Fear...

"Please, Abba, NO!" I screamed, my voice trying to reach the heavens.

"Shhhhh....it's okay, Raya. Everything will be okay. There is still hope. Just keep believing. Don't ever stop believing," Solo whispered into my hair.

I slumped to the ground, still crying out to the Most High, and Solo came down with me, never letting me go.

Juda skirted around us and ran for the stairs, not able to handle my emotional outburst. Clearly, after being reminded, he was not okay either.

Ryan glanced at me with a hint of remorse in his eyes then followed Juda out timidly.

FIFTEEN

Do We Really Believe?

Another way to tell someone to 'have faith' is to simply say to them 'believe'.

Admittedly, this is much easier said than done. However, believing is indeed something that we must – do– and not just something we feel or think in our hearts. Now, that statement may fly in the face of modern Christian thought, but it is most certainly the truth!

Believing is an action word – and so, it requires action on the part of every believer.

Many people ask "But doesn't the Bible tell us to just believe in our hearts and to confess with our mouths?" (Romans 10:9-11)

Yes, it does.

However, that is not all that the writer (the Apostle Paul) said. It is important that we keep reading down to verse 16 to get the understanding of what it means to believe:

ROMANS 10: 16 But they have not all obeyed the gospel. for Esaias saith, Lord, who hath believed our report?

You see!

In Romans 10: 9-11 we are simply told to believe but in verse 16 we are shown what that looks like.

Believing requires our obedience, and this fully agrees with the teachings of Christ:

LUKE 6: 46 And why call ye me, Lord, Lord, and do not the things which I say?

More people would be helped in their walk with Christ if this were better understood. Without this understanding, there is very little accountability and the danger of the believer being no better off than before they believed...

JAMES 2: 19 Thou believest that there is one God; thou doest well: the devils also believe, and tremble.

When we put our faith in Christ to be our Lord and Savior we are declaring that we believe so deeply in what he has done for us, that we are now willing to lay down our own way of living in order to take on his way of living:

James 2:26 *For as the body without the spirit is dead, so faith without works is dead also.*

—◦—

A FTER THE TEARS AND the screaming subsided, I felt a peaceful catharsis settle within me.

It felt like the tears had washed away all of my anxiety and in that same moment, I was resolved to remain strong and believe that everything would work out just the way the Most High intended it to.

My spirit was replenished.

My father lectured us all the time about remaining steadfast in our beliefs and showing it through our actions.

I knew God would get the glory from this situation...even if my dad was gone.

His message remained firm in my heart.

His mission would now become my mission.

Solo held me until all that was left was periodic sniffling.

He finally let me go when I began to pull away.

"You know...when we first came down here, I couldn't face you, Raya," he said softly.

"I remember, but why?" I lamented.

"I was ashamed and felt guilty because even though I don't see her much anymore, I still have a parent," he answered.

"Solo...that's nothing to feel guilty about. That's something to rejoice in. I rejoice in it! Praise the Most High for it! My parents will serve a different cause...even if they are gone...their values, hopes, and purpose live on in all of us. You were right, you know. I have to keep believing."

He looked away in thought, then back at me before saying, "I should call her. Let her know I'm safe. I'm sure she doesn't know what happened here and I'll let it stay that way…I just need to hear her voice. Tell her that I love her.”

I nodded.

“Tell Auntie Mei I love her, too.”

He pulled his phablet off the charger to dial his mom's number.

“I'm gonna go wash my face and find Juda. I'll see you later.” I paused, before ending with, “Thank you, Solo.”

“For what?”

“Always being there for me,” I replied.

He shook his head at me as if to say 'Why would you expect anything less'.

I walked down the steps to the bathrooms and went into my go-to purple stall. After looking into the mirror and seeing my swollen eyes and tear-stained face, I quickly turned on the faucet and splashed cold water on my face a few times. I forgot to grab a towel, so I took some tissue and got as much moisture off my face as I could, then blew my nose.

I was ready to face Juda, even if he wasn't ready to face me.

I went down to Juda's pod and was surprised to see it closed and locked by an accordion door.

The door was marked *4D*.

I didn't realize the pods had actual doors and turned around to the empty pod across from his. There was a handle latch barely visible in the folds of the doorway. I pulled on it and the door fanned out. The number on this one read *4C.*

Interesting.

I turned back to Juda's door and tapped on it lightly. He didn't answer at first, but continuously rapping on it for about thirty seconds seemed to do the trick.

He opened the door roughly.

"What?" he hissed.

"We need to talk, that's what," I snapped back.

He rubbed his eyes with the palms of his hands and walked back to his bunk, huffing at me.

My brother looked aged.

He fell back into his bed ragged and worn thin.

I cracked the door so it wasn't all the way shut. The atmosphere in here seemed negatively charged and having the door slightly ajar made me feel more at ease somehow.

"I know we don't see eye to eye right now, but we have to finish our conversation from earlier. Juda, if people need help, I'm going to help...and there are others here that feel the same way, whether you like it or not. I'm going to honor the vision Dad was given by DOING something.

He didn't build this huge place for a handful of people to play house in! Faith without works is dead!"

He remained uncomfortably silent for over a full minute.

"Hello?!" I snarked.

He finally sat up on his bed and replied calmly, "I heard what you said. But that's not happening. We can't risk our lives like that. It defeats the whole purpose of us being down here and I don't know if you realized this, Raya, but you almost died just a few days ago. You're lucky you even survived and now you wanna go back out there and put yourself in that same situation all over again?"

"Juda...people up there are going to actually die," I pleadingly said, while standing in the middle of the room. "Could you live with yourself knowing that we could have helped them but did absolutely nothing?"

"Y'all are just kids!" he snapped back, pointing out to the imaginary people in the hallway. "Going above ground to scope out the house was one thing. You're talking about constantly putting yourself in danger! What happens if someone follows you on your way back and you expose our location, hmm? What's gonna happen then? What's gonna happen to the rest of us?"

My voice caught in my throat, while Juda continued his rant.

"—Or what if you get to all these hypothetical people and they don't even listen to you?! Or they end up being a hate group after all and they try to hurt you?! Worst of all, what if you get shot again right along with the rest of them?!"

He gave a dramatic pause and put his hands to the top of his head, frustrated with the conversation.

"Am I just supposed to live with *that*?" he asked sneeringly.

"None of that's going to happen because the Most High will be with us, Juda," I responded, delicately.

He laughed sarcastically.

"You're too optimistic, Raya. Bad things happen to good people all the time. We weren't called to throw ourselves in harm's way on purpose and then hope the Most High'll save us when he's already given us shelter. Your pride will get you and everyone close to you killed...and I'm not losing anybody else. The answer is no..."

I felt my blood boiling and hot tears threatened to spill out, but I blinked them down rapidly.

As I turned to leave, I thought I saw the shadow of a person walking by the door in a hurry.

There was no point in continuing this discussion with Juda.

I said nothing further and walked out into the hallway, just as disparaged as I was during our first conversation about it.

I didn't know how to make Juda see reason but deep within my soul...I knew he was wrong this time.

Sixteen

I WENT UP TO my pod, which was one level above Juda's.

When I made it to my room, I pulled the latch handle to the accordion door I never noticed and read my room number. *3E.*

I went in, closed it, and locked it, in spite.

I didn't want to be bothered with anyone else tonight.

As I lay on my bunk bed, I replayed Juda's words in my head, over and over again.

What's gonna happen then? What if you get shot again? Am I just supposed to live with that?

I just wanted to sleep, but my mind wouldn't allow it.

About an hour later, someone lightly knocked on my door, so I dragged myself up out of bed to answer.

Once I got the door unlocked and folded back into the doorway, I saw that it was Naomi.

"Come on. It's dinner time and Ms. Lynn and Adina made potato soup, salad, and some rolls," she excitedly announced.

I couldn't even lie, I was starving.

All the adrenaline rushes and near-death experiences had me famished and all I had eaten in the past few days was light breakfast food and protein bars.

I nodded and tried my best to look unbothered.

It didn't work because Naomi intuitively asked, "What's wrong with you?"

"Nothing. I'm just tired," I responded.

She looked like she wanted to push me to spill the truth, but I guessed she decided against it.

She just nodded slowly as if saying 'sure' and left it alone.

I was grateful.

I wasn't looking forward to explaining that disheartening conversation I just had with my brother.

We walked up to the community room and I scanned the room looking for a good seat.

It seemed everyone was present except Juda and Ryan.

Adina was already sitting with the triplets so Naomi and I went over to their table. Once we sat down and said our greetings, Adina got up and grabbed me and Naomi a tray of food, which I thanked her for with a graciously genuine smile.

As they talked amongst themselves, I began to take note of everyone at the table.

Adina wasn't wearing her head scarf.

This was the first time I had seen her hair since meeting her. She had long pillowy curls, which she situated in a high bun. One curl was hanging loose in the front of her face.

She was beautiful.

If times were different, I might have even been a little jealous.

The triplets' skin tone ranged from a medium mocha to a rich, deep chocolate. They weren't exactly all identical, but very close. The shape and features of their faces were similar but Stalana was the smallest of the three, in stature, and she wore thick-rimmed glasses. Shoshanna seemed to be the leader amongst them, often speaking on behalf of them all. She mentioned that they were twenty-one years old, with Saraiah being born first, her second, and Stalana last.

They still had on their all-white wedding attire, which was starting to look a bit dingy, so I asked, "After this, would you ladies like to go through the storage room for some extra clothes? The showers down here are fully functional and the water is surprisingly nice. I think I saw some mini portable washing machines in storage and in the pantry, too. I need to wash some clothes myself, actually."

"That would be great!" Shoshanna exclaimed.

Just then, Solo walked up to the table and sat down next to Naomi and across from me but he didn't bring any food with him.

Since the triplets were done eating, they got up to leave after Solo joined us.

"We're in 3H when you get ready to show us the clothes," Shoshanna said. "We'll let you finish your food. See y'all later."

They all waved in unison and went towards the stairs, disappearing down the steps, like a gaggle of fluffy white geese.

Adina also said her goodbyes and went to make sure her little sister finished all her food.

After Naomi scarfed down her dinner, she said something about hitting the bathroom before anyone else decided to take a shower.

It was now just me and Solo.

"Where's your food?" I asked as I took a few small bites of my salad.

"I'm not hungry," he barely replied.

I knew my cousin.

If he wasn't inventing contraptions, tinkering with something mechanical, or playing video games…he was eating.

"I really thought we told each other everything. Don't switch up on me now, cuz. What's going on with you?"

He sighed loudly and looked down at his hands for a moment before looking up at me again.

"It's Shiri—" he started.

I winced at the unexpected mention of my best friend's name.

Shiri was always in our circle but she and Solo were never that close. They were only mutual friends because of me, so I didn't immediately understand why he brought her up all of a sudden.

"—I've lost my appetite because I feel like it's my fault she got taken. I have so much guilt about that day."

"What are you talking about? What's your fault?" I asked, confused.

"Remember when we were all sitting by the pond?" he questioned.

"Yeah..."

"And I was dead hungry, but they called her name first?"

"Solomon—" I gasped, but he didn't let me get a word in.

"Shiri would still be here if I'd gone first. It really should've been me. So, yeah, I can't eat because I feel like it's all my fault...and I know you miss her... but like, it hurts so bad because—" he hesitated, but eventually admitted, "—I might have liked her a little more than I let on. Everybody lost somebody that day...I lost Shiri and I feel like I could've prevented it."

I stared at Solo, dumbfounded at his words.

I would have never guessed in a million years he felt that way about my friend.

I would have to process that later.

"Look, you can't keep walking around telling yourself that what happened to Shiri was your fault, because it wasn't. I understand that you're grieving. I miss her, too. I miss a lot of people, but there's nothing that we could have done. There is nothing that *you* could have done. You're not the one who called her name and it's not that person's fault, either. She was just in the wrong place at the wrong time...don't blame yourself just because you were hungry, Solo. And definitely don't starve yourself thinking that it's gonna change anything because it's not. You're smarter than that..."

Without another word, I stood up and walked briskly towards the kitchen. I took another tray of food from the farmer's wife, thanked her before I walked back towards Solo, and then shoved the plates in front of him.

"Eat."

He looked at me in amazement for a second, then picked up his spoon.

SEVENTEEN

I OPENED MY EYES and stared up at the bottom rails to the top bunk. The smooth dark metal looked rather dull in the dim lighting of the room.

My bedroom at home was painted a shimmery silver and had purple accented furnishings throughout, which was a stark contrast to this room.

My room here was painted a muted gray and the furniture was black but my desk was white with gray legs. Unusual for me, but I quite liked the color scheme.

What day was it?

Wednesday…Thursday? I had completely lost track of time. It seemed like we had been down here for months.

I did happen to find a tiny digital alarm clock in the storage room and managed to snag it before anyone else. Solo confirmed the time for me and I set the alarm to 'recurring'.

'9:00 AM' it flashed and beeped, over and over.

I slung my right arm over lazily and smacked the off button on the top.

I forced myself out of bed, and stumbled around, grabbing everything I needed to go take a quick shower.

Solo had activated a timer on the showers yesterday, so we only got ten minutes apiece now. I knew it was for water conservation but still...annoying.

Last night, when I took the ladies to the storage room, I took the opportunity to grab a few more outfits for myself and was now trying to decide what I wanted to wear first.

Today, I planned on washing what I had compiled in my small, personal laundry bag. I originally found the bag neatly folded and hanging from my bed rail, the first night.

Each bed had one.

My bag was now full.

I was also looking forward to trying out the training room. I never went more than two days without sparring or working out.

I felt myself slipping slowly towards inactivity and that would not do.

As I made my way to the bathrooms, I wondered if Uncle Elijah was going to hold a prayer meeting at some point. We usually came together on Wednesday nights to pray. Sometimes we even held a corporate fast.

I made a mental note of all the things I needed to accomplish today. Hopefully, I could get everything done in time to help with whatever meal the ladies had planned for dinner tonight. The food prep always went by quicker when there was more than one set of hands in the kitchen.

I quickly completed my shower routine and decided to put on some loose black joggers and a knee-length orange tunic. To complete the outfit, I slipped on some black walking shoes.

I left my hair out so it could breathe.

I had managed to find some flax seed gel to slick my short crop down the best I could and once I was satisfied with the look, I went to find one of the portable washing machines.

I wanted to get an early start on my laundry.

After I left my pod, the hallway seemed a bit deserted to have twenty-five people there. I wondered where everyone was.

I went up to the community room and it had been completely rearranged. All the long tables that were in use were now in a classroom-style setup.

There was one table, separated, at the head of the room and the rest were facing it in two neatly spread out columns. Ms. Deborah was instructing Gabriel, James, Solo, and Juda on her preference for spacing them.

She would stand back, look, then say 'a little more to the left' or 'a little to the right' before she dismissed them altogether.

They all passed by me on the way out. Everyone grunted a 'good morning' except for Juda. He completely ignored me.

I wasn't sure if I was supposed to care.

When Ms. Deborah caught me walking through towards the pantry, she called out, "Raya..isn't it?"

"Yes, ma'am," I meekly replied.

"While you're in there, can you get me some snacks out for the kids? Put them in a basket, please."

"Yes, ma'am," I repeated.

She busied herself placing out some large tablet notebooks and some finger painting supplies.

She yelled down the room towards me again, "Oh! Get me some cups with a pitcher of water, too, please."

"Yes, ma'am," I repeated again.

The teacher inside of Ms. Deborah was taking over and I assumed she couldn't stand seeing the children idle for long periods of time. I thanked the Most High, under my breath, that He had seen fit to bring her to us. She would be able to relieve Adina from always watching the kids and had experience in keeping them reasonably engaged.

I grabbed her requested stockpile and brought everything out in one trip, barely able to grip everything.

"Thank you, young lady."

She smiled that toothy grin of hers and I felt an immediate bond growing between us.

Her honeyed skin, softly rounded body, and perfectly shaped afro reminded me of every elementary school teacher I had ever liked.

Today, she was wearing a denim jumper and a white t-shirt underneath. Her look embodied everything 'school' related.

Just then, Adina entered the large room with all seven of the children. Zara was clinging to her skirt as if to signal to the other children 'This is my sister'.

I smiled at Zara but she ducked out of view, to the other side of Adina's skirt, in response.

Adina hustled all the children to the tables, letting them spread out to any table they preferred.

"Ok, my babies! It's time to learn all about the joy of ART...," Ms. Deborah began, with her eyes wide and her arms flailing about dramatically.

I loved it.

I went back into the pantry to continue my mission for a collapsible washing machine. The ones I saw earlier were missing. I supposed someone had the same idea but I knew there were more in the storage room.

No big deal.

While I was already up here, I decided to check in on Solo.

I waved goodbye to everyone and continued up the stairs to Solo's Lookout.

When I got there, to my surprise, Big Man was standing with Solo pouring over some blueprints and maps. They were engrossed in conversation and pointing to various areas on the rolled-out papers.

I cleared my throat to get their attention.

They both turned around simultaneously and gawked at me like I was interrupting a very important meeting.

"Should I come back?" I asked, pointing behind me and shifting towards the door again.

"No, no...please join us," Big Man said, gesturing for me to come back in.

Big Man truly was a big man. When I walked in and stood next to him, I paled in comparison. I looked like a three-year-old standing next to a linebacker.

"How is Chava doing?" I asked sincerely.

"She still hasn't woken up," he responded dejectedly, but then he quickly changed the topic.

"We were just looking at the plans for this place. It's amazing what your dad was able to accomplish down here. I see some unfinished areas though that I would really like to explore and expand if it's cool with y'all," he continued.

"Like what?" I asked in guarded curiosity.

"Come look. Your dad designed six levels, total, that branch out and down like a beehive. Where we are now is the first level. It houses this room, your grow room, the training room, and the playground."

He pointed to the top portion of the design, to the left, as he spoke.

"Now look over here to the right. What do you see?"

I squinched up my face trying to make sense of what he wanted me to realize. I only saw more squares and a long hallway to the entrance. I pointed to the squares, hoping that was the correct observation.

"These?" I finally responded, more so in question form than an answer.

"Exactly!"

He shifted the blueprints so they faced more in my direction.

"These squares must be untapped rooms. I believe he placed containers throughout this long stretch of tunnel to modify in the future. I'm sure he thought he had more time," he said then paused, not wanting to seem unfeeling.

We nodded in unfazed understanding, and then he continued.

"They look to be shut up in the concrete walls but it's a thin layer blocking their entrances. I want to try and tap into one to confirm my theory. Maybe we can turn it into something useful."

"A laundry room would be nice..." I sarcastically muttered under my breath.

"Actually...that's a great idea!" Solo responded excitedly.

"I can reroute one of the water lines to the room, build a filtration system, and then direct the runoff through it. Maybe you can help me figure out the best way to get the recycled runoff water back through to the hydroponics room or the showers," he said towards Big Man, while he reached for his stylus pen that had been resting behind his right ear.

Solo was engrossed with the possibility of inventing something.

He cleared off one of his work tables and grabbed his phablet. He snapped a quick photo of the blueprints, then cast it to his largest monitor. He used the stylus to circle the area of interest and started doing calculations on the screen, which looked like hieroglyphics to me.

He ran around the room gathering trinkets.

He placed rubber hoses and clamps on the work table while glancing back at the screen periodically. He circled over to another computer screen and started typing schematics into it.

Some contraption's engine started beeping and humming. Then it began printing in the corner of the room but it wasn't printing on paper, though. I stared at it, trying to recognize what it was. Then it dawned on me..of course, he had a 3D printer.

Why wouldn't he?

I rolled my eyes at Solo and changed my focus back down to the blueprints.

I saw something I couldn't quite make out.

"What's this here?" I looked up and asked Big Man.

I was pointing to one of the covered-over areas on the right hallway but this one was rounded instead of square.

"I don't know. I don't see anything about it in the legend," he answered, his eyes searching the plans, perplexed as well.

"—but there is one way to find out."

He picked up a sledgehammer that was conveniently hanging from one of Solo's storage hooks on the wall and walked off with the blueprints in hand.

I watched him go, not wanting any part of the physical bit necessary to satisfy that inquiry.

I was sure he would tell me what he found after he had found it.

I turned back inside the Lookout to watch Solo work.

Finally, I got a chance to meticulously examine his space. Every other time I was in here, I was always distracted by horrible news, tedious meetings, or last-minute mission plans.

I tried to take it all in while I could.

Three of his walls were decked out in corkboard and had various instruments and tools neatly hung and organized throughout.

The room was filled with things that I could never explain. Solo's inventions, some of his tools, and his drone were all neatly displayed on tables or countertops.

There were monitors of all sizes that lined the last wall of the room. I glanced over at them briefly. Besides his casted blueprint and the 3D printer screen, there was security footage displaying for the exit, entrance, the storage 'boulders', the community room, the training room, and all the other common rooms and areas. They presented different shots from different angles every few seconds.

If I had to guess for the outside feeds, I would say that the cameras were embedded into the trees and maybe some were on artificial rocks, because some of the footage was from very low angles.

"Oh, by the way, Raya...when Big Man gets back with those blueprints, I need you to study them and come up with the best living arrangements for everyone. Elijah and Juda thought it best if you, maybe, did the room assignments," Solo finally said, breaking the silence.

"What's wrong with how they are now? Clearly, it's just going to be us down here," I quipped back.

I knew it wasn't Solo's fault Juda wasn't on board, but just the mention of the whole thing set me on edge.

"Well...about that...Big Man had quite the intervention with your bro last night after you left his room."

Solo's eyes got big and cut to the side as he talked like he was about to reveal something major.

"Intervention?" I questioned, thinking back to my heated argument with Juda.

I thought I saw someone pass by the door before I left. Maybe it was Big Man.

"Yeah, when I got to the room to lay it down, he was in there with Juda having a very deep heart-to-heart. He was giving his testimony about all the things him and his sister went through when they were younger and how he made a huge mistake by letting their individual beliefs separate them. He said they didn't speak for years until he finally came to the right understanding that he allowed the enemy to use him in a divisive way and it almost destroyed the love he had for her," Solo blurted out all at once.

"Wow," was the only response I could manage.

"Juda took it very seriously, Raya."

"Wow." Again, all I could think to say.

"He even went and found Elijah and we all prayed for guidance and understanding and that the Most High's will be done in all things. This morning, he told me to tell you to figure out the room assignments," he finished and shrugged, with eyes still wide.

Maybe this was confirmation.

"I just saw Juda and he didn't so much as nod in my direction," I responded, confused by all this new information.

"I don't know. I mean, he's probably still mad that we went to the wedding while he was stuck in the storage room. Give him a minute...he will get over it."

Solo went back to his work and his calculations.

I knew he was fully immersed in his filtration project now and I wasn't likely to get any more conversation out of him, so I told him I would catch up with him later and left.

I exited left out of his workshop and walked down until I reached the training room.

James was in there trying to do push-ups. His arms were wobbling but when he saw me come in, he pretended to straighten up, like his workout was no big deal.

I giggled to myself and shook my head.

Boys.

I went to the other corner and began to do some light stretching in the sparring ring.

I noticed some boxing gloves of various sizes hanging from the wall and immediately thought of my dad.

I had to fight back tears.

He had thought of everything...he had thought of me.

There were hand wraps hanging next to the gloves. I took a white pair down that looked to be my size and strapped them on, then put on the purple boxing gloves that were placed nearby.

Concentrate, Raya...

I began with my footwork, holding my fists up close to my chest and face, bouncing and stepping in place.

I extended my right foot...*JAB*...with my right arm. I ducked and turned my left hip...*CROSS*...with my left fist. I squared up again, extended my right elbow...*HOOK*...while throwing my entire right side into the move.

JAB...CROSS...HOOK. REPEAT.

JAB...CROSS...HOOK. REPEAT.

UPPERCUT.

I was in the zone.

Sweat started to drip down my face and back.

James had gladly disappeared after a few more embarrassingly difficult push-up attempts and I was grateful to finally be alone.

I was so focused, that I didn't notice when Juda came up behind me.

He had stealthily strapped on some focus mitts. He then walked around to face me, with his hands up in the air, ready to receive my blows.

He startled me and I hesitated in my reps.

"That won't do, little sis," he called out rather aggressively.

I looked at him in awe for a second before silently continuing my reps.

JAB...CROSS...HOOK. REPEAT.

UPPERCUT.

"If you plan on doing any more rescue missions, you're gonna have to be MORE than prepared..." he asserted while swinging an arm at my head.

I instinctively squatted, then rose back up, stepping out on a bent left knee, then swung back at him...*CROSS.* He caught my fist in his left mitt.

"...training starts tomorrow at 8 AM."

Eighteen

A**FTER WE WERE BOTH** tired from sparring, Juda gave me a sudden, unsolicited, big brotherly hug. It was a very sweaty hug and while I relished in the love and support, we were both stinky.

"Ok, ok. That's enough mushy stuff," I said, smiling and fighting back tears again.

I pushed him away, slightly.

"I love you, Raya...and I'm sorry....BUT if anyone ever asks...I will deny this conversation ever happened," he returned, playfully smiling down at me.

I smiled back at him and pointed to the camera in the corner of the ceiling behind me.

We both laughed because we knew Solo had seen.

"Oh, I have a witness," I teased, with a huge grin on my face.

"One that I can easily bribe or beat up," he countered.

We laughed some more, then he got serious.

"Today is Wednesday. I think Elijah wants to keep things as 'normal' as possible and have call to prayer at three o'clock."

"What time is it?" I asked.

"It's only a little after noon," he answered, looking at his wristwatch.

"Ok, good...cause I want another shower and I'm starving."

I still needed to do my laundry, too.

We both put up our equipment and walked through the tunnel, past Solo's room, towards the stairs. He was sitting in his swiveled chair facing the doorway, smiling.

"Not a word," Juda commanded laughingly, as we walked by.

Solo just grinned like an idiot and nodded.

I shook my head at both of them.

Big Man came jogging down the other leg of the tunnel towards us, with concrete dust and debris all over him.

"You won't believe what I found," he declared avidly, still clutching the blueprints in his massive hand.

Neither Juda nor I spoke, so he continued.

"—a vault!" he announced.

He waved us to come look, so Juda and I hurried to keep up with him. We had to walk about sixty paces before we made it to his demo site.

There were plumes of dust still wafting up in the air towards the small ventilation holes in the ceiling. I couldn't help but cough as we approached. The dust was getting caught in my throat and nose, and I felt choked immediately. I heard Juda coughing slightly, as well. We were both waving our hands back and forth in front of our faces to make it dissipate faster.

"Take a look," Big Man said while pointing to the right-hand side of the wall.

After adjusting to the cloudiness of the silica dust, I squinted at what appeared to be an actual vault door. It looked like the old-school kind that you would see on TV during a bank robbery scene. It had a round hand crank with six handles attached that were equally spaced. The entire door was a matte silver chrome. On the wall to the right of the door, at eye level, was a keypad.

I walked up to the keypad and tried punching in my birthday.

3712

It flashed red and produced a low sequence of beeps that sounded, to me, like an electronic rejection.

Well, that was disappointing.

Juda stepped up and typed another code into the keypad. I happened to still be standing right there, so I noticed the sequence he entered. It was his birthday.

2409

It flashed red again and beeped rejection for him, too.

He tried Mama's birthday.

Rejected.

Then, he tried Dad's.

Rejected.

We just stood there baffled, itching to know what was on the other side of this vaulted door.

Juda stared at the keypad for another moment, then looked down at his wristwatch before speaking.

"We have our call to prayer at three o'clock. Let's get prepared for that and come back later. We can try to figure this out again tonight. Thanks for showing us, David," my brother said, trying to sound all grown-up and official.

"Ah, call me Big Man...Little Man," David responded, half-humored by his own words.

I couldn't read Juda's stoney face. I wasn't sure if he was amused by this or not, and I wasn't going to ask either.

We all walked back to the stairs together, then parted ways to our separate pods.

Big Man turned back and handed me the blueprints before he prepared himself to check on Chava.

"I think you are going to need these?" he half said and half questioned, at the same time.

I nodded and told him I would give them back to him the following day so he and Solo could continue their renovation schemes. I gave him a big 'thank you for everything' smile before disappearing into my room.

I must have left my laundry bag in the middle of the walkway because I tripped over it as soon as I stepped inside.

Ughhhhh!

I bent over, picked it up, then tossed it on my bed. After prayer, I needed to help with dinner and then study these blueprints for room assignments.

Laundry would have to wait until tomorrow.

I quickly took another shower, then put on my last clean outfit. It was a long fringed denim jumper, similar to Ms. Deborah's, paired with a blue and white cotton striped shirt underneath. I slipped into some tan slides and headed to the community/dining room to scavenge for food.

I was determined to eat something before prayer.

Sometimes the brothers took turns praying and it could go on for a long time. I didn't want to be distracted by my empty stomach in the middle of it.

Ms. Lynn was already in the kitchen cleaning up.

She looked up at me while wiping down the oversized food prep table.

"Hungry, ain't cha?" she asked in a very southern drawl.

She looked back down to the table, then continued her task again without interruption.

"Yes, ma'am," I replied.

"Welp...you're in luck. I got one more thing of spaghetti no one claimed during lunch," she said.

She nodded her head over her left shoulder towards a covered bowl on the longest counter.

I reached for it, thanked her, then remarked, "I really appreciate you taking charge of the meal planning, Ms. Lynn...we all do...and I definitely wanna do my part. Is there anything I can help with for dinner?"

She threw her used dish towel over her right shoulder and wrung her hands together.

"Well, let me think—" she pondered, still kneading her hands together. "—I got some potatoes that need peelin' and some vegetables that need a choppin'," she concluded.

"Ok. Count me in. What are we having for dinner, by the way?" I asked in between large bites of spaghetti.

I was shoveling it down as fast as I could, thinking that I might have time to soak my clothes if I hurried.

"Mixed vegetables, ryycce, and scalloped potatoes," she responded. Her accent when she said 'rice' was long and drawn out.

I nodded and looked her over for a few moments while I stood there eating my food.

I was studying her features, trying to place who she reminded me of. She had a deep butter pecan brown skin tone and her hair was styled in a short coily coif. Her hair was just slightly longer than mine. She was about my height and on the plump side. If I had to guess, I would have figured her to be well into her late thirties or early forties.

From what I could tell in the few interactions we had, she could not sit still and hated to be idle. She was always shifting about the kitchen, cleaning the bathroom stalls, or checking in with her husband in the grow room. I wondered to myself if she missed the farm life she was forced to leave behind. Maybe she was trying to occupy herself as a distraction.

Then it hit me...she reminded me of Mama's cousin, Yasmine. Mama was very close to her all her life but Yasmine ended up getting married last year and moving to Louisiana with her husband. We all missed her dearly and hated to see her go.

I smiled at her memory while finishing my food.

"I'll just wash this and get out of your way," I announced to Ms. Lynn while heading toward the sink.

"Nonsense. Give me that bowl and go on now. Get," she quipped.

She took the bowl from me and turned back towards the sink, with the dish towel still hanging over her shoulder.

I thanked her again, grabbed a bottle of water, and then headed back towards the stairs leading down to my pod.

Once I got back in my room, I looked over at the clock. It was 2:45 PM.

No time to soak my clothes.

Oh, well.

After gulping down the entire bottle of water, I went over to the desk, took out one of the clean tan-colored headscarves, and wrapped my hair. I twisted the tail ends into a fabric bun at the nap of my neck, before tucking the ends in onto itself. After making sure it was secure on my head, I made an appearance back in the community room.

The long tables were still arranged as Ms. Deborah had requested them earlier and there was a sprinkle of people beginning to gather. They sat down in various places, making the place look extra big and empty.

I noticed Ms. Lynn had disappeared from the kitchen and the door was closed to the pantry. Maybe she and her family preferred not to participate in our call to prayer, which was their right.

As I sat waiting, Ryan appeared, still in his blue fatigues, and sat down as far away from everyone else as possible. He then put his head down into his folded arms on the table.

It looked like he was trying to make himself disappear.

I pondered to myself for a moment, trying to decide if I should go over there and speak to him.

I decided it couldn't hurt.

I moved fluidly to his table, sitting down directly in front of him. I made sure I sat down really hard so he would be jarred into attention. It worked because he jerked his head up immediately and stared wide-eyed at me.

"Hey," I simply said.

He looked left and then right as if he was questioning if it was really him I was speaking to.

"I haven't seen you around. What have you been doing with yourself?" I asked, not trying to hide my nosiness.

"I haven't been doing much of anything. Your brother thought it was a genius idea to lock me in one of your...rooms...or whatever it is. I just heard the door unlock but no one was on the other side when I opened it, so I just came up here. So...here I am," he responded, downheartedly.

"Well, to be fair, my brother wasn't there at the wedding. He didn't see how you helped us. Just give him some time. He will come around," I responded, trying to comfort him.

By his easy-to-read facial expressions, it hadn't worked.

Elijah and Juda walked into the room, with Big Man and Solo following behind.

Juda gave me a warning look like I was fraternizing with the enemy. I returned his look with a sneering smile.

Then Elijah cleared his throat to get everyone's attention. Once everyone settled down and a hushed silence fell over the room, he began to speak in his loud thundering way.

"I know this is all new and unfamiliar territory we have gotten ourselves into...but the one constant...the one unwavering factor...is our faith in the Most High," he began, wagging his pointer finger upwards in the air.

I could hear audible agreements resonating around the room.

"Now, I don't know how y'all do it in your gatherings, but we like to give glory and honor where glory and honor is due and the great I AM is WORTHY to be praised," he said in his sing-songy voice, clapping his hands while continuing.

Louder agreements and 'amens' echoed throughout.

"Juda, won't you lead us in prayer, today? If there is any brother who would like to pray also, feel free to continue when Juda has finished," Elijah announced.

Juda exhaled loudly in preparation, rubbing his hands together, visibly getting his thoughts together to come before the Lord.

We all faced Zion and lifted our hands up toward the heavens, in varying degrees.

Juda began to pray a powerful, uplifting prayer. It was a prayer of encouragement, for strength, and for mercy. It was for comfort, peace, and understanding.

It was a formidable prayer.

When he finished, there was a long pause before Big Man's voice rumbled forward.

He added to the prayer a request for healing for his wife, reminding the Most High that He is the greatest doctor and that there is no one thing too great for Him to accomplish or overturn.

As he continued petitioning the Father, I heard soft footsteps coming from the stairs behind me. They ceased suddenly after they reached the top step.

Curiosity got the better of me and I opened one eye, peeking over in that direction.

It was Chava!

She had on a flowing red and white sundress and a matching red headwrap. She was barefoot and her dress swished across her feet, as she rocked slightly back and forth.

She stopped walking when she realized a prayer was being said but she stared at her husband's back with luminous eyes, never breaking focus.

He, of course, did not see her behind him and as he finished his prayer, his voice began to break in anguish, pleading with the Most High to deliver his wife back to him.

When everyone ended with a unanimous 'ahman[1] ', Chava's voice filled the room with a slight rhythmic hum-

---

1. amen

ming before she transitioned into a crescendo of the Lord's Prayer in Paleo Hebrew.

Ahba-Nawa
Sha-Ba-Shamayam
Qadash Hayah
(Our Father Which is in heaven Holy Be) *Sham-Ka*
Ahayah
Malak-Wath-Ka
Tha-Baah *(Your name AHAYAH Your Kingdom Come)*
Ra-taza-wan-Ka
Hayah Isha
Ba-Arataza Kawa
(Your will Be Done In Earth As it) *Hayah*
Ba-Shamayam
Nathan-La-Nawa
Lachaam *(Be In Heaven Give to us Bread)* *Kal Yawam*

Wa-Salach-Nawa Chaawab-wath-Nawa (All Day And Forgive/Excuse Our d e b t s) *Ka-Salach-Nawa C h a a w a b - wath-Ya-Nawa Wa-La-ah* (As Forgive we Our Debtors And Not) *Tha-Ba-ya-ah-N a w a Ba-Nasayawan Ahbal* (Bring Us not In Temptation But) *Hawashi-Nawa Man Ri Kaya La-Ka*(Deliver Us From Evil For To You) *Ha-Malakwath Wa-Ha-Alah Wa-Ha-Tha-paarath* (The

kingdom   And   the
Power And the Glory)
La-Iwalam-Yam
Ah-(man)

Big Man turned around, facing her, as she sang in the most moving voice I had ever heard in my life.

He locked eyes with her and we all heard his voice rise up to meet hers.

It was as if they were singing a duet to the Most High and a love song to each other, at the same time.

My eyes were wet and a lump had developed in my throat. I tried to swallow it down but it didn't budge.

As their voices waned and faded at the very end, they closed the gap between themselves.

He scooped her up and swirled her around, laughing in joyous relief.

Not only was it breathtaking to hear them sing together but to witness Big Man's prayer be answered instantly...made me harbor deep awe and amazement at how good our God truly was.

Praise You, Father.

Nineteen

*B**EEP, BEEP, BEEP, BEEP...*

With my eyes still closed, I reached over to attack the little alarm clock with the palm of my right hand. I smacked at it over and over until my hand finally made contact with the button on top to shut it off.

I opened my groggy eyes but could still barely make out the tiny red illuminated numbers.

7:30 AM

Ughhhhhhhhh...Why couldn't Juda have chosen a more reasonable time to start training?

My body felt like a bag of cement bricks that I had to carry to the bathrooms and shower.

After showering and putting back on my now-dry joggers and orange tunic from yesterday, I wrapped my hair, quickly said my prayers, and then rushed off upstairs to the kitchen/pantry.

I saw Naomi had already beaten me to the protein bars.

When she noticed me coming, she nodded to me and tossed a bar at my face.

I caught it out of the air before it made any contact with my skin.

"Thanks...for the bar and for helping me with my laundry last night," I began.

"No problem. You looked a little stressed out after dinner so I figured you might have needed a hand. If you need anything else, just let me know," she responded.

I was about to tell her to do the same if she needed anything, when Big Man and James popped up, interrupting our conversation.

It surprised me to see Big Man wanting to take part in anything so soon, considering Chava was now conscious.

He must have seen this written on my face because he said, unprompted, "Chava needs to rest and fully recover. I heard through the grapevine y'all are training for rescue missions this morning. Like I said before, I'm all in."

James was staring up at Big Man with adoration in his eyes, then concurred in a deeper than usual voice, "Yeah, me too...I'm all in."

I smiled and shook my head at James, but I figured the more the merrier. One more person on standby couldn't hurt.

Naomi handed a protein bar to Big Man and one to James before we all walked up the stairs to the tunnels.

When we made it to the training room, it looked like we were the latecomers.

Everyone else was already there.

Juda was standing near the far left wall with Ryan slightly in front of him. He was boring an imaginary hole in the back of Ryan's head with his eyes as if he would vanish if he took his gaze off of him for even a second.

Solo was facing both of them, watching this weird encounter and shaking his head.

Besides the three of them, Elijah, John the farmer, and Gabriel were present.

This was definitely a rag-tag team if I had ever seen one.

John stepped forward into the center of the group and loudly announced, "If you don't know me, my name is John...and I will be your drill sergeant for the foreseeable future. If you have a problem with that, feel free to leave now."

He paced the room with his arms stiffly clasped behind his back. He raised his voice to an almost unnecessary yell.

"Today we will begin with endurance training. If you have a problem with that...leave. We will spend quite a lot of time learning discipline, endurance, and stealth. If you have a problem with that…leave. If you don't think you have what it takes to do this EVERY. SINGLE. DAY…you know the rest. Now…let's begin!" John boomed.

James leaned over to Big Man, on his tiptoes, and whispered loudly, "I thought your cousin was a farmer."

"He is now, but he is an ex-Marine. When he retired from the military, he bought a farm to lead a more…quiet lifestyle," Big Man loud-whispered back, while kneeling down towards James.

Solo raised his hand.

"What, son?!" John yelled.

Solo lowered his arm but still asked, "Every day…but the Sabbath, right?"

John looked at him annoyed.

"Hey…if y'all wanna lose a day, by all means—"

"—Yes, training will be suspended for the Sabbath. That goes without saying," Juda interjected, looking at John in a challenging manner.

"Okay, Little Man…this yo world, I'm just living in it," John said, throwing his hands up in the air, yielding.

We could all tell that John didn't have the patience nor the desire to assert his full authority over his younger counterpart, although he could have easily overtaken him physically.

John was also a big man, just not as worthy of that nickname as David.

We spent the next two hours running formations and doing exercise drills nonstop.

Gabriel tapped out after only thirty minutes.

James almost tapped out a few times but kept looking towards Big Man as if he was his inspiration for staying. I was proud of him for hanging in there, all the same.

Ryan was still slightly in front of Juda as he watched him run the drills. He didn't appear to be struggling physically but it seemed like his mind was far away from the training room.

I wondered what he was thinking about.

Farmer John finally dismissed us and reminded everyone to bring their 'A' game tomorrow because he would not go as easy on us as he had today.

Everyone groaned in pain.

John threw hand towels at everyone as they moved towards the exit. I graciously caught mine and dapped all the sweat from my face and neck.

Time for a second shower...

Everyone had gone their separate ways when Juda approached me with Ryan stuck by his side.

We had just made it to the stairs.

"We need to figure out how to get into the vault," Juda informed me.

I nodded and looked at Ryan.

"What about him? What are you about to do with him?"

Juda glared at Ryan again before saying, "Oh, he will be hanging out with me today. We still have a few things to...discuss."

Ryan lowered his gaze to the ground, then looked back up at me as if to plead for an escape, but he said nothing.

I was getting concerned about Ryan's treatment.

I got why Juda didn't fully trust him but I wasn't sure if all this was necessary. I felt in my spirit that he was being honest with us. I wasn't afraid of him.

I wasn't sure what Juda was seeing...or not seeing.

"Meet us at Solo's Lookout in an hour. Maybe he can work out how to get into the room. He probably has some tool or something we can use," Juda said, breaking my train of thought.

He slightly pushed Ryan forward after saying this, and then they descended the stairs together, out of my sight.

I quickly took my second shower for the day and changed into some other loose joggers and a long white shirt.

I had a little bit of time left and wanted to use it wisely so I plopped down at my desk intending to finalize the rooming assignments.

I had promised to return the blueprints today so I poured over the plans one last time and checked my written out notes. Everything seemed to be in order but I still said a brief prayer that I had considered everything to make the most sense and cause the least amount of discomfort.

I planned to house all the single women and children on the third level, the families on the fourth level, and the single brothers on the fifth level.

The storage pod was housed on the sixth level and would only be used in case of overflow. I didn't think that would ever be necessary since there were four hallways of pods that were offshooted to the main hall on each level.

There could be at least two hundred people here comfortably.

I looked at my clock and saw that it was about time for me to meet back up with Juda and Ryan.

When I got to Solo's Lookout, Solo was staring at feeds of security footage, checking his social media pages, and scouring through the news, all at once.

It hurt my eyes to try and follow everything that was popping up so I looked away towards his main work table.

Sitting there was a completely constructed water filtration system for the soon-to-be laundry room.

It was like Solo had just effortlessly finished painting a piece of art or put together a 1000-piece jigsaw puzzle overnight. Like it was nothing for him to build such a complex contraption in record timing.

The room hadn't even been uncovered yet and he was all ready to go with the designs. I laid the blueprints back down next to his invention.

I cleared my throat to get his attention suddenly and he jumped slightly in surprise.

"You know...it's baffling that you have all this camera footage, but still couldn't see me coming," I laughingly said.

"There's no fun in that," he replied jokingly.

Juda and Ryan appeared out of nowhere behind me and startled me, in return.

"That's what you get!" Solo quipped.

"We don't have time for whatever...this is," Juda said waving his hand from me to Solo and back. "Come on y'all. We need to get into this vault."

He then turned and walked down the right leg of the tunnel with Ryan at his heels.

Once we made it to the vault door, we stared at it again, trying to conjure up more number sequences to enter.

Solo asked to try, so we all stepped out of his way.

He began punching in combinations. He tried his birthday, first.

5910

We saw the red light flash and heard the familiar rejection beep.

7777

Rejected.

1234

Rejected.

The keypad was taunting us, denying us access to whatever mystery lay on the other side.

Ryan spoke up, "Your dad built this place right?"

"Yeah," Juda replied.

"Well, have you tried his birthday or anniversary or your birthdays?" Ryan asked.

Juda stared at him with malice as if to say 'Don't you think we would have tried all of that already' but did not reply.

Ryan looked despondently at the floor, then sat down Indian style against the wall to face away from us.

Solo stood at the keypad, leering at it, much like we had done the day before.

You could see in his face that his mind was whirling.

He was calculating, deriving, and analyzing with his methodical brain. He put his hand up to rub his smooth chin while deep in thought.

"Uncle Zeke told me a story when we first started coming down here to work. He would tell it to me every time we came...which was often. I was wondering if your dad was catching the dementia. It was the same story every time, line for line," Solo reminisced, while still eyeballing the keypad.

He stopped talking altogether and just continued to stare at the pad while rubbing his chin.

"Well?!" Juda impatiently demanded, after a long and uncomfortable silence.

"Oh! Sorry. He said 'Solomon...always remember your first major project. It's very important to remember. My first was this tiny home community in Alabama. It was my greatest accomplishment. I even saved one of the old mailbox plaques that the workers tried to throw away. I'll never forget that first house, the street number on the plaque read'..."

Solo reached up and typed.

2818

The keypad flashed green and hummed an electronic approval while releasing the door catch.

Juda, Solo, and I laughed happily amongst ourselves while Juda reached for the vault handle.

The stiff door creaked open slowly when he pulled on it.

It appeared to be a very solid, heavy door. As soon as it opened, a strip of lights overhead automatically turned on.

Juda and Solo went in without hesitation to check out the space. I stopped just short of the door and looked back to Ryan who was still sitting there on the ground, staring at the opposite wall.

"Hey...you coming?" I indirectly invited.

He turned towards me and looked up.

His eyes were blank and soulless. A chill ran down my spine.

He got up but said nothing, and walked into the vault before me.

I entered cautiously behind him. Something was not right with him. That, at least, I could easily discern.

I turned towards Juda and Solo while Ryan walked off behind me. There were rows and rows of more weapons and ammo lining every wall.

In the very back curvature of the room was a glass-encased shelf that had some journals and notebooks stacked up on it. Right above the small shelf full of notebooks were two large electronic buttons built right into the wall. One was green and the other red.

I walked over to the casement, unlatched it, and grabbed one of the journals.

When I opened the journal, I immediately recognized my father's unusually fancy handwriting but as I flipped through the pages, I couldn't decipher anything on them. It was a bunch of dots and lines, numbers, and random lettering. Some pages even had drawings but I couldn't tell if they were designs or maps or what.

I looked back towards Juda to ask him to check out Dad's writings but to my horror, he had a twelve gauge shotgun pointed right at my head.

He pumped it quickly, without breaking his aim.

My heart started to pound and my eyes got really big. I forgot that I was holding the journal in my hand and it slipped to the floor. I didn't even hear it hit the ground. I could only hear my heartbeat.

I stared at my brother pleading with my eyes for mercy.

What are you doing?

My brain could not comprehend Juda ever trying to hurt me on purpose, but as I peered into his eyes, I could see him looking through me.

No...I squinted.

He was looking behind me.

I turned around slowly and saw Ryan holding a .22 caliber handgun but it was pointing towards the floor.

"What do you think you're doing?" Juda spat out vehemently.

Ryan's eyes shifted from me to Juda nervously. They were full of confusion, but looked clearer, like he was back inside himself again.

"I...didn't mean any harm. I was just picking something up to look at it. I...I'm putting it back now...see..." he said, barely above a whisper.

He slowly placed the weapon back in its rightful place and held both hands up by his face to show he was fully unarmed.

Juda lowered the shotgun but made no effort to put his weapon away.

He then walked over to where I had just dropped the notebook. He picked it up with his free hand to examine its contents.

Ryan sighed and lowered his arms in relief.

I walked up to him and looked him in his eyes, searching for answers.

"What's going on with you? Are you okay?" I finally asked.

He sighed again but didn't break eye contact with me.

I could unmistakably see that his eyes were a clear emerald green. They looked almost dark brown when I asked him to come into the vault or maybe I had imagined it.

"I don't know. I mean this is all new to me but sometimes my brain feels...fried and stuffed in a box. I can't really describe it well but I don't feel like myself sometimes. Then being locked in my room all day or constantly followed by your brother isn't exactly helping me process my thoughts well."

I nodded my head.

"I get it. Do you think this has something to do with what they did to you at that retraining camp?"

"Most definitely, but I thought I was mentally stronger than this," he replied.

"You need to talk to Elijah. He can counsel you and pray with you," I automatically said.

I knew Uncle Elijah would be able to help and guide him.

"If your brother will allow it..." Ryan snided.

Juda looked up from the notebook and said, "...of course. We can go to Elijah as soon as we leave."

I rolled my eyes.

"Let him go alone. Where else is he gonna go, huh? There are cameras everywhere, Juda. It's not like he can sneak away," I countered.

Juda flipped through a few more pages before answering, "Fine...I'll just drop him off then."

He shrugged and sarcastically pretended to be unbothered by the thought of the strange soldier traipsing through our living spaces, unchecked.

I rolled my eyes again.

Solo picked up another one of the notebooks and flipped through the pages quickly before putting it back and picking up another. He repeated the same process until he had flipped through all of them.

"I don't understand a thing on these pages. You?" he asked while shifting his gaze between me and Juda.

We both shook our heads 'no'.

Then he stared behind the glass, at the buttons on the wall, with his arms folded.

"Well, I know for actual factual that you don't push random buttons on walls...ever...unless you know for sure what they do. That's Action Movies 101, right there," he continued.

"Yeah, no one is going to be pushing any buttons in the mysterious vault," I said in agreement.

Juda put the notebook he was holding back onto the shelf and closed the glass casement door.

He placed the shotgun back in its rightful spot, as well, before suggesting that we all leave.

I overheard him saying to Solo that it would probably be wise to move all the other weapons into the vault and out of the storage room where everyone could gain access to them. Solo verbally agreed, then we all walked out of the vault and Juda made sure the door *clicked* shut, was locked, and was fully secure.

"Now, let's go find Uncle Elijah," Juda commanded.

Ryan fell into step with him and Solo as they descended the stairs towards Elijah's pod.

I watched them go for a second and then headed to the community/dining room in hopes of a late lunch from Ms. Lynn.

TWENTY

FRIDAY'S TRAINING WAS BRUTAL.

My muscles were screaming in resistance to every command I gave them.

I barely made it through the two-hour session.

Elijah tapped out within fifteen minutes.

Even Big Man looked like he was struggling, but in his defense, he had just used most of his energy and exertion yesterday afternoon opening up the new laundry room.

It wasn't anywhere near finished yet but they got a lot done in order to fit the room with the filtration system. It needed some more work and testing before the washing tubs could be brought in and properly situated, though.

I wasn't sure how much more of this torture my body would permit me to endure, but Farmer John seemed well pleased with himself and his drills.

He pushed us, mentally and physically, to our limits.

I thought Naomi was going to tap out after the first hour but her resolve to be a part of the team was stronger than her wobbly knees.

I was proud of us, at least.

We were the only two girls that volunteered for the missions team and I wanted to make sure we could pull our own weight if need be.

After my shower, I went to the kitchen to get a meal from Ms. Lynn and started food prepping for the next day.

She greeted me with her warmest smile and pushed a plate of collard greens and cornbread my way.

"What y'all got planned for eating tomorrow?" she asked in that deeply southern drawl of hers.

"I'm thinking of a veggie taco bar. I saw some precooked cornmeal in the pantry and my mama taught me how to make homemade tortillas. We've got plenty cans of chickpeas, too. Adina said she knows how to make pico de gallo and salsa and even Drea promised to pitch in on the vegetable chopping if Ms. Deborah can watch her son," I exclaimed.

I was excited about the meal.

Tacos were my favorite.

"Do you miss ya mama?" she asked, not knowing that I had just lost her not even a week ago.

I looked her in the eyes and blabbered, "Like crazy. Everyday. It will be a week tomorrow since I've seen her last, but I know she is out there somewhere...probably trying to get back to me."

"Oh, baby, I'm sorry. I didn't realize that this was just a week ago. It seems like y'all been running this place for a lot longer than ya have. Well, if you want my two cents...talk about her as much as you can stand...to anyone who'll listen. Don't let her memory get pushed down into a forgotten place," she continued.

I nodded, mulling over her words of advice.

"I know it's hard but listen to me. I lost my mama some years back...and I tried to be strong for my brothers and sisters...I'm the oldest of six, by the way...I wouldn't talk about her because it hurt too deep and felt too hard. Now, when I try to think about her, I can't remember how her hair looked or what she smelled like. Sometimes I forget her completely. It's a painful thing. Don't make that same mistake, baby," she finished.

"Yes ma'am," I replied, grateful for her wisdom.

I hadn't ever contemplated the real possibility of forgetting my mama and thought immediately about her face, her smell, and her hair. Mama, with her beautifully long micro locs...and she smelled like lavender and lemongrass all the time. When she noticed me, she always had this look on her face, like everything I did was a wonder to her.

I knew I was loved.

Tears simmered up into the corners of my eyes.

Ms. Lynn noticed the mental reflections on my face. She scooped me up in a big cozy hug and held my face to her chest while rocking back and forth.

"That's it, child. You hold onto yo mama."

All the pent-up longing for my parent's arms and words rushed forth and I sobbed big wet tears of yearning into Ms. Lynn's brown cotton apron.

Just then, John came into the kitchen, nonchalantly.

He saw my untouched greens and cornbread and without hesitation asked if I was going to eat that.

Ms. Lynn shook her head and we both laughed quietly.

"Gone ahead. I'll fix her another plate," she replied to her husband.

He took the plate and fled just as quickly as he had entered.

I wiped my eyes with the back of my hands and inhaled deeply.

I felt so much solace from that simple, kind act of Ms. Lynn.

I woke up the next day glad it was the Sabbath and it couldn't have come soon enough.

I did not regret skipping Farmer John's ruthless drills today.

My thighs and arms were in necessary recovery and my mind was placid and at peace.

Elijah led the service while Juda volunteered to read for him.

There was a tinge of heartbreak in the inner depths of my soul at not hearing my father's voice ringing out when we began, but I was partially successful at suppressing it after a few moments.

After praying, Elijah began,

> There are many definitions for this word, *'life'*, but I believe that there is no greater way to define life than this: to exist with the Most High, for Him, and in His like-ness. When the Apostle Paul visited the city of Athens, he testified to the people there concerning the Most High, saying;

'For in him we live, and move, and have our being' (Acts 17:28).

Without the breath of life given to us from God Almighty then truly, what is life…what would we be, and what could we do? Therefore, true life is to be one with our Creator and to serve Him. As He Is, so should we be, and all to His glory. Because the Most High is the author of life, it only makes sense that we should live our lives to His glory. Get Isaiah 43:7–

Juda read loudly,

ISAIAH CHAPTER 43 VERSE 7…*Even every one that is called by my name: for I have created him for my glory, I have formed him; yea, I have made him.*

Elijah spoke,

If anyone desires any other way, and seeks only to please himself, then that man or woman, unknowingly, desires death, because they seek pleasure in things pertaining to it, and not God.

Juda read,

JAMES CHAPTER 1 VERSE 15...*Then, when desire has conceived, it gives birth to sin; and sin, when it is full-grown, brings forth death.*

Elijah continued with his lesson in great detail outlining how we should live for the Most High.

I listened intently while taking my notes.

I looked around the room and was pleasantly surprised to see John and his family attending.

The lesson seemed to resonate with both John and his wife and I saw that she was taking notes, too.

I smiled to myself.

Elijah concluded,

> So, in all these things we should seek to serve the Most High. Christ, quoting the law (*Deuteronomy 6:1-19*) lets us know that this is the very first rule of life, that our desires should be to the service of the Most High.

Juda read the final verse,

> MARK CHAPTER 12 VERSE 31... *And the second is like, namely this, thou shalt love thy neighbour as thyself. There is none other commandment greater than these.*

We were all sitting in the community room after the lesson, lounging, talking, sharing memories, and finishing our taco bowls when Solo sat down next to me.

He kept checking the time on his wrist watch and his leg was bouncing up and down impatiently.

The look in his eye was starting to make me nervous.

I tried to turn back to the conversation Shoshanna was in the middle of.

She and her sisters were telling us all about the praise dances they had coordinated for their church body. They were excitedly talking over each other and everyone could tell that dancing was their absolute passion.

"Maybe you can teach the kids a simple praise dance to practice. I'm sure Ms. Deborah would welcome some fresh ideas for activities. I know Zara would love that," Adina chimed in.

I was so astonished to hear her voice intermingling within the conversation. She seemed to be becoming more comfortable in everyone's presence and it made my heart glad.

I loved her newfound confidence.

Solo's leg bouncing was distracting me, so I finally turned to him and asked, "Everything okay? You got somewhere to be?"

He looked at his watch again and once he was satisfied that it was technically sundown, he grabbed my wrist and said, "We need to talk."

'We need to talk' was never a good conversation starter. That immediately gave me a sinking feeling in the pit of my stomach.

He gently pulled me by the wrist towards the stairs with no further explanation to the group at the table.

They gawked at us leaving for a few silent seconds before picking back up their discourse amongst themselves, gradually disregarding us completely.

Solo pulled me up the stairs behind him into his lookout room and closed the door once the lights came on.

There was red flashing on one of his monitors in a very menacing way.

It was hurting my eyes but yet I couldn't look away.

"We have a problem," Solo said, leaving me in temporary suspense.

"Okay...what?" I asked, getting very annoyed at him.

"I got an alert on my phablet during the lesson but couldn't really do anything about it," he replied.

"Okay...Solo, can you please just spit it out? All this dramatic pausing is killing me. You're starting to make my head hurt," I said, getting worked up.

I wondered if our solar-powered ventilation system was failing or if we had run out of water or something. If we didn't have enough air, maybe that's why I was getting the sudden headache.

"So, I programmed my social media feeds and police scanners to transcribe automatically into coding every second of every hour, so I don't have to sit here and listen all the time. Certain words trigger alarms and that's what happened, Raya. There is another attack coming. They plan on hitting a group tomorrow about an hour north of here and get this...it's not like it's the 'official' government doing it. It's some sanctioned group called the Syndicate," he blurted out as quickly as he could.

Solo was flailing his arms about, while he explained.

"Calm down. Maybe we should ask Ryan about this...and get Juda's input as well. Did they mention how many people are being targeted?" I asked, my headache starting to dissipate.

It was easier to breathe knowing the problem wasn't with the ventilation system.

"They didn't say...but I hacked into the Congress mainframe...you know to do some digging on this group. There was a federal bill that passed a few months ago that included like one or two sentences mentioning this group being sanctioned and funded by the government in case of 'ethnic' uprisings. Overall, the bill was related to increased healthcare benefits. It was weird how they just slipped that in there—" Solo tried to further explain.

"Yeah, that is weird. Look...I'll be right back. I'm gonna go grab Juda and Ryan. They need to hear this," I interrupted.

He nodded but looked antsy to finish his information dump. He sat down in his chair and started to bounce his leg nervously again.

I skipped some of the stairs trying to get to the community room faster.

When I got in, I scanned the room looking for Juda's face.

I saw the back of his head standing near the kitchen. It looked like he was going for seconds or maybe even thirds, at this point.

Ryan was right behind him, talking comfortably with Big Man about sports or something or the other.

There was no time to lose.

We only had hours to plan this next rescue attempt and I prayed that it went much better than our rushed wedding endeavor.

Only being able to recover ten out of fifty people was not exactly my version of triumph.

I walked up to my brother and said as quietly as I could, "Hey, Solo and I need you and Ryan for a sec. Can y'all come upstairs?"

"Yeah, in just a sec. I'm about to smash another taco bowl. These chips are good. You made these, Raya?

Ummm...tastes just like Mom's—" he started to reply before I cut him short.

"No! I mean...yes...I made those...but I need your help like right now...at this very moment...it's kinda important," I said, while he loudly crunched on the homemade chips.

He started to protest again, but my face and balled-up fists told him that he was about to get the 'Raya two-piece special' in front of all these people if he didn't hurry up and make a move.

He put his plate down and Ryan mechanically followed him towards the stairs.

"Everything okay?" Big Man asked.

I contemplated trusting David with Solo's developing information. My discernment was that he should be included. It would be nice to have a real adult present, which was no offense to Juda or Solo, but before, we always had Dad around to give us advice and steer us down the proper paths.

Now there was a gaping void left where wisdom should have been.

"Do you have a moment to come, too?" I asked.

He looked over to Chava and they had a facial conversation of sorts. She smiled at him in the end so it must have gone in his favor. He started for the stairs as well.

When we were all gathered in Solo's room, he started over with his rant about the Syndicate, the bill that gave them authority, and the attack planned for tomorrow.

Everyone was quietly taking it all in when Juda finally spoke up.

"I feel for those people. I really do…but there is no way we are going to travel that far and we aren't properly trained. We are not ready to take on more soldiers yet. We don't even know how many people will be there. What if we travel all that way and it's like three people?"

"Then we save three people, Juda," I said as if that was even a question.

"My decision is we stay and train until we are ready to do this. We aren't there yet," he said with finality.

"Am I allowed to speak on this?" Ryan pitched in.

All eyes were on Juda when he said, "Nope."

I muttered 'unbelievable' under my breath and shook my head in disbelief.

"No one is asking for your permission, Juda. If we go, we go. If you stay, you stay. Period," I fumed.

Juda had an incredulous look on his face towards me as if he was literally disgusted by my words.

He stormed out, even leaving his Ryan shadow behind.

We all stood there silently until Ryan asked very quietly, "So...can I go...grab some more food now...or—."

Big Man and Solo told him, at the same time, that it sounded like a great idea to them and that they wouldn't mind joining. They all dashed off towards the stairs, leaving me standing there with my frustrated thoughts.

I marched towards Juda's pod.

I wasn't going to let this fester between us, again. We both knew how to hold grudges and could each go for long periods of silent treatment.

I knew that was not Christ-like and had to resist the urge to stomp off to my room like an angry child.

His door was locked when I tried to push it open.

I exhaled loudly, checked my spirit, and then timidly knocked.

No answer.

I kept knocking and knocking until I heard forceful movement coming from behind the door. Juda pulled the door open with exaggerated force.

He looked down at me, clearly irritated that I had come at all. He then retreated back inside and plopped down angrily on his bunk.

I walked in, while Juda lay on his back, throwing what looked like a ball of socks up into the air, catching it over and over again.

I watched him do this a few times before I was able to swallow my pride and speak.

"We are going to leave in the morning to head to the attack site. I hope you change your mind and come."

"I thought I made it perfectly clear that no one was going back up there...not yet," he retorted.

I chuckled slightly under my breath before replying, "I meant what I said...I didn't come down here to beg your permission. This mission is happening with or without you, bro."

He sat straight up in his bunk, abandoning his sock ball beside him.

He looked at me then turned his face and scoffed.

I lowered my voice and humbly asked, "What are you really so afraid of, Juda?"

He stood abruptly.

"Losing you," he simply said. "I'm afraid of losing you and letting everyone else down. I keep trying to tell you that but you don't seem to be listening."

His countenance fell suddenly and his shoulders hunched forward. He looked like a wizen old man.

The pressure of it all was deflating him.

"I wanted to believe you, you know? About mom and dad...but you were wrong and it will be so much worse if I have to lose you, too...and everyone is looking up to me now...because I'm the 'pastor's son'. They think I just KNOW what to do when I don't. All I know right now is that I can keep y'all safe by staying down here...and I'm trying...I'm trying to do what is right and I feel like you're steadily trying to tear me down," Juda said, then sighed loudly.

He looked very close to tears but if he was, he didn't let them fall.

I shook my head at his confession and replied, "I'm not trying to tear you down, J. I'm trying to build us up. Why can't you see that?"

"Because you are reckless...and I can't lose anybody else, Raya. I cannot."

"Juda, you are afraid of something you can't control," I reasoned.

There was the real problem. He was afraid of death.

"People die, Juda," I started, swallowing the sob forming in my throat.

I thought of our parents, who may very well be dead after all.

I continued, trying to console my brother as best I could, "It hurts, but death is a part of life. You can't control who God has plans for...in that regard. You'll never be able to control that, and you'll never be able to properly lead us if you're constantly living in fear. I'm not afraid to die. Why are you?"

My brother stared at me in silence for a moment, pondering his thoughts, and for a second I thought maybe I had actually touched his rationality.

Then he spat out, "Because people who aren't afraid to die live foolishly and take innocent people out with them."

"No," I quickly countered, "people who don't live in fear have assurance in salvation and they know there's a better life waiting for them after this one...but you can hide down here like a coward if you want to! I know I'd 'rather die manfully for my brethren than stain my honor'...Judas Maccabees said something like that, didn't he? I can't believe you were named after him!"

That apparently struck a nerve with him because Juda shoved me like a little kid ready to brawl.

"Fight me," he challenged.

Once I regained my balance, I stepped up, closing the space in between us, and pushed him right back.

"Trust me, you don't want none of this..." I warned, recalling all the times I beat him in sparring practice.

We were then locked into an intense staring contest but no one was yielding.

Since I was shorter, I thought to stand on my tiptoes to match him and that sudden tiny gesture seemed to break the tension between us because we both began laughing.

Juda turned and sat back down on his bed and started throwing his sock ball in the air again.

"See. I knew you ain't want no smoke," I quipped, still laughing slightly.

He shook his head in agreement.

"Even Christ knew when to hide himself from a dispute," he snapped back.

Somehow, I perceived that he wasn't talking about us directly anymore.

"Yeah, well...you're running from the wrong fight," I countered.

Juda groaned, "There's nothing I can say to change your mind is there?"

"No," I answered, honestly.

"Well, then, I have nothing left to say to you. Please go away," he said, abruptly ending our conversation.

I had to admit, that dismissal cut deep, but I was determined to do the right thing with or without my brother and I could feel in my spirit that I had chosen wisely.

I quietly walked out of his pod, closing the door behind me.

TWENTY-ONE

The vision needed for where we desire to go can only be given to us by the son of God: No man, woman, or child can provide it unless it is what he has shown them in His word and at His mouth. PROVERBS 29: 18 Where there is no vision, the people perish: but he that keepeth the law, happy is he.

What allowing Christ to be our eyes in these last days means is being obedient and keeping the Law of Christ. For that is our sight, but many people look to man and other sources, which are not ordained of God in order to find direction for their lives, some ignorantly, and some knowingly, but all of them vainly...

I flipped through the little burgundy Bible that was tucked into my desk.

I imagined that it was something my father touched and placed here with great care. More than ever, I wanted to talk to him like we used to do at the kitchen table on late nights when I couldn't sleep and he was up studying.

He never turned down any of my random questions about anything. He never made me feel like I was wasting his time with my immature musings.

He listened and answered me, not as a child, but as a person who needed to be molded carefully and skillfully.

I looked over at the clock.

It was almost midnight, but my mind was churning and I couldn't sleep.

I pushed back my chair, trying to make as little noise as possible.

I decided to go sit at the park and read my Bible until maybe my brain would stop resisting, and sleep would take over.

After peeking both ways down the long corridor and confirming that no one would notice me, I started to walk toward the short stairway.

Noises coming from Drea's room stopped me in my tracks. I stood there outside her closed door listening for a moment, trying to distinguish what that sound was.

After a few seconds, I realized that Drea was wailing for her husband, asking God 'why'.

I wanted to go in and comfort her and let her know that she wasn't alone. I wanted to tell her that everything would be okay, but I quickly shoved the thought down and continued walking towards the stairs.

Empty words would only hurt worse and I didn't know how I could have approached her anyway, being that I'm only sixteen and not married yet.

I lost my parents, but she lost her husband.

Even I knew there was a major, unrelatable difference.

I said a quiet prayer for her as I continued on my short journey to the park.

As I approached Solo's room, I saw lights blinking and bright blue sparks flying. It was so noticeable against the stark dimness of the tunnel that it piqued my curiosity. Solo must have been up late working on another project.

I stepped into his doorway, clutching my little burgundy Bible loosely at my side.

He was wearing safety goggles and using a handheld welding torch, while hunched over one of his work benches. He was holding a skinny metal rod in his other hand.

The rod looked more like a thin, black metallic chopstick than anything else and he was touching something very flat with it while lighting the torch, periodically.

"What's up?" I asked, rather noisily.

He visibly jumped and almost torched a hole in the table.

"Geezus—" he breathed out.

Solo put the stick down and clutched at his chest like I had given him a heart attack.

"Don't be so dramatic, turd. What you doing there?" I bantered, trying to get a better glimpse of the project beside him.

After he finished his theatrics, he explained, "I'm making you a gift...and it's supposed to be a surprise, so be gone with you."

He used his elbow to cover up whatever small, flat thing he was manipulating.

I gave him a forced smile, disappointed that he had no intention of telling me right then and there.

I pushed away from the doorframe without saying goodbye and carried on toward my true destination.

As I got closer to the park, I began to hear muted voices coming from across the hall in the training room.

Why are there so many people up?

I drew near the entryway of the training room but didn't go in. I just lurked there for a few seconds, deciding if I should move on or enter. I didn't want to interrupt anyone else like I had done Solo.

I immediately recognized Big Man's strong voice and was going to dismiss the interaction and keep going, but I paused when I realized that Juda was his interlocutor.

I peeked, ever so slightly, around the corner of the doorway to get a better view of them.

Juda was standing at an angle, with his back to me, but I could still clearly see his hands entwined in boxing tape and he was wearing his wrist wraps. The large punching bag in front of him was still swinging slightly, as he'd just had a one-sided battle with it, only seconds before.

Big Man, detecting my movement at the doorway, glanced at me quickly, but then continued his conversation with Juda as if he hadn't noticed me at all. I then stepped back out of view, planning to walk away after being caught, but I heard him voice my name.

He said it in his sentence to Juda but the way he announced it had double meaning, like he was telling me to stay put.

"No, you don't understand —" Juda whined before Big Man cut him off.

"—Raya. You don't want to lose her…I do understand. I understand perfectly, but listen, Little Man…if you keep acting the way you're acting, you're going to lose her anyway. You have to handle your sister with humility. You think she'll want to keep dealing with you if you act like a hothead all the time?"

Big Man is right. I didn't like this new version of Juda.

My brother used to be easygoing. He would joke around a lot and he was fun to be around. Now, he was just too hard to reach and acted like the weight of everything was solely on him.

Juda lowered his gaze, clenching his jaw. He raised his fists again to punch at the bag some more.

Big Man continued, "Look, if those three hadn't come for us when they did… I don't know what would have happened to me and my family…my *wife*. I don't know where we would be now so I'm grateful. I praise the Most High for those kids and if He has called them to do what they're doing now, then the last thing you want to do is stand between them and their God-given purpose. You don't want to become an enemy of the Most High unknowingly...do you?"

Juda stopped his repetitive pounding of the bag and was quiet for a long time before I heard him sniffling in response. I watched as he lifted his wrapped hands to swipe violently at his face.

Is my brother...crying?

"No," he answered, finally, "I'm just scared, David. Her and Solo are all I have left...I've lost so many people that I care about already. I just feel like I want to set the whole world on fire!"

Big Man grabbed Juda cautiously by the shoulders, before pulling him into a lengthy, comforting hug. Juda seemed to melt into his arms, releasing all his tension onto Big Man.

"I know...I know, and it's okay to be scared sometimes. It's normal, but God hasn't given us the spirit of fear. Raya has come this far...I don't believe the Most High intends to leave her just now. Have a little faith, Little Man."

He let go of my brother, but there was something about him that clenched at my heart.

Maybe it was the way Big Man hugged him or the way he got Juda to finally release his pent-up tears. I couldn't place it, but he reminded me of...*Dad.*

Even though his words weren't directed at me, I still felt their effects.

I felt comforted and thankful as I blinked back the tears pooling in my eyes.

The Most High is giving back to us what we have lost.

He sent us a father figure.

I turned away and walked quietly back to my pod.

I no longer needed the solitude of the park to distract me. I could now welcome sleep and be fully prepared for whatever tomorrow's mission would bring.

Twenty-Two

— · —

I NSTEAD OF 8 AM training, the group went to Solo's Lookout hoping to get more details about today's raid attempt.

Everyone was on edge about going topside and the potential danger, but we all knew we had to at least try to get those innocent people out before it was too late.

Since Solo had been up late, I was concerned that he might have overslept, which he was known to do. Anytime he was hyper-focused on a project, he wouldn't rest until it was completed, literally.

I had hoped he would have checked all his feeds again to glean any new information that he could.

Anything at all would help us.

To my relief, he was already sitting at the monitors but with large, dark circles underneath his eyes. I immediately felt a tinge of guilt that we were asking so much of him all the time.

It appeared that I was the last one to arrive when I thought I had come early.

I had at least five minutes until training would have started.

When I stepped inside, I saw Elijah, Big Man, Farmer John, Naomi, Ryan, and James, but still no Juda.

Elijah was sitting in a chair next to Solo and seemed a bit too relaxed for someone who was about to risk his life. He also did not appear to be dressed properly to leave for any mission. I automatically assumed that he wanted to be in the 'know' but did not plan to be included in the actual execution of our rescue pursuit.

Everyone else stood in a semi-circle around the monitors and Solo, waiting for any updates he may have secured.

Solo rubbed sleep from his eyes and looked at me to signal to close the door.

I guess Juda really isn't coming.

I closed the door, but we all had enough space to remain standing comfortably, without being cramped by all the tools and devices inside.

When everyone had settled down, Solo began with his intel report.

"I was able to cross reference some social media feeds with the police scanner info and narrowed the time of the assault down to between one and three o'clock. It's gonna go down at the Wheelific Belle skating rink, which is roughly eighteen miles from our exit hatch. According to this lady's profile—" He swiveled around in his chair and pulled up the social media page of a very light-skinned female who appeared more Hispanic than anything.

She had medium-sized box braids that were partially covered by a hot pink bandana and her profile name read Lillian Yisrael[1] . I would have guessed she was in her late twenties or early thirties.

"She sent out an e-vite to at least forty people. I can only see that twenty-five or so RSVP'd an acceptance," he informed us.

"How are we going to get them all out of the skating rink without causing a scene though?" Naomi thoughtfully asked.

She was standing there with her arms folded across her chest. She looked like she was ready to shoot down any idiotic idea that could possibly be presented and she definitely did not disappoint.

---

1. word meaning people of Israelite descent

As soon as James raised his hand to give a suggestion, she immediately cut her eyes at him and simply said 'Nope' before he could even voice it.

His face instantly flattened and he blew out the breath that she wouldn't let him waste.

Big Man, without looking at him, patted him on the shoulders like he was proud of him anyway for trying.

Solo continued with his report, ignoring Naomi's question, indirectly, while seeming to answer it in the end.

"They are bringing in three Syndicate soldiers to pose as local officers. After the group is 'arrested' they will be transported off-site to God knows where. I don't think their goal is to cause a complete scene when other civilians are present. I'm sure they aren't gonna just pull up and start shooting like they did us. These operations are meant to be on the low and shooting up a skating rink isn't exactly anyone's definition of quiet."

Ryan's oddly deep voice reverberated throughout the room, "We will have to attack first. We are...I mean...they are trained to leave absolutely no one behind. Even if we somehow got to the people first, they aren't just gonna let us go on our merry little way and say 'Oh well'. If the quota is thirty...you bring back thirty...either dead or alive...or you don't come back until you do."

We let this new development marinate for a second before trying again to decide the best route to take.

"I have an idea," I finally uttered.

All eyes turned to me.

I swallowed down all the self-imposed pressure of being the one everyone relied on to come up with the most viable solution.

Then I suggested, "How about one or two of us go inside and pretend to be with the party...you know...to tell them we are going to get arrested? Hear me out...I know it sounds crazy, but...we let the 'officers' take us outside the skating rink...that way the whole group is together and not spread all over the place inside and we won't cause a huge scene...then the rest of the crew will ambush the Syndicate soldiers before they take us away—"

"Yes! I volunteer!" insisted Naomi right away, almost jumping with giddiness.

It seemed like she was too excited at the prospect of going skating one last time.

"Wait a second...just wait a second," Elijah spoke up, at last. "And just how do y'all plan on taking down three highly trained soldiers and it's just—" he began motioning his arms towards all of us collectively like we were the 'B' team.

"Don't worry bout it, sweetheart," John militantly countered, affronted by Elijah's lack of confidence in our abilities.

Solo rubbed at his eyes again, then said, "Okay, I think that's about the best plan we are gonna get under the circumstances. Let's go with that. I'll be right back with your Sanctuary-issued weapons...please check them back in upon return."

He said this like he was a flight attendant giving boarding instructions.

I couldn't help but smirk at him.

Solo got up and exited the room to go get the weapons from the vault.

Elijah left the room soon after, seeing that the planning part was complete. I was sure he wanted to go convey everything to Juda before we left.

While we waited for Solo to get back, I took the opportunity to question Ryan on how he was holding up down here. It had been almost a week since he practically begged to come with us, but I noticed that he was still in his ugly blue camo getup.

He looked unkempt and out of place.

I was sure that's exactly how my brother wanted it to remain, too.

I faced him and asked, privately, "How are you feeling?"

"—like a prisoner," he coldly replied, with his arms crossed like Naomi's.

"I'm sorry," I answered, remorsefully.

Solo returned before I could squeeze out any more sympathetic words.

Our heart-to-heart would have to wait.

Solo gave everyone a thin, black drawstring sports bag that could be worn like a mini backpack.

Everyone, except me.

He announced that guns equipped with silencers were already loaded inside, along with two bottles of water, a granola bar, and a compass.

He said with a sleepy grin, "Complimentary snacks...courtesy of Ms. Lynn."

Everyone took the bag that was given to them, put it on, and headed out the door.

Solo hesitated to hand me anything and waited until everyone had left the room, so I was forced to stay behind for a second.

With the room cleared out, he handed me the same black drawstring bag, but it felt incredibly light to have an automatic weapon loaded inside.

I lifted it up and down for a second to feel the weight.

"Where is my gun, Solo?" I asked, reactively.

"I didn't put one in. I have a feeling that you will be better off without it this time. Please, just trust me," he said.

He said it so convincingly, that I didn't even bother arguing with him. I just nodded my head and trusted that he had a good reason.

"But, hey...I did put a Taser in there, just in case. Oh, and this is for you. It's my top secret surprise...the one I stayed up all night working on...just for you," he said, trying to make me feel guilty that he was so tired.

He had succeeded.

He looked terrible and I felt completely responsible.

Solo handed me a holographic-looking piece of paper that had two, barely visible dots on it. They were a matted black color and I did not understand the relevance.

Solo looked beside himself with pride before explaining quickly, "These are moles."

He just stood there smiling like an idiot and bouncing on the balls of his feet.

I waited for more of an explanation but it didn't come.

"You really gotta stop with the dramatic scene breaks, Solo," I finally said.

I was beginning to feel like everyone else was too far ahead of us now.

We would have to hoof it to catch up if he kept this up.

"These are moles! You know, for your face, or whatever. But they are also...special long-range comms. You wear one near your mouth and the other near your ear, so you can talk to me and hear me responding. It will look like you have two tiny...normal...run-of-the-mill moles and no one will ever know the difference!" he eagerly explained.

"That's pretty cool, Solo, but why do I need these?" I asked, concerned.

"Well...because I'm not going—"

Again, with the pausing.

" —I did a lot of thinking and I prayed about it and I'm being led to 'wait'," he responded.

I was perplexed by this sudden change of heart, but I didn't dare question his purpose.

I didn't want to do the very thing Juda accused me of doing...being reckless and taking innocent people down with me.

"I will be with you every step of the way on the comms...besides, I have access to the CCTV for the rink and all the surrounding businesses...and now, I get to use my drone to help guide you there and back safely."

Solo was starting to 'nerd' out on me.

When he got like that, it was best to slowly walk away, which I started to do.

I took a few steps backward with each word he spoke until I made it past his door's threshold.

I was just about to turn and bolt, when he added, "The keys to the ATVs are in your bag, Raya. And the code to the storage boulder is your birthday."

I couldn't resist a few more questions.

"Why my birthday?" I asked, genuinely curious.

"All of our birthdays work, but when you use your own, I get an alert that it's you that's accessing whatever it is. It's so there is a record of who is coming and going, that's all," he explained.

"Oh...and one more thing. How 'long' exactly is long-range for these...moles?" I asked, hoping to myself, that I could resist the urge to ask anything else.

I was falling behind and would have to run at full speed to catch up with the others.

I started to jog down the tunnel towards the exit.

I wasn't exactly waiting for his answer when he called out his reply from the door, and I heard him in the distance.

"You can go all the way to Africa and I will still hear you."

Good to know.

TWENTY-THREE

ALTHOUGH SOLO DELAYED ME considerably, I was able to catch up to the team within a few minutes and we made it out of the exit hatch without a hitch.

Big Man climbed the hatch railings first and swiveled the door open. Bright morning light poured down on us.

At first, it was unnerving but after our eyes adjusted, the light became a welcomed shower of sunshine.

Once Ryan made it up and over the opening, he took in a deep breath of fresh air in a manner that conveyed *'ah, freedom'*.

The gesture was not lost on me and I felt deep embarrassment that we had caused him to feel like he had traded in one captivity for another.

I heard a slight whirring sound above us, so I looked up to find the source.

It was Solo's drone.

I almost couldn't see it because it was painted sky blue. He must have brought it out last night or earlier this morning.

After securing the exit, John and Big Man acted as our lookout points. John was in front, with me, while Big Man brought up the rear.

I tried to pass the time by conversing with Farmer John but his facial expressions upon hearing my voice made it abundantly clear that he was not interested in chitchat, only survival.

We made it to the storage boulders with no interference and I successfully opened them using my birthday code.

I thought about what Solo said about keeping records and just then remembered to put on the moles.

While I did that, the rest of the team began connecting the two trailers to ATVs, leaving two standalones.

"Hello, hello…testing, testing," I said loudly to myself, after putting one mole on the right corner of my upper lip and the other on my left temple, closest to my ear.

Everyone turned to look at me like I was insane.

I just smiled apologetically and pointed to my ear like I had on a Bluetooth earpiece.

"Solo gave me comms. He's gonna talk us through everything," I eagerly explained.

"Oh, cool...we got 'a guy in the chair'," James said, excitedly.

No doubt, he had been watching too many action thrillers.

I turned away from him and rolled my eyes.

Then I heard Solo's worn-out voice invading my headspace, coming through crystal clear.

His genius never ceased to amaze me.

"I'm here. Everything is clear. Y'all will need to head west towards the interstate but stay off the road like before. I'll let you know when to veer north. The skating rink will be off an exit of I-75 N. Oh...and you don't have to yell, Raya. I can hear you just as clearly as you can hear yourself," he explained.

"Oops...sorry," I said, lowering my voice.

I gave John, Big Man, and Naomi a key for their ATVs.

I figured Ryan could ride behind one of us and so could James. Big Man and John took up most of the seats on theirs so that only left me and Naomi.

Naomi gave Ryan a look that needed no words.

He immediately walked towards me and hopped on the back of mine.

"Just like old times, huh?" he nervously said.

I gave him a polite half-smile, not wanting to tell him that the comment was ill-timed and weird.

"—Okay, let's move out. Stick by the interstate until I signal for us to head north. Solo will get us near I-75 and we can go from there," I instructed.

I was on one of the standalones and Big Man was on the other.

I led this time and Big Man brought up the rear. Naomi and John were hauling the trailers and made up the center of our convoy.

We rode in silence, but every once in a while, Solo popped in a comment to stop or slow down or veer this way or that way.

It freaked me out every time he spoke.

He came through so clearly, that it was almost like he was an extra voice in my thoughts.

We rode like that for at least twenty minutes before I felt comfortable breaking the silence with Ryan.

I turned my head slightly, while driving full speed and started, "So...how old are you?"

It seemed like I had broken his concentration on something, but he eventually responded, "I'm eighteen...just old enough to be drafted into service. Why?"

"You just...sound...a lot older than you look," I admitted.

He chuckled at that.

"Yeah...well...I get that a lot. Genetics, I guess. My dad has a really deep voice, too," he explained.

His face stayed neutral at the mention of his father so I dared to ask, "Where is your dad?"

"In jail," he bluntly replied.

That shut me up for a moment and we continued our ride in silence.

"That was dark," Solo said in my thoughts, but I couldn't respond without sounding crazy to Ryan.

"Tell me more about your mom, then," I picked back up after the silence became unbearable.

"I don't know where she is, but I think they took her to Mississippi," he replied, looking disheartened.

"What makes you say that?" I questioned.

This could have been the development we needed to help find the others.

"When we were en route to the wedding, I overheard one of the senior soldiers mention a facility in Mississippi. He said that's where the 'pretty engineer' went. My mom is an engineer, so I assumed they were talking about her. If

I hadn't come with y'all...that's where I would have been headed next," he explained.

He looked off in the distance with a longing expression and I wondered if he was reconsidering his choice. We weren't exactly the most hospitable of hosts thus far.

"Maybe if your mom is in Mississippi...that could be the Southeastern TRP! My family could be there, too!" I audibly realized, connecting the dots between the information he had just given and what Solo had learned previously.

"I don't know...maybe," he offered.

After that comment, we continued without further conversation.

I had my thoughts to keep me company and I was sure he did, too.

Solo navigating with the drone's help was quite effective.

We remained unnoticed the entire way, even when we crossed over the main roadways.

Once we made it to the wooded area behind the skating rink, we stopped and dismounted the ATVs.

"Okay, so me and Naomi will go inside and find this Lillian lady—" I tried to suggest before Solo came through on the comms.

"Actually, I just pulled up the skating rink rules of entry and anyone under seventeen has to be accompanied by an adult over the age of twenty-one. Naomi can't go with you."

"—Well, Solo just informed me that I need to take an adult over twenty-one or they won't let me in," I corrected.

Naomi's whole countenance fell into disappointed envy, but she didn't try to combat what needed to be done. She checked herself quickly and submitted to the plan without debate.

Big Man agreed to go in with me since John was the one with actual militant experience and we needed him to take out the soldiers once we got out into the parking lot.

"Raya...tell Big Man to leave his gun. I can see metal detectors at the front door," Solo said, scaring me a little.

It wouldn't have been so weird to hear his voice in my head if I had some kind of warning that it was about to happen.

I relayed Solo's message to Big Man and he reluctantly handed his bag over to James.

"Don't eat my granola bar," Big Man said to James.

James gave him a look like he couldn't make any promises.

"Take your taser, Raya, just in case. It's not made out of metal. It's a hard polymer," Solo voiced.

I took the taser out of my bag, put it in my pocket, and then handed the bag to Naomi for safekeeping. She begrudgingly took it and threw it into the trailer of her ATV.

Big Man and I casually walked out of the woods when Solo gave us the go-ahead. We maneuvered through the back parking lot to the front entrance, staying within the blind spots of the cameras.

Once we got to the front, we both cautiously looked at the ground the entire time until we made it past their CCTVs and faced the lady at the ticket counter.

A loud wave of music hit us and even Solo balked at the noise through the comms.

The older woman sitting behind the glass ticket window was so pale that her skin looked almost translucent. I could see the blue network of veins underneath her eyes and in the creases of her nose.

She seemed to redden deeply, though, at the sight of us.

She flipped her straightened, blonde ponytail over her shoulder before remembering her manners.

She spoke to us with a great deal of forced politeness and said, "Hi, welcome to the Wheelific Belle, how can I help you today?"

"Me and my niece are here with a party...we're just running late," Big Man spoke up, with a polite smile plastered on his face.

We weren't late though, it had just turned one o'clock.

The woman frowned and stared at us while chewing her gum loudly. Her eyes trained on the head covering I had wrapped around my hair with the bun of fabric in the back.

She finally looked away from us and down to her clipboard, flipping a page before lifting accusatory eyes back up at us.

"Is your party under the name...Yisrael?"

My stomach dropped.

The way she said the name with such unwarranted animosity, gave me leave to think, if anyone had turned these people in, she most definitely had something to do with it.

If this Lillian lady thought they were just coming for a day of fun, she had chosen the wrong skating rink.

"Yes, that's us," Big Man said, while I remained speechless.

"Okay...seems they do have a few more people running late today. There are four more people left on their list...you can go on inside," she unnecessarily offered.

She feigned a smile and handed both of us a small pink ticket. She then went back to chewing and popping her bubble gum while looking down at her phone.

I held my breath as we walked through the metal detectors, hoping Solo was right about the taser. No alarms rang out when I passed through, so I exhaled in relief.

"Should we split up?" I yelled at Big Man, over the music.

He nodded in the affirmative and moved off towards the right where the lockers and game room sat.

I went towards the rink and the booths near the concession stand.

The music attacked my ears as I scanned the crowded area. I loved loud music but this was an actual assault.

There was cussing in every other lyrical bar and the bass rattled my chest at every treble.

I used to love going skating with Shiri. The whole atmosphere, down to the smell of overly deodorized skates, brought back comforting memories.

We would go as often as we could during the summer, to this rink called 'Sparkles'. The music there was decent because the parents would complain, otherwise. I got a sudden nostalgic feeling thinking back on me and Shiri taking our tickets and exchanging them for a pair of skates.

I missed skating rinks, in general, but this one was not my idea of a good time.

Especially knowing what was to come.

Quite a few children were skating around on the floor, as well as adults and they were all mixed in different shades and ethnicities.

It would be really hard to tell who's who unless we found the lady that Solo had researched. More than likely, she was the one who coordinated this whole event.

I quickly scanned all the booths that were occupied but I was having a hard time discerning faces.

When I moved closer to the concession stand, I did a double take at a girl standing there ordering a soda.

She had her head wrapped in a long, yellow headscarf with the tail end of fabric twisted and hanging down to resemble a ponytail.

From the side, she looked almost like the woman we were looking for, but this was a young girl, maybe thirteen or fourteen years old.

I decided to try anyway.

"Lillian?" I cautiously asked once I was within earshot.

She turned towards me and was about to respond when she just stopped and stared, open-mouthed.

She forgot all about her soda that was just placed on the counter. She grabbed my arm and pulled me towards the bathroom while she skated.

I had to jog awkwardly to keep up.

It all happened so quickly, that I had no time to make sense of what was going on or to offer up any resistance.

Once she swung open the bathroom door, she stooped down to see if there were any legs occupying the stalls. She saw a pair but seemed to recognize their owner.

She called out, "Ya-el...is that you?"

After an embarrassing second or two, a voice responded from the stall, "Yeah..."

The girl with the yellow scarf then said, astonished, "Ya-el...you won't believe this! It's the girl from my dream. She's here. Literally...like right now."

I heard the toilet flush.

Then a short, plump yellow-skinned girl with two long, dark plaits stepped out of the stall. If I didn't know any better, I would have assumed that she was Native American.

She peered over at me and then went to wash her hands, nonchalantly.

"Okay, so now what?" Ya-el asked, sarcastically.

Yellow Scarf looked at me eagerly, waiting for an answer.

This whole interaction was surreal and I could only think to say, "My name is Raya."

Yellow Scarf repeated it as if she were taste-testing my name in her mouth.

This child was strange and I felt anxious to leave this whole encounter behind. I subconsciously started backing up towards the door.

"You're looking for Lil right...Lillian, I mean?" she finally asked, noticing my visible discomfort.

"Yeah. Do you know her?" I responded, still not too sure about this girl.

"That's her oldest sister," Ya-el threw in. "And I'm her cousin. She is strange, but don't worry...she doesn't bite...often."

Yellow Scarf cheesed at her cousin's words and gawked at me again.

"—I see a prison bus headed your direction, off I-75, Raya. Seeing how there aren't any prisons within a hundred miles of here...I'd say they're most def Syndicate soldiers coming for y'all. You got less than 5 minutes. Hurry!" I heard Solo say into my ear.

"I can take you to Lil. My name is Maya, by the way. I saw you in my dream the other night...you were standing on one side of a barbed wire fence looking out towards this weird bush with white flowers on it," Yellow Scarf blurted out.

"Oh? Um...okay. Uh...we don't have much time, we need to find your sister," I declared.

I felt my adrenaline rising with each passing second. I didn't have time to comprehend whatever dream she was trying to explain.

Maya nodded in agreement and happily swung the bathroom door open, looking left then right, before choosing to head left.

She skated up to her sister who was already standing next to Big Man.

"It's her, Lil! It's Raya!" she blurted out, excitedly, to her much older sister.

"—the bus just pulled up in the parking lot. Look alive, Raya," I got from Solo, over the comms.

"Listen, please—" I pleaded with Lillian, interrupting whatever response she was about to give her little sister. "—we are about to get arrested. Gather your entire group together RIGHT NOW and stay calm. We are here to help you."

Lillian looked over at Big Man and he gave her a reassuring nod.

She didn't hesitate.

She put her arms up in the air and motioned in all directions for her people to bring it in.

Everyone came up to her in less than a minute but seemed confused at being summoned so abruptly.

She cupped her hands to her mouth and yelled so everyone could hear her over the music. She told them to remove their skates...that they were leaving.

Some of the younger children looked heartbroken but still complied.

"—here they come, Raya. Stick to the plan. Make sure you get everyone outside. John, Naomi, and James are all in position. It's gonna be fine," Solo declared.

"Is this everyone?" I asked Lillian.

She looked and did a mental count, then nodded 'yes'.

"Okay, good. Everyone, stay calm and comply with the officers. Please...you have to trust me," I said, just as the music came to a sudden halt.

The see-through lady's voice came on over the intercom and she announced that there would be a brief interruption. She asked that all skaters exit the skating rink floor.

She also apologized for any inconvenience.

I rolled my eyes, knowing that the only inconvenience to her was our presence.

I knew that the three 'officers' had entered the building when I heard the metal detectors alerting.

Without thought, I touched my pocket housing the taser to reassure myself.

The pretend officers burst through the entry doors and singled us out immediately.

One took off his cop-ish-looking sunglasses and glared at us, trying to decide who was in charge.

Big Man impulsively stepped forward, as well as a slightly toned, medium-built Hispanic man. He looked to be in his early forties.

The lead soldier said loudly in our direction, "We received a report of fraternization of unauthorized personnel. Please present your chipped passports to prevent any further criminal charges."

The Hispanic man spoke up first, "We don't carry around our passports, sir. It's our right to not do so. What's this really about?"

The officer looked outraged that he was publicly questioned. He promptly marched up to the man and punched him in the gut, without hesitation.

The man doubled over to the floor, coughing and trying to catch his breath.

I heard gasps coming from all over the building and detected a small flicker of light coming from the right side of me. I turned to see what was the source and noticed someone had their phone camera out with the flashlight on, recording the whole scene.

I quickly turned my head away from the camera. The last thing we needed was for our faces to end up on the news for all the world to see.

The pretend officer was thoroughly satisfied with himself. He smirked and put his hands on his hips, looking out to us to see if there would be any more challengers for him to publicly assault.

When no one else stepped forward, he loudly told his counterparts to round everyone up and load them onto the bus.

He still had that vile smirk on his face when he caught notice of me.

He did a double take and locked eyes with me.

I instantly started to sweat.

He stalked over and demanded, "What's your name, girl?"

I said the first thing that popped into my head.

"Stephanie."

"I know you...yeah...I know you. Hey, Clay—" he turned and addressed the bald man to his left.

"This is one of the South Passage ones that got away," he excitedly explained to Clay.

My heart sank into my shoes.

That was our street name.

"Oh, you have no idea how much trouble you caused me, girl. The Commander will get off my neck when I bring you in...and I'm sure once we get you to the TRP, you will be singing like a canary about the rest of them's location."

His accent sounded southern, with Creole mixed in. He was a bright shade of sunburnt red like he had been camping outside for weeks.

They all pulled out a plethora of zip ties and cuffed all the adults and teenagers, leaving the smaller children to follow freely behind.

Ringleader Cop tightly placed a zip tie onto my wrists, then grabbed the space in between my bound hands.

He dragged me out beside him.

"I'm not gonna let you out of my sight until I make quota," he whispered in my ear.

He was so close I could feel the heat of his breath on the side of my face.

I hoped Solo was getting all of this.

If something went wrong, at least he could give Juda the details of what happened.

As if his Spidey senses were activated, I heard Solo's calming voice over the comms.

He wasn't exactly talking to me though.

He was talking to the Most High, praying for our safe delivery.

I whispered a quick '*amen*' when he finished.

When we were all forced out through the front door, the blonde lady sneered at us as we passed.

I couldn't, for the life of me, understand how some people could be so hateful, even when no one had done anything wrong to them.

Once we reached the parking lot, we were made to stand in a tight circle, in the hot afternoon sun, whilst the three soldiers decided the best way to usher us into the white prison bus. The bus was parked almost to the front door of the skating rink but offered no shade to us.

They were minutely arguing over if the children should sit in the front or the back or if they should put females on one side and males on the other, like that even mattered.

Just then, a stray bullet struck the asphalt near Ringleader's foot. When it penetrated the ground, a small plume of asphalt particles and dust rose slightly in the air.

Ringleader noticed right away that it didn't have that loud POP sound of a regular gun and immediately screamed out, "SNIPERS IN THE WOODS!"

They rushed everyone onto the bus and told them to stay down. I moved to get into the back with everyone else, but Ringleader yanked my zip-tied wrists towards himself.

"Where do you think you're going?" he questioned, rhetorically.

He opened the driver's side door and pushed me aggressively up into the front of the bus. I almost fell across the driver's seat and when I quickly gained my bearings, moved over to the passenger side bucket seat, since that was the only other place to sit.

I glanced back toward all the scared faces.

The cab and chassis of the bus were separated by thick metal bars. I saw that I couldn't get to my people and it was pointless to try.

The other two soldiers were standing near the metal bars on the other side and had their guns drawn, trained on the group.

I could hear quiet whimpers and crying coming from some of the terrified children. Older ones were asking their parents what was happening.

When I caught a glimpse of Big Man's face in the back, he looked at me with outright determination.

I knew, without a shadow of a doubt, that whatever move I made, he would back it.

I felt a weird tranquility in sensing that and I recognized that I had to do something, quick.

"—Raya, you gotta do something...cause a distraction...something. Don't let them get to the interstate. The team won't be able to keep up from there and there's no tree cover," Solo instructed before Ringleader's words distracted me.

After he abruptly put the bus in drive and swung us onto the main road, he continued driving like a bat out of hades, barreling towards the interstate.

"I can't wait for you to see the TRP. Ohhhh...you're gonna love it! It's just what you people need...all y'all are disgusting...like cockroaches. The more we eradicate, the better...but before that, a little torture and manual labor won't hurt, right? It's what y'all are built for, anyway. Yeah...I'm gonna have fun playing target practice with you, girlie. I'm getting pretty good, too. You should have seen how I picked off y'all's wannabe pastor. It was so smooth...POW...right to the chest."

He laughed maniacally and my blood began to boil, as I stared at him in disbelief.

Angry tears welled up in my eyes and all I could see was my father, lying there limp on the ground, and my mother screaming his name over and over.

Ezekiel...Ezekiel...Ezekiel!

I wanted to rip this man's tongue out of his mouth.

I wanted his blood to spill.

I wanted revenge.

I needed a weapon, and in my anger, I remembered the taser, wishing that it was an actual gun.

If it had been, I wouldn't have given a second thought to shooting him in the face.

While still glaring at him in revulsion, I reached into my pocket and in one untroubled motion, had the stun gun up to the side of his neck, pressing the activation button.

He convulsed to the electrical currents humming through his body and started to foam at the mouth.

I had no mercy.

I never let up.

Ringleader uncontrollably jerked the wheel towards the right; towards the woods.

When we suddenly flew off the road, the two other soldiers, while grabbing for the metal bars, turned around to see what was all the commotion.

Big Man and two of the other men rushed them like linebackers as soon as their backs were turned, screaming their war cries at them.

Big Man targeted the one Ringleader had called Clay. When Big Man made contact with him, I heard the side of his head crunch against the metal bars.

I felt no sympathy.

The other soldier-officer was trying to grapple his gun away from the two that had rushed him. He was fighting desperately, trying to point it in their direction to discharge.

At the same moment this was happening, we abruptly hit a tree, knocking everyone forward violently.

"—Raya...Raya...they're almost there. Hold tight! Raya—" I could hear Solo saying in my thoughts.

Or is this a dream?

My vision was clouded with smoke and I could see white starry dots dancing across my eyes.

As I lifted the side of my head from the dash, I remembered being on the ATV talking to Ryan and smiling at his awkward joke.

Everything was starting to come into focus.

A man was slumped over the steering wheel, not moving...not speaking.

I heard moans coming from behind me so I painfully turned towards the sounds.

"Is everyone okay?" I heard Big Man asking the group in the back.

There was some more groaning but no one seemed too bad off.

Smoke wafted throughout the bus and I could hear the hissing of the damaged radiator.

Something was trickling down my face.

I put my hand to my forehead.

It seemed like I was sweating profusely, but I wasn't remotely hot.

I touched the pouring liquid and then looked at my now damp, red fingers.

I'm bleeding.

I instantly felt faint, but then I saw a blue figure moving toward the front of the bus, out of the corner of my eye.

He stopped to confront the figure of that third soldier-cop, who I supposed had gotten away from the two men that attacked him.

I could hear them briefly talking.

The soldier-cop said something about calling the others for backup.

The Syndicate soldier, in dingy blue camo, replied that he had already called for help. He then lifted his right hand, which was holding a gun equipped with a silencer, and shot the cop point blank.

The blue figure came towards the driver's side of the bus and forced open the door.

It was all over for me.

I was too weak to fight and I had lost my taser upon impact with the tree.

The blue figure reached up and pulled the dead driver out of the bus, then climbed into his seat, closing the door behind him.

I mustered all my remaining strength to feign an attack.

"Raya...I'm gonna get us out of here...Raya!" Ryan said, from the driver's seat. He was reaching over towards me, while his voice fading in and out of my head like a long-distance call.

Then another voice invaded my mind as Ryan caught me waning back towards the dash.

"Solo said...follow the drone," was the last thing I remembered saying before his arms and the darkness took me.

Twenty-Four

SOMETHING JARRED ME AWAKE.

I opened my eyes slowly.

I felt grass and brush under my hands while I sat, leaning up against a tree.

My vision was still blurred, so I blinked rapidly, willing my useless eyes to focus.

Once my brain and vision aligned with one another, John was my immediate focal point.

I saw him rummaging under the hood of the white prison bus and pulling at a small hose inside the engine compartment. He snatched at it violently, several times, before it ripped free.

He then stomped over to the ATVs and started searching through his drawstring bag. He pulled out the two bottles of water and drank hurriedly out of one while pouring the other one out onto the wooded ground.

With both bottles emptied, he threw them on the ground along with the hose.

He demanded Naomi and James' water bottles, as well. They rushed to pull them out of their black bags, then handed them over, without question.

He poured them out onto the ground, too, making sure he shook out every remnant of water that he could.

Finally, he scooped up all the remaining bottles from the ground, along with the hose, and walked over to the gas tank of the bus.

He unscrewed the gas cap and shimmied the hose down into the reservoir. John put the other end of the hose into his mouth for a second, then spit out some yellowish but clear-looking liquid.

Once the fluid was flowing freely, he began to fill all six bottles.

He left the hose hanging out of the tank and it continued dripping fluid onto the ground, around the back tire.

He then went inside the bus and let down all the windows that would open.

I watched him spread the bottled gasoline all over the seats and walls, saturating the entire bus, as much as possible.

He finally walked back to the engine compartment and started yanking on wires. I saw some electrical sparking, and then he quickly poured gasoline on the wires and a fire flared up instantaneously.

The fire traveled up the cab of the bus with lightning speed. Flames licked up the gasoline like a parched marathon runner.

It got really hot, really fast.

I tried to move away from the heat by lifting myself off the ground, pushing against the tree, when Big Man stooped down and picked me up as if I was nothing more than a plastic grocery bag.

As he lifted me into his arms, I closed my eyes and retreated back into oblivion.

<hr>

Ugh...my head hurts.

The wind was rushing against the side of my face as I leaned forward against something warm and solid.

I opened my eyes and saw bushes and trees rushing past me. I stared out for a few seconds, mindlessly enjoying the passing scenery.

My arms were limply hanging at my sides, but when I was rattled by a quick descending sensation, I immediately reached forward and wrapped my arms around whatever I was leaning against.

As realization started to formulate in my mind, the ATV slowed to a complete stop.

I looked up to see who I had been riding with and to figure out why we were stopping so suddenly.

Juda rotated his body around in the extended seat, unlocking my arms from across his chest with his movement.

"Raya...oh my God...you're awake—" he exclaimed, while wrapping his arms around me now, and laughing to himself. "—praise the Most High," he said into the wind.

Ryan pulled up beside us in an ATV that had a trailer attached.

A few of the skating rink people were sitting in it, patiently waiting to press forward.

I noticed Lillian, Ya-el, and Maya were part of this group. They were huddled together for comfort and familiarity.

Lillian looked over at me and cautiously smiled.

"You good?" Juda asked Ryan.

"Yeah, yeah...I think I got the hang of it now," he replied.

"Okay, we're almost there. Hang on guys," Juda looked over and declared to everyone in the trailer.

Juda pressed the clutch down with his foot and accelerated toward the direction of the Franklin tree.

He consistently changed gears until we reached a good, steady speed of 35 mph.

Ryan was a little slower, but he kept us within sight.

Although he looked to be struggling a little with the clutch-acceleration combo, he was still mobile, and that's all that mattered at the moment.

Juda turned slightly and looked at me from the corner of his eye, before saying, "I've never met a white boy in South Georgia that has never once driven a four-wheeler."

I smiled at his joke and replied, "Well...now you have."

We rode on in silence and I wrapped my arms back around my brother's chest and squeezed him in a playful hug.

When our group finally made it to the exit hatch, Maya gasped and squealed with excitement as if she had been given a brand-new pony for her birthday.

"It's the tree, Ya-el! The tree from my dream!" she exclaimed frantically while pointing towards the Franklin.

Ya-el just nodded her head and collectively jumped down from the trailer.

She and her cousin were complete polar opposites.

Ya-el seemed reserved and logical while Maya was giddy and unnervingly optimistic.

Lillian patted her sister on the head before helping her down.

It seemed like she was more than used to her little sister's exclamations and animated outbursts.

As I curiously watched their interaction from the back of my ATV, Lillian knowingly, explained in my direction, "She has visions often. They are always accurate, if not timely. Sometimes it takes years for anything to come of them but when they do, she gets...overly energized. Sorry."

"No apologies necessary," I replied, feebly.

After Juda jumped off the ATV, he told Ryan to escort everyone down to the community room where Adina would be waiting.

He wanted everyone to be looked over for injuries.

He walked over to the hatch door, put in his code, and swiveled it open for us.

Ryan helped me down from the ATV and I was thankful because although the faintness had passed, I was still feeling weak from the blood loss.

Lillian and Maya rushed over, each putting one of my arms across their shoulders to help me walk upright to the opened hole under the tree.

Lillian went down a few rungs first and held onto my waist while Ryan lowered me in.

I heard Juda driving the standalone ATV up onto the trailer. There was a pause then I heard him drive away.

Once our group got into the tunnel, Ryan swiveled the hatch door closed until that precious *click* sounded.

We all made the journey to the heart of the sanctuary with hushed sniffles, very few conversations, and dragging feet.

No one asked any exploratory questions about the interesting rooms we passed.

I was sure that time would come later, once the shock of today's events wore off.

Ryan led us to the community room where Adina was already tending to a small boy who had a gash above his left eyebrow. She was just finishing cleaning him up when she saw our rag-tag team enter.

She rushed over to do a quick triage and saw that everyone was on their feet, so that was a good sign for her.

When she eventually noticed that my face was caked on both sides with partially dried blood, she practically mowed everyone aside to get to me. She then asked what happened.

"I hit my head pretty good on the dashboard of a bus," I said, right away.

I did not share Solo's flair for the theatrical pauses and suspense.

"Let me see," she replied while pulling my headscarf away.

I was shocked that it had remained secure on my head the entire time.

I sat in the nearest chair, while Adina continued to look for the source of the bled.

I noticed Lillian, Maya, and Ya-el politely moving away towards a table to have a seat.

Naomi was standing a good distance from us, conversing with some of the new group, while holding what looked to be my notebook in her hand.

She must have been giving out the room assignments I had detailed in case we had more people join.

When she noticed more people walking by her, she turned and looked in my direction.

Naomi practically threw the notebook at an unsuspecting bystander and sprinted towards us.

"Raya...oh my God...you're okay!" she abruptly said.

"Yeah...I keep getting that today for some reason. Of course, I'm okay. What else would I be?" I responded, trying not to sound frail.

"Be still," Adina ordered.

"Yo...that whole thing was crazy! It was like straight out of a movie scene. How did you get that bus to crash? Tell me everything..." Naomi rapidly requested.

"How about you tell me something first? How...in the world...did I end up on that bus in the first place, huh?" I balked.

Naomi looked at me with a sudden shadow of latent anger hidden behind her eyes.

"I would say 'ask James' but he is probably in time-out somewhere," she sarcastically replied.

"What did he have to do with it?" I asked, curiously.

Adina was cleaning the blood from my scalp but her eyes read as if she was just as interested in hearing Naomi's answer as I was.

"Well, John was giving him a quick lesson on how to aim. He took the safety off for him and everything, just in case he needed to shoot. When y'all stepped outside, Mr. Trigger Happy got...overwhelmed with nerves. He said he 'slipped' and fired. I guess that's what spooked your guy,"

Naomi blurted out, still caustic about the whole situation.

"Ahhhh... so I owe James a beat-down," I said while trying to squeeze out an unbothered chuckle, but it turned into a wincing cough.

I was just content with being back in the Sanctuary in one piece, with everyone that we intended to warn.

How we got here made no difference to me as long as we were all safe.

"Where is Solo?" I suddenly asked.

Adina told me that she believed he had gone to sleep after Juda left to come get me.

"Why did Juda come for me?" I innocently asked Adina.

"Why wouldn't he, is a better question, Raya," she responded thoughtfully while dabbing at my head still.

I had no definitive answer for that, so I kept silent and let that reverberate through my thoughts.

When she was done checking and cleaning my wound, she asked a thousand questions about my symptoms.

Once she was finally satisfied that I had not suffered a concussion, she moved on to other patients.

"I gave out room assignments from your book. I hope you don't mind. I put Adina and me in your room. We need to start conserving space for newcomers," Naomi volunteered.

I nodded my head.

"That's cool but what about the little kids?" I asked.

"They will be in the room right across from us and Ms. Deborah and Drea will be nearby as well. Drea wants her own room still and argued up and down when I tried to bunk her with Ms. Deborah...I didn't feel like fighting her on it anymore and caved. Maybe you can try?" she continued.

I nodded again, thoughtlessly.

I just wanted to take a shower and sleep.

I kept reflecting on my encounter with Ringleader while on the bus.

I had so much hatred in my heart towards that man when he spoke to me the way he did, it made me shudder.

I needed to pray for forgiveness.

I never want to feel that way again.

I got up to head towards my pod when I heard Naomi say over her shoulder, "Oh... by the way, I won't forget. I want all the juicy details on the bus crash later."

I smiled weakly then headed down to the safety and solitude of my pod, ready to repent and wash away my sins, literally and figuratively.

Ryan had stayed standing at the entrance of the massive room the entire time and when I passed him to go down the stairs, I breathed a *'thank you'* to him.

Remaining composed, he nodded in my direction.

Just then, Juda came down the tunnel stairs, announcing himself by his loud, clopping feet.

He took one look at Ryan standing there and immediately grabbed his arm. He commanded 'Let's go' while pushing Ryan aggressively towards the stairs to the lower pods.

"What are you doing, Juda?" I practically yelled behind them.

Juda didn't stop shoving Ryan while taking the stairs.

Ryan almost tripped a few times going down them.

"What do you think? It's time for soldier-boy to go back to his room," he retorted.

Once they made it to the fifth level, Ryan jerked his arm away and turned to face my brother with a stoic look plastered on his face.

He looked like he was about to square up with him.

Juda was slightly taller and more built than him and was by no means intimidated.

"Oh...you ready to go, huh?" Juda taunted while getting up in Ryan's face so they could lock eyes.

"Stop it! If it wasn't for him, I wouldn't be standing here right now. None of those people would be either! Why do you keep treating him like this?" I shouted at him.

Juda ignored me completely and addressed Ryan.

"I don't care nothing about your little attitude. You were never supposed to be down here in the first place!"

After he said this, he shoved Ryan into a set-apart pod, then locked the accordion door behind him.

I could hear Ryan punch the door once before retreating further into the room.

I spun around and looked at my brother with confused horror.

He turned to casually walk back up the stairs.

"He is not our prisoner! You can't just lock him up whenever you don't feel like dealing with him!" I screamed at Juda's back.

He turned quickly towards me, then vehemently spat out, "Don't get too attached, Raya...as soon as it's safe to get rid of him...we're doing it."

"If he looked like you and me, you would be throwing him a party. Admit it! You're racist," I quipped.

"No...I'm not racist! It's not about his skin. He is one of 'them', Raya! Stop being so naive! He's playing some game with us and you are falling head over heels for it! I'm only trying to make sure everybody here is safe! I don't know why I have to keep explaining that to you, but I'm not going to anymore and I'm not arguing with you either. You're going to stop going behind my back and doing stupid stuff and that's the end of it!"

And with that, he stalked off with the key.

TWENTY-FIVE

— · —

"*B*ABY, ANGER IS A *natural response to feeling violated in some way or another. Being angry is not the sin...it's usually what follows that is," Dad said, as we sat at the kitchen counter.*

"But you weren't there, Daddy. That boy said I was black, baldheaded, and ugly. He had it coming," seven-year-old me responded, matter-of-factly.

"Listen...when our anger goes unchecked and we act on it in a way that gets others hurt, that's when we are no longer just a victim...then we've also turned into the violator. Do you understand?" Dad retorted while tousling my extremely short hair.

"You don't get it, Daddy. I had to show him better than

I could tell 'em. He can't just get away with saying mean things to people," I tried to reason.

"I know it's much easier said than done in some instances...HOWEVER, we must learn to control our anger, so we don't cause more harm to ourselves and others, in the heat of the moment. Proverbs 25:28 says 'He that hath no rule over his own spirit is like a city that is broken down, and without walls'," he explained.

"I'm not a city though. I have feelings," I said, still trying to make him see things my way.

"I know, baby girl...but even if we feel justified in our anger to respond a certain way, we have to first examine whether or not that action is justifiable with the Most High. Most times, we'll find that it's not..."

"So...I should have just walked away and let the Most High deal with it, right?" I asked, defeated.

Daddy nodded and said, before he faded away into vapors, "We must learn to get control over anger and leave judgment to God, who will always judge righteously..."

7:30 AM flashed on the alarm clock and the constant beeping made my head swim.

Before I could reach over to smack the off button, Adina walked over and tapped it effortlessly.

For a second, I was confused as to why she was in my room so early.

When I glanced over to my left, Naomi was moaning and complaining about the little alarm clock being a dream killer, while rolling out of her bottom bunk.

"How are you feeling this morning?" Adina asked me, bending down to examine my scalp.

She didn't wait for a reply when she said, "You need to rest for a few days. I'll bring you some turmeric and lavender tea. Are you hungry?"

I shook my head 'no'.

I planned to fast for a day or two.

I needed to refocus myself on the righteous path and deal with the anger that had caused me to sin.

I also needed to spend some time in prayer on the Ryan/Juda situation.

I was determined not to make him feel belittled or undermined by me, but Juda was wrong and I wanted Ryan out of his room-prison. I just didn't know how to accomplish that without going behind Juda's back and physically breaking him out.

I would have to get over myself and leave that in the Most High's hands, though.

After Adina and Naomi left the room and I was all alone, I said my prayers and then tried to go back to sleep.

Not even an hour later, I was prodded awake, just as I was slipping into a deep sleep.

Adina was sitting on my bed with a cup of steaming hot tea when I opened my eyes.

After placing the tea on the little white and gray desk, she said, "You have some visitors. Is it okay to let them in?"

"Sure, that's fine," I replied and forced myself to sit up.

Lillian and Maya entered our pod after Adina called out for them to come in.

"How are you feeling? You took such a nasty hit when we crashed yesterday," Lillian asked.

"I'm doing good. My head hardly hurts anymore. By the way, I'm sorry about yesterday. That's not really how everything was supposed to go down. We had a plan...it just didn't—" I tried to say before Lillian interrupted me.

"Please...don't work yourself up over that. We are here and we are safe. Everyone has been so welcoming and this place is amazing. I was told it was your dad's design. Yah...I mean, the Most High...has used him for a great work and we are so grateful," she said, meticulous with her words.

Picking up on her subtle apprehension, I replied, "Don't worry...we were taught not to judge what name other people call God by. My dad taught us that we are so far removed from our heritage, that now everyone is just doing the best they can, to be as close to the right thing as possible."

"I think I like your dad more and more..." She smiled deeply before continuing, "Oh, I actually came because I had a question for you...How exactly did you know to come get us? I've been thinking about it and I just don't get it. I was so careful to invite only people that I knew and it was a private e-vite."

I thought about it briefly and remembered.

"Someone called in and reported your party to the Syndicate. That's the government-sanctioned group that's rounding up ethnic believers. They think we are all part of some conspiracy hate group or something to justify what they are doing," I explained.

"Ahhhhhh...I bet it was that lady at the ticket counter. When I called to reserve the place, she was less than helpful as soon as I gave her my name," she reckoned.

I nodded.

"Could have been. I didn't get a good vibe from her either when we got there, but I don't know for sure," I explained.

After a few more minutes of small talk, she and Maya said that they were going to go help Ms. Lynn prepare lunch, and then left.

Adina checked my head again before she slinked out of the room, closing the door behind her.

Finally, I would be able to sleep.

I started to mull over Lillian's words about the ticket counter lady when realization hit me like a ton of bricks.

She called in to reserve the public skating rink and got reported that way.

The wedding party called in to reserve the banquet hall area and got reported that way.

Our event was a private sabbath service, same as always, so who could have reported us?

Whoever reported us had to still be among us and there was only one person that it could have possibly been.

I tossed off my covers and barely got dressed fast enough to run upstairs to Solo's Lookout.

He wasn't there.

I rushed back down the stairwell to the fifth-level pods where Solo and Juda shared a room.

The door was partially opened and I heard Elijah's voice quoting 1 John 4:8, "He that loveth NOT knoweth not God; for God is love".

"—but I can't just let him roam free around here. That has nothing to do with love...it has everything to do with safety. He could be a mole, for all we know, and she just let him in like it was nothing," I heard Juda respond.

"You are missing the point, son. You can't treat others like they are undeserving of the same grace and mercy that the Most High grants you. That's not your call. You know what you need to do..." Elijah said with finality.

It sounded like Elijah was about to exit the room and I didn't want him to see me, so I ducked into the unoccupied room across the hallway.

I heard Elijah traverse back up the stairs towards the community room.

When I was sure that he was completely out of earshot, I moved back across the hall and went into Juda and Solo's room.

Juda sat at his desk with his hands on his head, deep in thought.

"Hey…" I said, lowly.

He turned around and replied, "Hey."

"I'm looking for Solo. Do you know where he is?" I asked quickly, not wanting to stay any longer than necessary.

"Uh, yeah, I think him and Naomi went to get the drone from outside and readjust a camera that got knocked over by a deer," he replied, just as quickly.

The energy surrounding us was weird and I didn't like it, but I had to deal with myself before I could face anyone else.

I turned to leave when Juda pushed his chair back and said, "I'll go with you. I need to talk to him about something, too."

I gave him a nod and waited while he walked towards the door. He followed close behind and we went the whole way towards the exit hatch in awkward silence.

After barely passing the park and training room, we ran into Solo and Naomi.

They both seemed surprised to see us together but didn't verbalize it.

"You go ahead, Raya. I need to talk to Solo in private when you're done," Juda offered.

"Well, actually, it might be better if you all hear what I have to say," I replied.

I looked behind me and saw no one else in the tunnel.

Believing that it was safe to talk, I began, "I think we do have a mole down here—"

"Who?" blurted out Naomi.

"I already told you. It's that Ryan kid," Juda threw in.

"—just listen for a sec. Geez! Someone called in and reported the skating rink event...and the wedding event. Those were public functions in public places. We got attacked during the Sabbath service...a private event on private property. So who called them on us?"

Everyone looked at each other, in turn, while digesting my words.

"Think about it...who didn't get caught or chased that day? Who didn't have anyone of their own family there? Who still emitted a signal from the house and was visibly disappointed when they learned their phone wouldn't work down here?" I guided.

"No, it can't be Elijah," Juda said, without further thought.

"He attacked Naomi at the house, Juda! Wouldn't he have recognized y'all's voices? Think about it..." I reasoned.

"But it was dark in there, Raya. I mean...you didn't recognize his voice before you attacked him," Solo countered.

I shook my head before saying, "If I had enough time, I would have figured it out, though. He did sound familiar but I wasn't gonna take any chances... he had Naomi."

"I just can't believe Elijah could do that to us. I mean, why would he? What's the motive?" Juda questioned.

"I don't know, but maybe we don't know him as well as we think we do," I replied, folding my arms in defense.

"Look...I don't want to believe it at all," Solo started, "but even if you are right, and it was Elijah...it still doesn't matter."

"What? Why?" I countered.

"Because Elijah has been down here for weeks...if he wanted to hurt anybody, he would have done it already. And it's not like he can call anyone since his phone doesn't work down here. So why poke the bear?" Solo reasoned.

Everyone, other than me, nodded their heads in agreement.

"No. Y'all don't get it," I groaned, frustrated at their ignorance. "Elijah can leave! And once he gets out, his phone is gonna work just fine."

"Even if he does leave, he can't get back in without one of us," Juda snapped back.

"Yes...he can! We have two tunnels, remember? And we brought him in through the one that doesn't need a code. He knows exactly where to find it and he knows how to get in because he watched you pull that flower lever. As long as we don't do anything about it, everybody here will be at risk!" I returned, getting more frustrated by the second.

There was a collective silence while everyone reflected on my words.

"Guys, we have to confront him about this," I finally demanded.

Juda glanced at me abruptly, as if he were being challenged.

"No," he said sharply, "that's dangerous. What if you're right, huh? You wouldn't walk up to a killer and tell him that you know he's a killer, would you?"

Without another word, I shook my head 'no'.

"Exactly, and if you're wrong, you're gonna start something that we don't need down here. We'll have to do some more digging first to find out the truth. Until then, we keep this between us. Don't go around telling anybody about this. The last thing we need is to sow discord or raise panic in everyone. People will want to leave then, and we don't know them enough to trust them yet."

Solo and Naomi nodded in agreement, but when I didn't acknowledge him, Juda's countenance became grave.

He leaned down to match my height and looked me square in the eyes.

"Raya, promise me," he exhorted, "This doesn't get out. You haven't really been listening to me lately and if you never listen again, I need you to listen now...Promise."

I sighed in defeat.

I wasn't going to tell anybody but Elijah anyway, but I knew Juda was right.

"Fine," I agreed. "I'm not gonna say anything. But when we do find out the truth, we have to do something about it. We shouldn't have to spare feelings when people are at risk."

Juda crossed his arms, satisfied with my response.

"Okay," he ended.

Everyone, again, agreed.

I could try to sleep now that was off my chest.

I gave Solo an unsolicited hug, then walked away quickly, before he could protest.

I heard the rest of the group still quietly chatting concerning what to do about Elijah. Solo said something about getting his phone before I was finally out of earshot.

I went back to my room and laid on my bottom bunk, not able to sleep for hours. When dinner time rolled around, Adina came and asked if I wanted her to bring me anything and I declined.

She took the untouched cold tea from the desk and walked out of the room downcast.

I wanted to explain to her that I had chosen to fast but decided against it.

I said my prayers and was finally able to sleep.

⚊⚊◆⚊⚊

The next day went much the same.

I mostly stayed in my pod but this time Adina didn't attempt to bring me food or tea.

I was sure she discerned that I was fasting by now.

I wanted to go check in with Solo to see if he had made any progress on my Elijah theory, so I quietly left the room and went upstairs.

To my surprise, not only was Solo and Juda in the Look-out, but Ryan was also sitting in a chair near one of the monitors. He had on a fresh pair of jeans and a yellow T-shirt that complimented his dark auburn hair.

I rapped at the door frame before coming inside, not waiting for a response to enter.

They all turned around and acknowledged me before promptly turning back to the monitors.

Juda and Solo looked to be scouring through texts of some sort. They were quickly reading, then tabbing through more pages.

I stood there quietly, for what seemed like forever, while they were each engrossed in their tasks.

"Here!" Ryan said abruptly while pointing at his monitor.

We all looked over to what he was pointing to with interest.

It was Naomi's social media page.

Her very last post was a selfie of her holding up the peace sign, with duck lips poking out of her face, while she posed.

The tent was in the background, filled with the entire congregation. I could see the back of my own head under the tent and my dad's face turned towards her camera.

In the description, it read 'Shabbat Shalawam[1] y'all!'

Right underneath, it had the location turned on, which showed our full address on South Passage.

The post was marked 'public'.

My eyes got really big and I clasped my hands over my fully gaped mouth.

I was wrong.

"So what are we gonna do?" Solo asked, dismayed.

He turned to face Juda, looking for an answer but Juda just stood there with his arms crossed, staring blankly at the screen. The screen represented the undeniable evidence against Naomi.

Of course, we knew that it wasn't intentional, but my dad always told everyone to be extra cautious with what they put on social media.

There was no reason my family's home address should have been sprawled out underneath her picture like that.... now everyone was gone.

After truly comprehending what he witnessed, Juda shook his head at the ground, not knowing what to do next.

---

1. meaning 'peaceful sabbath'

"I think we should just keep this to ourselves, don't y'all?" Solo offered. "We'll have to tell Naomi, of course, but there is no reason for anyone else to know about any of this. We can slip Elijah's phone back in his room and go on with our lives...no harm, no foul."

"I guess..." Juda accepted, before saying, "I'll go find Naomi and have a talk with her. Raya...you coming?"

"Um, I don't really have a choice do I?" I reluctantly questioned.

Juda peered over at me with an earnest look on his face and I knew that was a 'no'.

When we finally found Naomi, she was in the training room doing some aerobics by herself.

The conversation was very brief.

I did not comment while Juda broke the news to her that she was the undeniable cause of bringing the Syndicate down on us that fateful Sabbath.

She was in such shock that she couldn't even verbalize an apology or any words at all, for that matter.

After Juda was done explaining, she promptly walked out and I automatically followed her to our pod, leaving him alone in the training room.

I still didn't offer her any words.

I had no idea what to say that would take that weight off of her.

She crawled into her bunk, sweaty clothes and all, and rolled facing the wall. I sat and listened to her pitiful wailing for hours before eventually falling asleep.

<hr>

When Wednesday rolled around, I hastily went into the community room right at three o'clock, thinking I was late for call to prayer.

I had stayed with Naomi all day hoping that she would snap out of her acute depression, but she had not moved from her same position in her bunk bed.

I had to make a decision to stay with her longer or go pray and I believed that a prayer request was in order, so I left her there and hurried off to the community room.

Besides Adina putting away washed containers and dishes, the room was completely empty.

"Where is everyone?" I asked her, dumbfounded.

Just about everyone attended last week.

This didn't make any sense.

"Everyone is in their assigned pods," she replied, nonchalantly.

"Why?" I inquired.

She turned around and slammed a container down.

"Because everyone thinks Elijah works for the government and is gonna turn us all in for money," she said angrily.

I gave her a surprised look.

"Why are you so shocked? You're the one who put it in Drea's head...now she won't shut up about it to anyone who will listen," she retorted.

"I didn't tell Drea that!" I replied, trying to defend myself. "I've been in our room this entire time!"

"She was in the park when she overheard you, Raya," she said, then went back to putting up dishes.

My stomach dropped to the floor.

"Does Juda know?" I asked after I got my thoughts together.

"Like I said...everybody knows. Even Elijah knows," she answered.

"Your brother is with Solo upstairs. You may wanna go try and help fix this mess before it's too late," she added, vexed.

I didn't say anything else, just turned and walked up the stairs, with lead for feet.

I was dreading Juda's contempt, and if Adina was that displeased, I could only imagine Juda's reaction.

I walked loudly into Solo's Lookout.

"Raya...before you even say anything...it's not your fault and nobody's mad at you," Juda said, while turned away from me still.

"Adina seems to be mad at me," I quipped.

"Ok, well...everyone else isn't mad at you," he said, correcting himself.

He finally looked back at me to continue his speech, when Ryan's unexpected voice startled all of us. It seemed like we always forgot that he was even there until he spoke.

"I think you need to tell everybody," he said meditatively.

Juda didn't provide any immediate input.

He seemed to be dealing with something and I was pretty sure it was the fact that Ryan even spoke...or maybe it was something else.

I didn't know, but I did know that telling everybody Naomi was the actual 'mole' was a terrible idea.

"Because," Ryan explained further, "everybody is on edge right now. With what Drea has been spreading...it makes Elijah look like a real threat...but it's obvious Naomi didn't mean any harm. If people know the truth, they won't target Elijah anymore, but they also won't target Naomi because she's just a kid who made a mistake."

Juda took a long pause to contemplate this.

"You go get Naomi. I'll go get Elijah," Juda instructed Solo.

"What about Drea? What do we do about her?" I asked.

Juda deliberated, "We should hold a meeting with all three of them and another adult maybe. Then we need to tell everybody the truth…"

He avoided Ryan's eyes, all while verbally agreeing to his plan.

Am I detecting progress?

After they left the room, I turned to Ryan, remembering my manners, and asked him if he was okay.

This was the second time I saw him 'free'.

"Yeah…I'm fine, I guess. For some reason, your brother decided I didn't have to be locked up anymore. Not sure what took him so long to figure that out…but hey, beggars can't be choosers," he replied.

I smiled to myself, grateful that the Most High worked it out.

Everything would have been perfect now if only I hadn't opened my big mouth and falsely accused Uncle Elijah.

TWENTY-SIX

S OLO BROUGHT A DISHEARTENED-LOOKING Nao-mi into the Lookout. She still wore her workout clothes from yesterday and had a slightly tangy smell clinging to her, like musty sadness.

She dragged a chair into the corner and plopped down in it, visibly signaling that she wanted to be as far away from the general population as possible.

Shortly thereafter, Juda returned with Elijah, Big Man, and Drea in tow.

Elijah looked demoralized as well.

I could only imagine the seriously unwarranted rejection he was feeling...all because of me and my big mouth.

He didn't make eye contact with me when I desperately wanted him to. I needed him to see just how apologetic I truly was. I felt the size of an ant and wished I could shrink inside my headscarf and disappear.

Everyone took a seat while Juda remained standing.

He cleared his throat and looked like his thoughts were muddled but he got straight to the point.

"To my understanding, there have been rumors and wild accusations floating through the Sanctuary about Elijah being a double agent and a betrayer. Everyone is anxious about it and I have to say I'm a bit disappointed in this whole situation," he voiced.

Elijah quickly chimed in, "I would NEVER put this body in harm's way on purpose. Frankly, I'm hurt that anyone would think otherwise."

He said this while glancing over at me. I held my head down humbly, no longer brave enough to meet his gaze.

"Uncle Elijah, we know and we owe you a public apology for this. We will hold an assembly today after we are done here. This will be set right," Juda resolved.

"Also, we have to address the issue of spreading false information, even if you think you had it on good authority," Elijah established while looking over at Drea.

She held her head up proudly and glared back at him before insisting, "I didn't do anything wrong...people have the right to know what's going on and what they're dealing with. Raya and the 'Three Stooges' shouldn't have said all those things if they didn't want it getting out."

I was appalled at her words.

This wasn't the sweet, easygoing person I once knew. Her voice even sounded corrupt.

I could see paralleled looks coming from the rest of the group.

"If you heard us talking, you would have heard the part where we all agreed to find out first before making any public accusations. You did what was in your heart to do and that was to stir up trouble," Naomi bitterly spat.

"Drea, this is your final...private...warning. If you do anything like this again or anything remotely detrimental to the wellbeing of the whole, you will be publicly rebuked," Juda boomed.

At this, even I sat back in my chair, with full attention.

"Please leave...we will speak to you about this again later," he said, waving Drea out.

She sneered at him and said something under her breath about not testing her before she skulked out of Solo's Lookout.

Juda stood at the doorway and made sure she completely descended the stairs before returning to the conversation.

He closed the door behind him, then instructed, "We will have everyone gather in thirty minutes to explain the entire situation. Solo, can you gather everyone on levels four and five? Raya, you get everyone on three."

We nodded before leaving him, Elijah, Big Man, and Naomi in the room.

I wondered what they had left to talk about, but didn't want to seem nosey by taking my sweet, precious time to leave.

I walked quickly downstairs to let everyone on three know about the mandatory meeting.

Thirty minutes passed by slowly, but when it was finally time, everyone appeared to be present, except Drea.

I looked to Juda when I didn't see her and he gave me a knowing look to just leave it alone so I sat down to wait.

I sat with Lillian, Maya, Ya-el, and the triplets and made small talk with them.

Adina came and slid down into the seat next to mine and I was so glad that she did because I thought she was still mad at me.

"I hope everything goes well," she whispered to me.

"Me, too," I replied and gave her a slight smile.

Juda, Big Man, Elijah, and Naomi walked in and went over by the kitchen. They stood almost shoulder to shoulder and everyone gave their full and undivided attention.

There was only a slight cough from somewhere in the back of the crowd.

Big Man looked thoughtfully at each full table and loudly began:

> Each and every human being is born with an innate ability to know the difference between right and wrong. God has wired us in such a way that when we do wrong we know that it is INDEED wrong. When that same injustice is committed against us...we feel it...and we respond to it. This natural occurrence does two things: it leaves mankind without an excuse before Almighty God and it justifies God when He judges...who has also given us His laws. So, since we know better, let us show better! We are responsible for the truth that we receive....we will be held accountable if we do not respond in time with sincere repentance.

He paused and made eye contact with many individuals in the group, before continuing:

Some people will argue that right and wrong is subjective...but God, from the very beginning, has made it extremely clear to mankind where He stands concerning sin and unrighteousness. ROMANS 1:19 says 'Because that which may be known of God is manifest in them; for God hath shewed *it* unto them'. So, no matter how we try to justify ourselves in the flesh, the spirit of God within us will seek to convince us otherwise! If we refuse to respond to the prompting of the Holy Spirit, then the consequences of the sin will soon follow. Right now, our righteous wiring has become frayed by sin...and every ungodly influence. But the Most High, has given unto us many tools by which we can and should be repaired...His laws, His prophets, His Son, and lastly, the unseen help of His Holy Spirit within us, which provides us with that knowing...which we just KNOW.

Juda stepped forward and roared:

It has come to our attention that one amongst us stands accused and wrongfully so. We called this gathering to set the record straight regarding one of our elders, Brother Elijah. He has labored with you...for you...and it's an unjustifiable sin to turn against him in the manner that we have. Elijah was NOT the cause of our original group coming under attack, as it was so wrongfully put forth...and he is by no means a double agent or a spy or whatever you have been falsely told. My sister, Raya, had a valid concern and brought it up privately...and that private concern was flamed throughout this body prematurely and without merit by someone who was not privy to that conversation...someone who should have excused themselves as soon as they realized the message was not intended for them. I would personally like to apologize for my family's role in this false accusation and rumor. Moving forward, we will not tolerate this type of behavior in the Sanctuary! Gossiping and back biting is against the word of the Most High and we were all called to be a set apart, holy people. I pray the bonds of brotherhood and sisterhood will be unbreakable between us all, because right now...WE ARE ALL WE GOT...and it would be a shame to allow the spirit of the enemy even one inch between us!

There were a few handclaps and 'amens' that resonated throughout the room.

Then Drea stepped forward from the stairwell holding her son on her hip.

"I saw my husband, lying on the ground, bleeding from his neck. He had turned towards me and Little Isaiah...trying to get to us by the pond before the guns did. He was unconscious, facedown in the dirt, when they drug him away like a trophy animal. He was RIPPED from me! I want to know who...who was it, huh? If it wasn't Elijah, then WHO DID THIS TO ME?!" she all but screamed.

Juda tried to clarify that we can't change the past and that even if she knew, it wouldn't change what happened, but before they got into a very nasty public back and forth, Naomi quietly stepped forward and answered, "It was me."

Everyone looked towards Naomi like a soap opera was playing out in front of them. Audible gasps were filling the space.

"I took a picture and posted it on my social media page. I didn't realize that the location control was on. I'm sorry, Drea....I'm sorry everyone," she said remorsefully. She burst into tears and brushed past Drea who made no effort to move out of her way.

Adina got up and grazed past Drea, following Naomi down to our room.

Everyone stared at Drea with disdain, when I was sure she intended to obtain sympathy. She looked out of place all of a sudden, then stomped back down to her pod to everyone's relief.

After the commotion, Juda asked for everyone's attention once again.

He apologized again before he and Elijah went over the 'house rules' and asked that everyone be respectful and mindful of each other.

He also announced the need for volunteers for future rescue missions before dismissing the crowd, stating that training was daily at 8 AM, except on the Sabbath.

I couldn't believe my ears. Juda was still on board with the training.

I couldn't wait until the next morning, but I was feeling lightheaded from fasting.

I had planned on breaking my fast as soon as the call to prayer was over but since that got canceled for the meeting, I would eat something when everyone dispersed.

I didn't have it in me to sit with Naomi right away and hoped Adina had more encouraging words for her than I could ever think up. Hopefully, she would be up to praying together later.

After most of the people left, I went to the kitchen to see if there were any quick leftovers I could scrounge up.

True to nature, Ms. Lynn was in there preparing for dinner.

She handed me a thick piece of cornbread with a tall glass of almond milk and told me not to rush eating or I would make myself sick.

Apparently, she noticed right away when I stopped eating.

I sat back down at my table, began tearing off the crumbly corners of the bread, and stuffed them in my mouth.

Solo pulled up a chair and sat across from me.

"Hey," he said, briskly.

I glanced up at him before focusing back on my corn-bread.

"Wassup..." I answered, dismally.

My mind still lingered on Naomi's words and I had yet to offer my apologies to Elijah.

Somehow, I knew 'sorry' just wasn't going to cut it this time.

I popped another piece of the sweet bread in my mouth before Solo decided to respond.

"So, there's something we need to talk about," he said.

I groaned mentally.

Please...no more drama.

Solo detected my mood and quickly added, "Nothing like that. It's something else."

In that infuriating way of his, he left me lingering, as I tried to guess what was on his mind.

"Are you ever going to stop doing that?" I asked teasingly, although I meant to only say it in my head.

"Stop what?" he asked, confused, but I guessed the question was rhetorical because he didn't let me answer.

"Whatchu been up to, Raya?"

He asked it like he was a detective conducting an interrogation.

He narrowed his eyes at me and leaned forward as if he would be able to detect a lie if I decided to offer one.

In return, I squinted my eyes in concentration and genuine confusion.

"What do you mean?" I asked, cautiously.

"I mean...nobody's really seen you around that much lately. I'm...just curious," he retorts, skeptically.

"I've been resting, Solo. What's this about?" I blurted out, pushing the rest of my cornbread away in annoyance.

He leaned even closer, searching my face for any hint of deception.

Great...what else have I done now?

"Listen, Raya...I overheard your whole conversation with Ryan while y'all were out on the ATVs."

"Oh yeah, I totally forgot about that," I replied, almost relieved that this was the topic he chose to discuss.

"Right....I'm just trying to make sure you weren't off somewhere devising any crazy schemes," he admitted, sounding genuinely concerned.

That made me laugh out loud.

"What? Like me running off to Mississippi when nobody's looking?" I smiled, still slightly chuckling at his insinuations.

I pulled my plate back towards me and returned to popping more bread in my mouth.

Solo gave me a look like that's exactly what he was thinking.

I laughed again before taking a sip of my milk.

"Oh...I'm definitely going to Mississippi," I assured him, once I set the glass down.

He raised his eyebrows at that, but not in an amused way.

"But you don't even know exactly where this place is," he started to debate.

"True...I don't...but I do have a genius for a cousin," I smirked over at him.

He started to protest again when I cut him off.

"—Look, I know my dad probably didn't make it," I offered, trying to remain logical, "but I never saw my mom get shot and if they took her, then she's there. If there's even a remote chance that I can find her, I'm going to take it or die trying."

Solo sighed heavily and looked to be deep in thought before speaking again.

"I miss them too, you know...especially Uncle Zeke. He always supported my crazy schemes and literally pulled me out of a dangerously foolish lifestyle."

He looked down at his hands underneath the table, taking a long pause before he continued.

"I want to help you...and I'm going to, but we're going to have to take our time with this one."

He looked up and into my eyes without breaking contact, "And you have to tell your brother. Me and him might disagree about a lot of stuff, but your safety isn't one of them. I can't let you go all the way to Mississippi by yourself, because of course, you know...Juda would kill me."

I nodded, hesitantly.

I agreed that Juda should know, but I knew for a fact that now would not be a good time to bring it up.

I didn't have to explain that to Solo though. He understood.

"I'll tell him...eventually," I replied.

"I really hope y'all fix...whatever y'all got going on," he volunteered. "Things have gotten really weird around here for me."

He huffed, before pushing back his chair to leave.

I laughed anxiously at that last comment.

Back when things were still normal, it was usually Juda and Solo who got into constant disputes and it was always over something dumb. Like who stole whose T-shirt or who beat who in a video game. Juda and I hardly ever got into it about anything, so things felt weird for me, too.

As Solo began walking away, his pocket started chirping excessively. He stopped mid-stride and pulled out his ph-ablet to investigate it.

I playfully called after him that his…thing sounded like someone was ringing a doorbell.

He turned back to me and said, "That's because some-one is at the door…"

Twenty-Seven

I ABANDONED THE CORNER of bread that was left and stood up so fast, that my chair dramatically flipped backwards. Not seeming to care about the chair or the remaining bread, I rushed after Solo.

We both bounded for the stairs. His long legs carried him quicker to our destination and when he reached the Lookout seconds before me, he opened up all his screen feeds eagerly.

When I ultimately made it inside, my eyes frantically searched for the entrance and exit surveillance feeds.

The entrance cameras reflected a serene scene, with little more activity than the wind rustling slightly through the trees.

The exit looked the complete opposite. There was movement and activity in every exit-related feed.

Every few seconds, when the screens switched camera angles, I caught a new glimpse of different types of occupations. People were setting up tents near the Franklin tree and pulling out camping equipment to, maybe, start a meal.

Involuntary heat started radiating through my body.

My armpits spontaneously perspired in anxious sweat.

"Are you seeing this?" Solo asked, rhetorically.

His eyes never turned from the screens as he spoke.

He pressed some keys and manipulated the angles of the feed, enlarging them, so we could get a closer look.

Nine or ten people were invading the monitors, walking around like they were hosting Tabernacles[1] but in summer. From what I could tell, there seemed to be a grouping of a family of four, then a smaller family of three. The rest didn't appear to be attached to anyone else, by my count of tents. They were shaded all different variations of brown; all the way from slightly tanned to deep mahogany.

"Solo, these are our people!" I exclaimed, ready to run to the exit and invite them in.

"Hold up there now, Turbo," Solo started. "Before we go offering them afternoon tea, we need to figure out why

---

1. biblical feast lasting a week, while dwelling in booths/tents: Lev 23:33,34 Zech 14:16

they are here...specifically. This could be a ruse or a decoy to flush us out."

I looked at him in disbelief.

Why would he think these people had ulterior motives?

They looked like they were about to grill some burgers and hotdogs, not execute some elaborate plan to overthrow the Sanctuary.

"Go get Juda and Elijah," he facetiously ordered.

I cringed slightly at the mention of Elijah but knew I needed to comply.

I ran out in search of my brother and Elijah.

I went left to see if maybe they were at the park or training room, but no luck. I went down to the fifth level, knocked slightly on Elijah's door, and listened for any sounds coming from inside.

Still nothing.

The same results at Juda's door.

The only other place I could think to look was in the sixth-level storage bunker. I scrambled down the last set of stairs and saw that the storage room bunk bed door was opened.

Finally, I caught a glimpse of Juda, standing with Elijah and Ryan. They were apparently collecting clothes to wear for the rest of the week.

"People are camping near our exit hatch. Come quick!" I exclaimed to the wind, not caring who all caught it.

Elijah and Juda looked at each other before promptly abandoning the clothes and moving quickly towards the stairs.

As I turned to leave after them, I heard Ryan groan loudly while bending down to pick up the left-behind clothes.

"Guess I'll just put these in your rooms then," he uttered to himself.

I looked back at him and gave him a commiserating smirk before leaving him there alone.

I followed Juda and Elijah up to Solo's Lookout but they were already in discussion when I made it back.

"These people are from Florida...or at least this man and his family are," Solo explained while pointing to the family of three.

They had a toddler with them; a girl.

"How do you know that?" Elijah asked, incredulously.

Solo turned to face Uncle Elijah with his right hand over his chest like Elijah had just punched him in the heart.

Oh, boy...here we go.

While deepening his voice like a not-so-subtle villain, Solo replied, with his fists clutched in the air, "I am the master of all things tech...every device...every instrument must bow down to my will, my genius, my demand. Muhahahaha!"

Then he burst out laughing at himself, keeling over from the low belly chortling and snorting.

When he caught his breath, he said, "I'm just kidding. Most social media sites have facial recognition. I just screenshot one of the surveillance pictures and cross-referenced it through my page. Bing, bang, boop."

Elijah blinked slowly.

His facial features read as disinterested, at best.

He was not amused.

Solo sat down swiftly, putting himself in a self-imposed timeout.

"Anyways...what do you think we should do?" Juda asked Elijah, completely ignoring Solo's antics.

They both stared at the screens, watching the people make their dinner.

Everyone on the monitors looked tired but in good spirits.

"I think we should stay quiet on this for a few days. Maybe observe them for a little bit, before deciding what to do about it. Maybe they are just passing through," Elijah finally determined.

Juda nodded.

They must have forgotten that I was even in the room.

"Why can't we go ahead and make ourselves known and just...ask...them what they are doing here?" I inserted into the conversation.

Everyone turned to me and stared, their faces questioning why I was even standing there.

Again, I felt that anxious heat rising within.

I was out of place, as told by their facial scrutiny.

"We have to use wisdom about this, baby girl. It's what Ezekiel would have wanted," Elijah answered, calmly.

For a second, I reeled in disoriented emotion at the mention of my father's name. I could not think of any reasonable response and was completely muted by his words.

I nodded my head in submission and turned to go when Elijah asked me to wait for him.

We walked down the stairs together and headed toward my pod.

He asked me if Adina and Naomi were in there and I nodded in the affirmative.

"Good...I would like to talk to all of you young ladies," he said.

I turned and looked up at him while we took the short walk to my shared room.

Before we entered, I felt compelled to apologize.

"Uncle Elijah...I'm really sorry about accusing you. It's just that...at the time, it only made the most sense. I—" was all I could get out before he stopped me with a raised hand.

"I understand, Raya. And I forgive you. I love you like my own daughter...but we will talk about this in just a moment. Your friends must hear what I have to say, too."

When we got to the pod, I peeked in, making sure both girls were decently dressed and then announced that Elijah was coming in to talk to us.

Adina had been sitting at the desk, reading a book. Naomi was rolled over in her bed, but at the mention of Elijah's name, she quickly sat up.

When he came in, Adina offered him her chair and she sat on my bunk. I sat next to her and Elijah settled into the seat, facing us all.

"I want to be very careful with my words with you right now," Elijah began while looking at us, in turn. "Christ makes it clear in Matthew chapter six, that if we do not forgive others, then we cannot expect to be forgiven....that means that our very own salvation depends on forgiving others. Do you understand? Unforgiveness is an offense to the Most High God."

We all nodded in understanding.

"—We have to realize the power that we have in moments of offense, okay? In some cases, the offender may sincerely be remorseful, which I believe is the case now...but until we have forgiven, we all remain bound by what has been done to us. In these moments, we have the power to show the love of Christ and to set others free, as we also set ourselves free...so please know that if you have caused any offense to me, knowingly or otherwise...it is forgiven."

A lump of emotion formed in my throat and tears threatened my vision.

Without thought, I reached out and hugged Elijah.

I felt such relief to hear his wisdom pouring forth.

Naomi slowly came forward and joined us in a group hug.

Adina sat on my bunk still and looked clueless.

I silently motioned for her to join us and she timidly stood up and hugged my back, making the circle complete.

After Elijah left, we all began talking amongst ourselves about what we planned to do the next day.

Anything to get our minds off of all the recent drama.

It was time to move past it.

"You never told me what happened after James accidentally misfired. I wanna hear the details," I put forth to Naomi, trying to coerce her into getting her mind off her self-imposed guilt.

She looked as if she was deciding whether she wanted to play into my trap of distraction or not, but she finally gave in and began describing the part I had not known about.

"Well, after they started loading y'all onto the bus, John and I drove you and Big Man's ATVs onto the back of our trailers before they even pulled out of the parking lot. Then we high-tailed it out of there, following Solo's drone through the woods," she started.

"Wait...how did y'all know to follow the drone?" I asked.

"He made it pretty obvious when he kept flying up and down in our faces. It was like an electronic 'Lassie' situation," she said, forgetting her grief for a second, laughing naturally.

"What's that, girl...Timmy fell down a well?" Adina reenacted while slapping her knees with both hands.

We all howled in a fit of laughter.

Once we all calmed down somewhat, Naomi continued, "We followed drone Lassie until we saw the bus come flying into the woods in front of us. Me and John had to swerve to avoid getting hit...the only thing that stopped the bus from barreling through the woods and into us was that huge pine tree y'all hit. It was crazy cause then one of the soldiers fell out the door of the bus and Ryan ran over to him and put him out of his misery."

My stomach lurched a little at the mention of that part.

I vaguely remembered witnessing it.

"I wish he hadn't done that," I added, somberly.

"He had to, Raya. It was a mercy to him," Naomi explained. "He told me and Big Man while John was getting rid of the bus. He said that if the Syndicate found him or any of the other soldiers alive after losing over thirty people...they would have been tortured to death for their failure. He said that they have to stay in the field without any provisions or help if they lose one or two...but thirty...that's a death sentence."

I reflected on her words.

I still felt somewhat indifferent to the role I played in Ringleader's death and I knew that I had to rely on the Most High's forgiveness instead of my feelings, in that regard, but I started to think maybe his death was a mercy, too.

His fate would have been much worse if he had lived and we all got away...especially with losing me, twice.

"Well...while that was a very fascinating story, Naomi...I think you are long overdue for a shower now. You got our room smelling like a swap meet," Adina jested.

"Yeah...I wasn't gonna say anything...I was just gonna go down to the storage and get some candles or something," I teased, as well.

Naomi laughed at us, threw her arms up in the air, and shook her armpits, so we could better enjoy her aroma.

"Yeah, yeah, yeah...I'm going," she said while grabbing her towel and toiletry bag from the bunk above her.

Adina and I looked at each other and laughed some more before she went back to her book and I left to go get another thick piece of cornbread from Ms. Lynn.

Twenty-Eight

7:30 AM. Thursday.

I yawned wide when the alarm clock started going off, stretching my arms out into the air.

Adina was above me in the top bunk, groaning at being woken up so early.

Naomi turned off the alarm and rolled back over as if she planned to sleep in again.

I needed to use the bathroom badly and didn't want to be distracted by my bladder when I said my morning prayers, so I hopped out of bed and whipped the door open, ready to bolt for the bathroom.

I only had on a tank top and some shorts and didn't plan on starting any more drama with my attire.

As soon as I stepped foot out into the hallway, I noticed a baby with chunky legs and a cherub face, sitting in the middle of the floor. I rubbed the sleep out of my eyes to make sure I wasn't seeing things.

It was Little Isaiah.

He had on nothing more than a full diaper and looked like he was ready to cry out in distress.

I wandered over to him and scooped the little boy up, shushing and rocking him once he was in my arms.

That seemed to suffice for the moment because he began babbling and cooing, instead of continuing to whimper loudly.

I walked up to Drea's open door and peered into the dark room.

I didn't see her immediately, so I turned the light dimmer up to make it brighter. Once I could fully see, I noticed that the room was devoid of life and in complete disarray.

I scanned the pod for the diaper bag I handed her a while back. Once I found it strewn open in the corner of the room, I dug through it for a clean diaper. I found exactly one, along with some wipes. I then took Isaiah back to my room.

After asking Adina to hold him for a second, I finally ran over to the bathroom to relieve myself.

When I got back to the pod, Adina had already changed Little Isaiah's diaper and was playing with him on the floor.

I got dressed quickly and picked up the baby to try and find his mother.

On my way to the community room, Chava and Big Man appeared on the stairs, walking up from the level below me.

"Shalom, little achwath[1]," Chava greeted.

"Shalom. Good morning. Have y'all seen Drea?" I asked.

They both shook their heads in the negative.

I continued up, searching the massive community room and kitchen. Then I tried all the areas above in the tunnel.

I couldn't find her.

I quickly made my way down to the storage room but it was closed and the lights were off.

I got a sick feeling and hoped she hadn't abandoned Little Isaiah by leaving the Sanctuary.

I went back up the stairs and felt winded like I had already had enough exercise to last me the rest of the day.

Searching for Drea made me run late for drills and when I stepped into the training room, John already had everyone doing several sets of jumping jacks.

He glared at me holding the near-naked baby.

---

1. Hebraic word meaning sister

"ATTENTION!" he boomed.

Everyone stopped mid-stride.

"Today I see we have our youngest volunteer yet...what exactly is this BABY doing in my training room, young lady? If you plan on multitasking today, you will have to do that elsewhere!" he commanded, rather aggressively.

"Actually, sir...I can't find his mother," I replied.

He looked at me annoyed, dismissing me with his eyes.

"I'll take him to Chava. She is setting up the final touches in the laundry room and I'm sure she won't mind hanging out with him for a little while," Big Man offered.

I handed him the baby and he walked out into the tunnel. I supposed Big Man was safer from John's wrath than I was and he was trying to spare me any further embarrassment.

I went and stood near Solo in the back of the room before the training picked back up. Juda was in the very front, next to Ryan. It seemed like they both were doing their best to avoid me this morning.

"You couldn't find Drea anywhere?" Solo leaned over and whispered.

I shook my head 'no' and whispered back, "He was just sitting in the hallway, outside of their pod, when I went out this morning."

Solo looked shocked and concerned.

"I'm sure she is somewhere around here....I hope," I said, before starting my jumping jacks.

I could visibly see the wheels in his head turning, but didn't think much more of it.

In between swinging my arms up and down, I looked at the growing volunteer group.

We had three more men from Lillian's circle join.

I recognized the forty-something-year-old man who was gut-punched by Ringleader a few days ago. When John called out to him to pick up the pace, he called him Jose.

The other two were much younger men but I didn't catch their names.

Naomi was nowhere to be seen, leaving me the only female in the room.

I hoped she wasn't giving up on going out on the missions. I didn't think she realized just how much I needed her presence. Without her, I felt completely out of place.

Once training concluded, I popped into the new laundry room to get Little Isaiah, but Chava was alone.

When I entered, she was setting up the final portable washing machine on the east side of the room.

The room had a total of eight machines and she had strung up cording to make clotheslines for people to hang their garments to dry on the opposite side of the space.

"You found Drea?" I asked her, curiously.

"Well, actually, no...she found me...and went off on me. I had to let her know real quick that I'm holy...and hood. We hashed it out though. It's all good," Chava replied, bluntly.

I chuckled a little under my breath, wishing I had been a fly on the wall for that conversation.

I asked her if she needed any help with anything and once she declined, I went over to Solo's Lookout to check the campers' activity.

Solo was sitting in his swivel chair, swaying his legs from side to side, while examining the monitors.

"Any new developments?" I asked him, coming into the room and pulling up my own chair.

He shook his head, then asked me if we found Drea.

"Yeah, she popped up eventually. I'm not really sure where she was in the first place but I don't like the fact that her baby was just left all by himself like that," I ranted.

He made a 'hmm' sound and again, I could see, in his face, the wheels and gears in his head churning, like he was thinking up an invention.

"Welp...I have work to do," Solo said, before eyeing the door.

I knew he was telling me, without telling me, to leave.

I caught the hint and got up to go to the kitchen to see if I could help with any food prep for the day.

I also wanted a snack.

He closed the door behind me and I could hear him turning the lock.

That signaled to me that he was about to be spending a lot of alone time with a new project. I tried to speculate to myself what it would turn out to be, but I couldn't think of a single thing we needed him to create, so it must have been something personal.

When I made it down to the community room, Ms. Deborah and Lillian had the little children in a circle on the floor.

It sounded like they were working on a biblical skit.

There were handcrafted props for the kids to use, while they went over their short lines in the story of Noah. Some of the smaller children were playing the animal parts and their dialogue consisted of grunts and roars. Everyone looked to be enjoying the activity.

I smiled over at them and to my surprise, Zara caught my eye and smiled back.

She was starting to become quite the social butterfly, now that she didn't have her sister always coddling her. The other kids didn't ask as many questions about her facial differences as before, either.

She was just...Zara.

I moved past them and entered the kitchen, searching for a piece of fruit to snack on.

As I reached for an apple, Ms. Lynn, with her dish towel draped across her right shoulder, volunteered me to come help her peel some carrots for a salad.

I gladly accepted the task and sat in the kitchen with her for a good while, talking about her farm and what crops she would be harvesting right now with John and her boys.

Maya and Ya-el came in to grab apples, as well, but before they could escape the kitchen, Ms. Lynn had them rolling silverware into napkins for dinner. They looked like miniature servers, wrapping the forks and spoons into the many white napkins.

Neither one of them did the task begrudgingly, though. Maya even sang a little song to herself, while Ya-el glared at her, annoyed at the song's repetition.

Maya suddenly stopped singing, to Ya-el's relief, and said, "Raya, guess what?"

"Wassup?" I replied.

"I had another dream about you. You were picking flowers off that weird tree and giving them to a little girl with a blonde streak in her hair. She was smiling up at you...then suddenly ran back into a red hut," she said.

She didn't give me a chance to respond before skipping off into the community room, with Ya-el dragging her feet in tow.

I shook my head cheerfully at Maya's light and bubbly mannerisms.

When I had finished with the carrots, Ms. Lynn dismissed me, saying, "Ok, nah. Go ahead and have yourself a good time with everybody else. I'll see y'all at dinnertime."

"Yes, ma'am," I politely responded, before heading back to my pod.

I wanted to get Naomi out of the room. Maybe she would agree to go to the park with me or to spar, just the two of us.

I was bewildered to find that she wasn't even in the room.

I started gathering our laundry bags, hoping to be one of the first to test out the new laundry room.

Out of nowhere, Naomi flew into the room and hurriedly blurted out, "Guess where Drea was this morning..."

I looked at her like I could care less at this point, but she did not take the hint.

"Well, I don't know exactly where she was when YOU went looking for her but after you left...she ended up in here."

That caught my attention.

"—She had a fork and was trying to stab me with it. She was screaming something about me taking her baby and, oh yeah, revenge," Naomi explained.

"What?" I asked, incredulously.

What she explained made no sense to me. Drea just got called out for spreading rumors and now she was resorting to attacking people?

"She blames me...and she's right. It was my fault. I know everyone is blaming me...but to attack me with a fork?" Naomi tried to reason but with a heavy heart and a look of shame on her face.

I saw something else behind her eyes, too.

It looked like a glimmer of rage.

"Naomi, you didn't do it on purpose. That could have happened to any one of us. You have to stop this! It's not healthy. Forgive yourself and re-pent...please...we need you...I need you," I begged sincerely.

Naomi sat back on her bunk silently, mulling over my words before responding, "I just went and talked to Elijah about the whole thing. He agreed to counsel me for as long as I need. I think I'm going to sit out on the rescue missions for a little while until I can get my head straight."

My heart sank.

I couldn't articulate why, but I needed her presence on those missions. I felt like she had just abandoned me, even though I knew she had a valid reason.

I tried to stuff my disappointment down and not let it show on my face or in my body language.

"I'm gonna go do a few loads. Wanna come?" I asked, instead of continuing a fruitless conversation.

She nodded and we both went up to the new laundry room, carrying our bags.

When we entered the tunnel, there was a fresh plume of dust wafting in the air past the vault.

We curiously went over to investigate and Big Man was swinging his sledgehammer at the tunnel wall, knocking away bits of concrete covering the next free space.

He had the blueprints rolled up in his back pocket.

Adina was standing nearby, waving the dust smoke out of her face as Big Man made quick work out of the wall.

Soon, there was an opening showing and he pulled away large chunks of concrete pieces to reveal an empty interior.

"This will be my new infirmary room," Adina called out to us, eagerly.

I looked at Naomi and said under my breath, "We are definitely gonna need it..."

TWENTY-NINE

— · —

FRIDAY MORNING CAME AND went.

Training was awkward again, without Naomi there, but I muscled through it. I kept looking towards the door, hoping that it would be like in the movies and she would burst in, fashionably late, to save the day.

But she never did.

After our typical drills were over, I asked Juda to spar with me for a little while, because I was starting to feel rusty again. He agreed and his Ryan shadow decided to go get a late breakfast, leaving us alone in the training room.

As I wrapped my hands in preparation, he taunted me by saying, "Today is gonna be different. You won't be getting the best of me...watch. You're gonna be laid out in five minutes, tops."

I raised my eyebrows at him and gave him a look like he was talking a bunch of nonsense.

Juda was all bark and no bite.

I knew it and most importantly, he knew it.

I stretched my arms and rolled my neck from side to side, preparing to whoop him just like all the times before.

He bounced on the balls of his feet and put his fists up in the air, preparing for an attack.

Today, we were going to slap-box...my favorite.

We did not go lightly on each other, either. Sometimes, until one of us yielded, we would sport a bloodied lip or a cut cheek, dealt from the other contender.

"Do you have a plan for the people up top?" I asked while lunging toward the right side of his head.

He narrowly escaped contact and responded, "I was thinking we could go get them tonight. They don't appear to be a threat."

He kneed me with tremendous force on the left side.

I staggered for a second but quickly regained my balance and completed a cross with my right open hand.

I made a nice contact point with the left side of his face.

He sprayed a little cloud of spit when my hand swiped heavily across his cheek.

He stumbled to the side, then put his fists back up in defense, while wiping at his mouth.

He circled me waiting for another blow or an opportunity to strike.

"I would like to go," I mentioned, then attempted a roundhouse kick to his left shoulder.

He leaned into the kick, faltering for only a second. Then he jabbed at my face with his open palm.

Contact.

I tasted fire as his hand met my chin.

"Why not? It's not like you would take 'no' for an answer anyways," he retorted, circling me again.

"Hey...I do listen...but only when you're right," I teased, preparing myself for his next assault.

When it didn't come, I completed an open-handed cross-jab combo to the left side of his head and swiveled in a hook kick, finishing him off.

He fell to the floor of the sparring mat, landing on his back.

He gave the hand signal for 'yield' and I extended my arm to help him up.

"Yo...why you always gotta do that combo on me like that?" he asked, in exasperation.

"The better question is why do you never see it coming?" I laughed while pulling him up from the floor.

"What time are we going tonight?" I asked when he was back on his feet.

"Right before the sun goes down," Juda answered, holding his jaw like he needed an alignment.

"—Geez, Raya..." he sneered.

Juda squeezed my shoulders and we walked out together.

Even though things were not quite the same as before, I was cautiously optimistic about our progress.

After I took a quick shower, hoping to beat Solo's ten-minute timer, I walked to the community room, looking for leftover salad.

Ryan was still sitting there, people-watching.

"Hey," I started, then sat down in front of him.

He looked up briefly and returned my greeting.

"Are you avoiding me or something?" I bluntly asked.

"Um...no...and yes," his deep voice responded.

"Ugh, what does that even mean?"

"I'm not avoiding you in a sense, but Solo warned me to stay away from you and your Mississippi schemes or I would get sucked in without realizing it," Ryan blurted out, honestly.

"Well, my cousin does have a valid point. I do plan on going to Mississippi and I was thinking that you would want to go, too...to find your mom," I enticed.

He looked at me wide-eyed with his hazel eyes. They were more green than brown today.

He looked to his left and right to see if anyone was paying us any attention or perhaps eavesdropping.

When he was satisfied that neither was a possibility, he whispered, "I'm in."

I nodded my head and responded, "Good. So here's my thoughts...what if we find a car or something and I stow away in the backseat or trunk or whatever and you drive us to Mississippi? Once we find the TRP, you can turn me in and I can scout the place out. You bust us out in three days—"

"Wait...what? How am I supposed to do that? And even if we did get a car or whatever...we don't even know where this place is exactly," he tried to reason.

I looked at him seriously, before saying, "Solo is going to help us find this place. He told me to give him some time but I believe in him...and we can work on the rest of the details in the meantime. Just think about it, okay?"

I got up to get the salad I had intended to eat in the first place and left Ryan with his thoughts.

I was determined to find my mom and reunite with my people. I just needed to be patient.

If anyone could find them, I knew it would be Solo.

True to nature, as soon as I thought about him or mentioned him, he popped up.

I saw him out of the corner of my eye, talking to Drea privately at one of the long tables furthest from the kitchen. That seemed out of place to me, so I honed in.

It looked like he was handing her something delicate. It looked like a...necklace.

She was clutching at it, looking down into what must have been a locket attached to the small chain. She had a forlorn look in her eye but she was smiling through it.

I, unfortunately, couldn't hear their conversation and decided to continue with my salad mission.

I probably should mind my own business when it came to Drea, anyway. She was starting to strike me as an antagonist to our otherwise decent existence down here.

When I came out of the kitchen with my prize, Ryan was gone and so was Solo.

Drea remained at her table, now donning the necklace and rubbing it mindlessly with her fingers over and over again. She looked like she was ready to shed reminiscent tears.

When she finally recognized my presence, she walked over proudly.

Without letting go of the necklace between her fingers, she began to brag, "Look what Solo made for me. Isn't it beautiful?"

I nodded and replied, as politely as possible, "Yes, it's very pretty. That was very nice of him."

I plopped down in my chair, ready to devour my salad. I was stabbing at it repetitively with my fork, while she stood there in front of me, uninvited.

"It's a locket...with a picture of both my Isaiahs," she further explained, without any prompting on my part.

She bent down towards me so I could get a better look at the tiny reflections of her miniature husband and son.

I paused mid-bite, with lettuce and tomatoes impaled on my fork, and smiled silently at her before she went on, "It's the nicest thing anyone has done for me since we got down into this god-awful place."

I put my fork down aggressively and made a clanging sound against the bowl at her badly timed reference to my dad's design of this breathtaking underground haven.

I inwardly tried my hardest not to become easily offended, but I'm sure my face read as if I was thoroughly insulted.

If it did, she did not care to catch the hint, because she continued, "You should have told Deac Zeke to spend his time doing something much better than this."

She motioned her arms all around her.

I took a long, deep breath to calm myself and tried to focus on holding my peace.

I picked up my fork again with the intent to continue enjoying my salad, but I was quickly losing my appetite at every echoing of her words against the recesses of my brain.

Each bite began to feel like gravel in my throat and swallowing was increasingly unbearable.

I eventually abandoned the endeavor, silently apologizing to Ms. Lynn for wasting her food. I got up to put the rest of my salad in the compost bucket outside the kitchen.

John usually came and emptied it every evening into the compost tumbler he had constructed in the hydroponics room.

I noticed a few days ago that he was attempting to reintroduce organic soil into one section of the grow room. I wondered how long it would take for the rotting food to become usable dirt.

Drea, still fondling her recently acquired treasure, sat down in my abandoned chair.

She kept opening and closing the locket, asininely.

I wondered what was running through her head as she stared at the mini pictures, but didn't care enough to audibly ask.

I was fairly out of the room when I heard her calling out to me, "Oh...Raya, can you tell Ms. Deborah to watch Little Isaiah for me for a few more hours? I'm tired."

With an exasperated sigh and without turning back around, I nodded my head.

After entering the dimly lit stairwell, I slumped my shoulders forward and exhaled deeply.

I was grateful to be out of that draining conversation with Drea. It was like she intentionally sucked all the motivation and harmony from the spaces she inhabited.

As I slowly made my way to the park to be the bearer of contentious messages, I whispered a quiet prayer for my fortitude and her emotional healing.

⸺◆⸺

It didn't seem to take long for Elijah, Juda, and me to make it to the exit hatch. Each time I made the trek, it became a mindless routine, and the time flitted by effortlessly.

I had on my mole comms, so Solo could let us know if there was any trouble headed our way or if any developments occurred before we made it out of the hatch hole.

Initially, when we left for the exit tunnel, I peeked into Solo's Lookout.

He was captivated, watching the security feeds. His head kept turning from screen to screen every few seconds. He looked like he was engrossed in a riveting TV show or a fascinating movie.

The only thing he was missing was a bucket of popcorn.

I had to swallow down a giggle as we passed by.

He heard my stifled laughter giving off echoing feedback on his end of the comms and turned to give us a wave. The sound of it was so unnerving, that I almost took off the mole nearest my ear because I could hear the echoing of him hearing my echoing.

Weird...

Now that we were at the exit hatch, I started to feel knee-jerk nervousness.

I said a silent prayer that we were making the right move concerning inviting these campers to join us. I didn't doubt that it was, but I'd been proven wrong too many times to be fully reassured.

After Solo voiced the go-ahead, I relayed it and Juda went up first.

The hatch door groaned and clicked as he stood on the extended ladder rungs, then he swiveled it open. It sounded a lot heavier and older than it actually was. Juda disappeared over the ledge of the gaped opening. I went up the piped rungs next and squinted at the setting of the sun when my head peaked over the ridge of the hole.

The light, scattering through the trees, showed a twinkling of tangerine and blood-red coloring. It was stunning to witness. It was a brief reminder of some of the things I took for granted when we were freely above ground.

Juda reached his hand out to me and I grabbed it, anticipating him hoisting me out. He had no trouble slinging me up and out of the hatch. I landed, gleeful-ly, on my feet. This exchange evoked memories of him pushing me on the swings when we begged to go to the park every Sunday and our parents caved.

My nervousness was instantly replaced with courage, knowing that my brother was there and would always make sure that I was safe and secure.

Elijah grunted in stiffness as he climbed the stepladder. Juda and I had to each grab one of his hands to distribute his weight and help pull him out.

Oddly, no one seemed to notice three black people popping out of the earth, from under a tree.

The tents were scattered only a few feet from each other and all of them were occupied with their owners. It appeared that they were getting ready to hunker down for the Sabbath.

Before we even got a chance to think up the best way to approach them, Elijah bellowed out a "Hello."

We heard cautious whispering coming from inside the tents and suddenly a man unzipped the front flap to his burgundy-colored one and stepped out with a hunter's knife.

A few more tent flaps unzipped and we were faced with three grown variations of men, each brandishing some kind of weapon.

My small party put our hands up slowly to show that we had no weapons and that we were no immediate threat.

"Shalawam ahyam[1] . We mean you no harm," Juda cautiously offered.

---

1. Hebraic word meaning family

"Who are you, brother? How did you find us?" the original man with the knife questioned, suspiciously.

Taking turns, we each gave our names, and then Elijah answered him more fully, "We've seen you camping here for a few days now and wanted to offer you sanctuary...a place of refuge. I'm not sure if you came here intending on staying or passing through but if you need...more permanent lodging, you are more than welcome to come with us."

The main brother eyed us carefully, probably wondering where we had set up camp and how they could have missed seeing other people so close nearby.

He glanced at the two other men for some unspoken consensus, and after being satisfied with their nodded agreement, he eventually clarified, "My brother had a vision that led us to this spot all the way from Florida. It's getting real crazy out here, man. Our church group got attacked a few weeks ago. From what I heard, some soldiers took everybody who showed up. My wife happened to be sick that Saturday...she's pregnant...so we stayed at home. My brother was visiting another congregation and Luke...over there...had a bad feeling, so that's what kept him away. My name is Leon. My brother over there is William—" He pointed to the slender, dark-skinned man with a faded, short afro that was closest to my left side. William put his hand up in greeting but did not offer any actual words to us. "—And that's Luke," he said, pointing to the man directly across from Juda.

He gave a quick 'shalom' before putting his rifle back inside his small, two-person tent.

Elijah described in brief detail what had happened to our congregation and told him that the offer of refuge still stood if they wanted to move out before the sun went down.

The men, again, looked at each other and nodded in agreement amongst themselves.

The single brothers began gathering their belongings and breaking down their tents.

Leon was about to duck back into his tent to do the same when his daughter dashed out of the tent opening.

She couldn't have been more than two years old. She was giggling uncontrollably and had a bright yellow streak in her coily loose curls. Her skin was the color of a dusky almond hull. Her smile made me want to reach out and pinch her full cheeks.

She ran right into my arms as her mother called out, "Leon! Stop that child...she squirted mustard all in her hair and took off when I reached for the wipes..."

I smiled down at the baby sprawled in my arms and immediately gave in to my desire to pinch her cheeks.

Leon gave me a knowing smile before he reached for his daughter with outstretched arms. I reluctantly passed her over. She ran back into the burgundy-red tent after he put her down in front of the door flap and gave her a slight nudge to go back inside.

I could distinctly hear her mother huff and say "I'm too big for this."

"So...where are we headed? Where's your campsite?" Leon asked us inquisitively, afterward.

Juda walked just a few steps over to the open hole in the ground; the one they were too busy not noticing while talking with us. He jumped in for dramatic effect.

I watched Leon's face as it contorted into wild disbelief and I smiled deeply to myself at Juda's momentary flair for the theatrics.

"—Looks like something I would have done."

Solo's voice startled me right out of my smile and I jumped sweirdly in panicky agitation.

"I'm gonna get you back for that..." I hissed under my breath, so no one thought I was indirectly talking to them.

"—You know vengeance is the Lord's," he replied while howling in laughter.

Juda climbed back up and out of the hatch, then we all helped grab the campers' belongings before descending into the tranquil safety of the Sanctuary.

Thirty

— · —

Three Months Later

There are many religions in the world today, some of which have different denominations within them...But the thing that all religions have in common is each of them has some outward identifying marker to express who they are, and what god they serve...whether it's their doctrine, their rituals, the way they dress, or some form of symbolism that sets them apart from others. Those who subscribe to a particular religion can often be easily identified as a follower by some of those markers. So...here is the question, Do you know how to properly identify with Christ?

I WAS FULLY ATTENTIVE to Elijah's sabbath lesson, but I could also hear the sniffling of a child near me, the scooching of a chair by someone near the back, and the 'mm-hmm' and 'Kan'[1] verbiage floating through the air like dust particles.

I broke concentration from Elijah briefly and studied the faces in the crowded room.

There were over 150 people in the Sanctuary, of all different backgrounds and hues within our community.

Most of them were extracted right from under the Syndicate's nose, while others pilgrimaged here through dreams or visions of the Franklin tree.

Since the Syndicate had set up daily patrols in our woods and commandeered our old house for one of their base camps, it was getting more dangerous to go out on missions now.

They were constantly searching for us.

Too many people had disappeared from their clutches and they were getting sent back out to find us, at all costs.

We had to adapt our plans each time we left, but it was getting easier to cause distractions and decoys, with three mission teams in place. When everyone played their rou-

---

1. Hebraic word articulating agreement

tine parts, we ended up increasing in numbers each time. I couldn't even remember the last time we had a hiccup.

I abruptly recalled my surroundings and tuned back into the lesson.

> The Messiah, himself, has left for us the only acceptable answer to that question. John 13:35 says 'By this shall all men know that ye are my disciples, if ye have love one to another.'

> It's not the gold necklace with a cross hanging down. It's not the T-shirt with your favorite Bible verse or tribe printed on it. It's not the fringes or some little fish symbol on the back of your car...or the Bible collecting dust sitting on the dashboard...or any other outward expression for that matter. None of those things truly point to the Messiah, but rather to the men who use them.

Neither do they justify us with the Most High. They only justify us unto other men.

Big Man read,

> Luke 16:15 'And he said unto them, Ye are they which justify yourselves before men; but God knoweth your hearts: for that which is highly esteemed among men is abomination in the sight of God.'

Elijah continued,

> You see, it's not what other people have to say about us, but what the Most High has to say. We would all like to wear the designation of 'a child of God' but that title can only be true when we operate in the character of Christ who is the express image of his Father. 'God is love' and we should be too...

Big Man read the corresponding scripture,

1 John 4:16 'And we have known and believed the love that God hath to us. God is love; and he that dwelleth in love dwelleth in God, and God in him.'

As Big Man quoted the scripture, my gaze fell to Juda.

He and Solo were sitting near Elijah and they both looked so aged, but in a wisdom kind of way, not a haggard kind of way.

I smiled inwardly, thinking about how far we've come in the past few months, but my smile quickly faded into apprehension when I reflected on how I've kept my Mississippi plans from Juda.

Every day I meant to tell him, but my nerves wrestled me into silent submission whenever I gained an opportunity to voice my intentions.

I picked up Elijah's voice again,

Before leaving the world, Christ prayed to his Father. In his prayer, several times, he requests that those who have believed on him in this world be made one with the Father and with him.

He ends that prayer, requesting that we be filled with that same love that was in him so that the world might also come to know our God.

Big Man read,

John 17:25, 26 'O righteous Father, the world hath not known thee: but I have known thee, and these have known that thou hast sent me. And I have declared unto them thy name, and will declare *it*: that the love wherewith thou hast loved me may be in them, and I in them.'

Elijah concluded,

Let us, therefore, seek to be identified by our love. As He is, so let us be!

Big Man boomed,

1 John 4:17 'Herein is our love made perfect, that we may have boldness in the day of judgment: because as he is, so are we in this world.'

A few seconds of silence passed before Chava stood up in the middle of the community room and sang a beautiful rendition of Psalms 103, acapella.

Her voice was like sweet honey dripping into a cup of warm tea. The range she mastered vibrated somewhere deep within my soul and a tear coerced its way out of my left eye.

I swiped at it briskly, hoping no one saw me get even remotely emotional over a song.

I had gained quite the reputation as an unbreakable and resilient figure amongst the mission volunteers...being that I was the only girl for quite some time.

Naomi finally rejoined us a few weeks ago and I could hardly contain my elation when she walked in that morning. She was late for training, but it was like she hadn't missed a beat. I even clapped a little when I saw her step through the doorway, to John's immense disapproval.

He did not take exception to his drills being interrupted.

After we concluded service with prayer, I got up and maneuvered my way through the crowded room to speak to the triplets about the praise dance practice they planned to hold every Sunday afternoon.

Stalana had asked me specifically to join and I told her, in our room, that I would let her know by the end of the day.

Since we had so many newcomers lately, the triplets got relocated into my pod, to make way for the others.

It was quite interesting to have three variations of the same person bunking with us, but I also thought it was a good learning experience to be around older women, even if they weren't that much older than us.

"Shabbat shalom, sis," Stalana greeted when she saw me approaching.

"Shabbat shalawam," I returned. "I just wanted to let you know that I think I will join you guys tomorrow for practice. I'm not the best dancer, but I guess I'll give it a try and see how it goes."

"Praise the Most High!" she said, before getting distracted with something Shoshanna was mentioning to someone else.

I waited a second but when it became abundantly clear that her attention was fully engaged in her sister's conversation now, I started to shuffle towards the back of the line of people waiting to be served from the kitchen.

Ms. Lynn, Ms. Deborah, and Lillian were serving plates of lettuce wraps, pasta salad, and fruit bowls.

I was the last person in line for a while before Solo sauntered over and stood behind me.

He checked the time on his watch, then looked around distrustfully before grabbing my arm.

He was holding me back from stepping forward when the line began to move.

"I think I've finally figured it out," he said, in a hushed voice.

"Figured out what?" I whispered back, smiling playfully.

I had gotten so used to Solo's theatrics, that I felt compelled to play along this time.

"Mississippi...the camp...where they took all our people...you know," he said, even lower.

I looked him in the eyes with anticipation written all over my face, waiting for the details.

He stared back at me, waiting for the suspense to build.

At this point, I was beyond playfulness.

I balled up my right fist and was just getting ready to pop him in the mouth and cause a whole scene, when he finally blurted out, "It's right on the edge of Ocean Springs. I created an algorithm months ago to cross-triangulate certain trigger words and I finally got a hit!"

As he started to further explain, he noticed Drea had jumped me in line.

"—Come to the Lookout later and I'll show you."

I nodded my head in agreement and turned around to focus on the queue in front of me.

Solo stayed behind me and we waited in silence for our plates. Drea glanced back at me momentarily like she wanted to comment on something I had on or had done or had said. Who knew with her, but she didn't attempt any conversation and turned boorishly back around.

I was thankful for it.

I didn't have the proper energy for any more shenanigans.

Lately, Drea was really starting to abuse the system and order we had created for efficiency. After her attempted attack on Naomi, Elijah quietly moved her down to the fifth level where she has since remained. Elijah thought she and Naomi needed to be shown a little grace after all the trauma that had occurred, but Drea apparently did not appreciate that mercy.

I felt she was given an inch and was now trying to take a mile.

By this time, she had quite a few marks against her and I was, frankly, wondering when it would be addressed.

For starters, she flatly refused to share her room anytime a new person was assigned to it. Secondly, even though everyone was given chores to complete, she often disregarded hers or feigned like she was too tired to be bothered. Then, she never had charge of her son anymore.

The baby was passed around like a hot potato and was frequently seen in the arms of people we didn't even know the names of.

She didn't care, as long as she didn't have to deal with him herself.

The only things she seemed to care about was her freedom and her frivolous locket.

She held onto it, while it dangled from her neck, and caressed it between her fingers whenever she spoke or did any other mindless thing that didn't involve her hands.

It was like her self-soothing blankie.

I never brought these concerns up to Juda because I was sure that he was seeing all of it for himself.

How could he not?

After Lillian handed me a generous plate of food, she smiled at me and told me that she really enjoyed the lesson today.

I nodded in agreement and said "Me, too" before turning back towards the room, searching for an empty seat.

I saw Adina sitting at the end of a long table, somewhat alone. There were people at her table but not actively engaging with her so I went over and swiftly sat next to her, like I was playing an imaginary game of musical chairs and this was the last seat open. I almost missed it entirely and had to reposition myself in the crooked chair, before I landed on the floor.

She looked over at me oddly and laughed.

"I don't even want to know," she quipped.

I laughed, too, and did not explain, while regaining my balance.

I said a quick blessing over my food before digging into the spicy pasta salad. Whoever made it needed to keep making it and often. I sampled everything on my plate and was not disappointed. Even the fruit tasted sweeter than usual.

"Are you going over to the park tonight?" I asked her while scraping the last bit of salad off my plate.

"Yeah, I think it'll be fun to have a game night, finally. I haven't seen much of anyone lately since y'all got me so busy playing nursemaid to everyone," she said while rolling her eyes at me, but smiling at the same time.

"Okay, well...you can always help in the laundry room instead or shovel compost for John...whichever you prefer," I answered, amused at her fake complaining.

We were giggling in conversation when James walked up and leaned against the table. He was standing across from where I was sitting and looked rather nervous.

"What's up?" I asked him.

"Juda asked me...to tell you...that there's another group up top by the tree. He wanted to know if you were going," he spat out.

I shook my head 'no' and when he didn't leave right away, I stared at him expressionlessly, blinking slowly.

James had grown about an inch or so, over the past few months, and was starting to slim down considerably. I was sure it had a lot to do with all the extra training he was putting himself through.

I knew he felt really bad after the skating rink mishap and since then he was often found in the training room, running laps or doing exercises in the middle of the day. He had become quite skilled with a blade, too.

Juda spent as much time as he could spare, teaching James the correct form and attack points and techniques.

He had gained a lot of respect from the group since the incident and no one teased him much about it anymore.

"Are y'all going to the park tonight?" he finally asked, shyly.

"Yeah, we'll be there in a little while. Why? You trying to challenge me in a game of darts or something?" I jokingly questioned. "Because...you know...the reigning champ doesn't plan on losing her title tonight."

"Naw, naw...nothing like that. I was just asking," he responded awkwardly.

He turned his head towards the kitchen and we all noticed Juda glaring at him in an unspoken warning, while Ms. Deborah scooped globs of pasta salad onto his plate.

James gave me a timid wave goodbye after that and escaped to the other side of the community room, where the other young brothers were cracking up about something in conversation.

As soon as James was outside of earshot, me and Adina looked knowingly at each other and shrieked in laughter, garnering a few sour looks from the other people sitting at our table.

We calmed down immediately and got up to clear our area. We both wanted to go change clothes before heading to the park and I needed to meet up with Solo at some point, too, to find out more about the TRP located in Mississippi.

Soon, I would be forced to tell Juda, but I reasoned within myself that it didn't have to be tonight.

One more day won't hurt anything.

THIRTY-ONE

I HAD BOTH FEET firmly planted behind the throw line. The makeshift dart 'balls' had a little bit of weight to them, so I aimed a smidge higher than the intended bullseye. With my right hand holding the ball up near the side of my face, I turned my right foot towards the left side of the room slightly and threw.

I just barely missed the bullseye but I was proud of my attempt.

Each time, I got closer and closer.

"Looks like the reigning champ will remain undefeated tonight," Naomi bantered.

She kept up pretty well in our group tournament though and made it to a solid second place.

Good thing she wasn't a sore loser.

She gleefully slapped me on my left shoulder and turned to meander towards the rest of the regular crew that were standing by the playground equipment.

I was more than grateful that she decided to join the rest of us for a little R & R because earlier she had told me that she wasn't sure if she was feeling up to it.

I couldn't stand it when she wallowed in the room for long periods.

I looked over at the small cliques that were present.

Each group occupied their time with a different activity.

There were about thirteen of us teenagers that came to hang out. A few faces I did not recognize right away and I was generally terrible with names, so I stopped trying.

We kept rapidly gaining people and it was so hard to keep up with them all.

Elijah seemed to know, not only everyone's names but who their children were and where they hailed from.

That was completely bewildering to me.

Ryan and Solo were immersed in an oversized game of chess, while James and Gabriel looked on. Naomi ended up joining the spectators and rooting for Solo.

Figures...

Adina was getting her swing on at the swing set. She looked way too big for it though and I was about to go tell her to chill out or else Big Man would have something else to repair.

But before I could make it across the park to where she was, out of the corner of my eye, I caught Juda walking by.

He was traversing through the tunnel with a small group of five in tow. They were headed to the community room for debriefing and room assignments.

I had made a chart for Juda weeks ago when we had to rearrange again, due to a large number of families joining all at once.

I heard, in their passing, that they had come from Alabama from a tiny home community that got overrun by the Syndicate.

That made my ears perk up and I walked stealthily towards the doorway to glean any more nuggets of information that I could obtain.

Anything that they offered, by way of intelligence, could help me and Ryan on our trip through Alabama to get to Mississippi.

One of them asked Juda if he was related to someone named Angel, from Alabama. The woman mentioned that his eyes and mannerisms reminded her of the one she had called Angel.

Juda shook his head quickly, but offered that we did have some distant cousins on our Mama's side from there, so who knew.

The woman then told Juda that Angel was the organizer of their last camp but she disappeared and when she did, everything fell apart.

Juda asked her what she meant by 'fell apart'.

She explained to him, in short detail, that with the leadership vacuum, people started disagreeing and causing riffs, and a few people's reckless behavior got them noticed by the Syndicate.

I could hear the bitter tears starting to form from the shakiness in her voice.

I said a quick prayer, hoping that the Most High would not allow that same fate to happen to the Sanctuary.

I wanted to run after them to ask the disheartened, older woman more about their community setup and where, exactly, was it located, but my brain conveniently turned my legs into jelly.

I thought about the questions Juda would eventually ask me afterwards, about my specific curiosity, so I let it go.

When I regained the use of my limp limbs, I went over to Adina and sat in the swing next to her. We talked a little bit and it was starting to get boring in the park.

Juda finally came in, by himself, and there was a renewed challenge of darts, but I bowed out this time.

If anyone could give me a run for my money in darts, it was my brother.

Naomi re-entered the competition and so did Adina. She glided off to the darts tournament, leaving her swing swaying after her.

I sat on my swing, alone, dangling my legs out and arbitrarily pushing around the rubber mulch with the toe of my shoes.

I started twisting the seat of the swing while holding the chains to keep myself steady. As I twisted, my shoes made a dull scraping sound against the rubber mulch, popping some of the smaller pieces out of place. I watched the pieces hop like artificial frogs.

I liked the mulch placement.

It mostly kept the swingset in place when the big kids weren't purposely trying to get the poles to lift off the ground, and it kept the little kids from knocking their teeth out if they fell from the swings accidentally.

It was fun to pick up and throw, too, as evident from it all scattered about the place.

I subconsciously smiled to myself, thinking of all the good times I had with my family when my parents used to take us to the local park.

I bounced slightly up and down when Ryan flopped the full force of his weight into the swing to my left.

I looked over at him, irked that he had broken my happy musings.

"Solo mentioned some news," he said while looking straight ahead at the others.

He seemed to be avoiding eye contact with me on purpose.

I hoped this wasn't his attempt at being an undercover agent. I wondered if he was going to slide me a black briefcase next.

I shook my head at him and giggled.

"Yeah, but did he actually tell you the news or did he intermission you to death?" I retorted.

He chuckled at that and replied, "You already know."

I chortled some more, before gaining back my seriousness.

"But for real, though...he found out the TRP in Mississippi is located on the edge of Ocean Springs. We have our location. I just need to tell Juda and then maybe he will come, too," I quickly stated.

He turned to earnestly study my facial features when I mentioned Juda possibly agreeing to come.

"You think he'll go for it? I mean, we still don't have a solid plan. Stealing a car is not a plan," he stated, logically.

"Let me worry about my brother. You, on the other hand, need to worry about a haircut. You can't go anywhere with me looking like a whole Komondor."

We both burst out laughing again, before he countered, "Well...if y'all would figure out how to rescue a barber that can deal with my kind of hair, I would."

"And here I was...thinking that all you needed was a pair of scissors and a bowl," I was barely able to get out, in between the giggles.

"Hey! That's a bit below the belt," he yielded, but still smiled deeply at my comment.

It got really quiet all of a sudden, so we both looked towards the darts tournament and everyone was staring at us, trying to figure out what was so funny.

Juda was wearing a disparaged look on his face.

"Meet me at 7:30 AM in the training room to go over our plan," I breathed out.

Ryan nodded once then quickly got up from the swing and walked over towards the chess game Solo was now engaged in with Gabriel.

Juda turned around triumphantly and went back to focusing on his darts challenger.

I shook my head at him and got off the swing to leave the park. I said my goodbyes to everyone and walked slowly towards my pod.

I would definitely require a good night's sleep tonight if I was going to wake myself up before the alarm did.

THIRTY-TWO

— · —

The dark, gloomy sky pressed down on me like an anchor in the middle of the ocean. I struggled to stand under the weight of it, hands clasped tightly to the metal wiring of a barbed fence, searching for another body... anybody. I swayed, involuntarily, in the wind, the fence being the only thing grounding me. Cold rain began to pour down mercilessly, leaving me not only alone but soaked through...without any shelter in sight. I clung to the fence...still looking out towards the deep, endless woods...sprawled out far beyond the freedom I was denied. A tall, shadowed figure twists and contorts, before materializing fully...just at the discernable treeline. I cried out, hoping to be heard over the thundering rain and howling wind, but there was no voice to be heard. I tried to scream. Louder. Louder. Th e figure finally ascends from the shriveled-up trees. It was Juda...but not my brother. His face was ashen, his eyes hollow, and there was blood...so much blood.

My eyes flung open and I shot straight up in my bed. I heard myself gasping for air, before realizing where I was.

The dim lights cast shadows over all the other girls who were fast asleep in their bunks.

I exhaled deeply while listening to Adina's soft snoring coming from above me.

It was just a dream.

I laid back, buried my face in my hands, and said a quick prayer, before looking over to check the time.

It was 7 AM.

I slid on a short-sleeved hoodie and some loose-fitting sweatpants, before retreating out of the room to complete my bathroom routine.

The hallways and bathrooms were eerily quiet.

With over 150 souls occupying the Sanctuary, the washrooms were usually the most trafficked in the mornings and right after dinner.

I decided to skip the shower since I managed to get one in last night.

When I was done, I crossed the spacious hallway back to my pod, then threw my toiletry bag on my bed as quietly as I could.

I held my breath as I did this, hoping not to wake anyone, especially the triplets.

They were well-versed in the language of dull interrogation; always asking where we were headed and what we were planning on doing when we got there.

It could be quite exhausting.

When none of the girls stirred, I left the room and traipsed, unbothered, up the stairwell toward the training room.

The massively empty room had a draft wafting through it, and with the lights dimmed, it was amazingly unnerving. I shivered from the cool October air permeating from the ventilation network and turned up the light dimmers.

I hoped that the unearthly feel of the room would dissipate in the brighter glow of the lights.

I wondered if my dad and Solo had figured out a heating system for the coming winters but quickly dismissed the thought, knowing that Dad usually thought about everything in his designs.

As I taped up my wrists, I wondered how long Ryan would keep me waiting. Even though it was innocent, I didn't want to be caught alone with him.

As I started stretching my arms and rolling my neck back and forth, I was startled by someone clearing their throat.

I nervously flinched, then turned to confront Ryan for sneaking up on me like that.

He needed to be properly educated on how to make some noise when he walked up on people first thing in the morning, and I fully intended to give him a lesson with my fists.

As I spun around to square up with him, I was further frightened by the figure before me.

To my astonishment, it was Juda.

He was standing there, much like the silhouette in my dream, except he was in his own flesh and there was no outpouring of blood.

He looked a bit on edge, too, at the sight of me.

"I see you left your clumsy feet behind in bed…I didn't even hear you come in. What are you doing up so early anyways?" I started.

"Couldn't sleep…had a bad dream. You?" he loosely replied.

He rubbed into the sockets of his eyes with the backside of his hands and groaned loudly.

"Same," I answered softly, recalling the nightmare involving my brother.

Not wanting to discuss it further, I turned to choose which punching bag I would focus on this morning.

Deciding on the speed bag, I moved over to it and prepared my stance. I lifted my fists to eye level and started striking the bag with the sides of my closed fists. I went faster, circling down and then back, concentrating on the dim repetition of it all.

"I know, Raya," Juda's voice rang throughout the empty room, as he walked closer towards me.

"Know what?" I hypocritically asked, when I already knew the answer.

"Ryan and Solo confessed everything last night. I can't believe you thought you had to hide that from me," he continued, his expression still groggy, but perfectly neutral.

"Well, things haven't exactly been the same with us since we got down here, so...what did you expect? Half the time, I don't even know what all I can say to you anymore," I returned, but before I could say anything else, Ryan walked in, letting out a forcefully loud yawn.

He sounded as if he was trying to imitate a lion.

He didn't look alarmed to see Juda in here like I did.

"Morning," was all he offered, before squatting down onto the empty sparring mat.

Juda ignored him completely and turned back to our conversation, "You could have told me. I would have helped come up with a better plan, for starters. Your idea has holes and you're gonna get yourselves caught."

I kept silent, all the while trying to think up a reasonable comeback.

The only sound I did manage was the crack of the bag being hit over and over again.

"Seriously, Raya. I can come up with a solid plan and in a few weeks, we can leave. Elijah's got this place under control and they don't need us like that. We can go find Mom—" he resumed, but at the mention of our mother, I lost it.

"I can't wait a few more weeks, Juda! It's been three months and those soldiers are doing God-knows-what with our people. Every day is probably torture for them...and you wanna wait a FEW MORE WEEKS?!"

He stared at me in muted resentment, then quickly regained his composure.

"If you come up with something doable, we can go sooner, but I'm not rushing out there on a whim and a prayer," he retorted.

With hands now on my hips, I was opening my mouth, about to go off on Juda regarding the power of prayer.

"—Can I say something?" Ryan tried to interject before we both shut him down at the same time.

He threw his hands up in defeat and got up from the mat, walking awkwardly over to the standalone punching bag. He took a few pathetic-looking jabs at it.

I watched him out of the corner of my eye, distracted by his sloppy form.

His wrists looked weak as he jabbed at the bag and he hadn't bothered wrapping them for protection.

I couldn't take it anymore.

"Do you even know how to fight?" I seriously questioned.

Juda snickered loudly.

Ryan put his fists down and looked nervously over at me.

"I'm okay," he replied, shrugging his shoulders.

"How can you be a soldier and not know basic self-defense and form?" Juda threw in, with his arms folded across his chest.

Ryan glanced between the two of us, trying to figure out how all of a sudden he was under attack when we were just arguing with each other a second ago.

We were instantly united against his lack of fighting skills, teasing him relentlessly.

"Wow...okay. It's because I'm white, right? I'm always getting treated differently because of my skin color and I'm sick of it," he responded, disgruntled.

"Oh...yeah...you know the struggle, huh?" Juda retorted, immediately.

I covered my mouth to hide the laughter.

Suddenly, we heard shouting echoing through the tunnel.

Without hesitation, we all took off in the direction of the commotion.

The shouts were that of a female's voice and it originated from Solo's Lookout, which was strange because it was usually locked this early in the day.

Juda and Ryan made it there first, compliments of their longer legs. As I approached the doorway, I heard Juda ask loudly what was going on.

Solo, standing near the monitors, cried out that Drea had broken into his room and was about to expose their location.

He had her tightly by the arm and was shaking her slightly as he spoke.

"She was going for the Incognito button…if she would have turned it off, everybody and their mama would have been able to see our digital footprint!"

Solo looked like he was in the throws of a panic attack but he didn't release his grip on Drea's arm.

She was struggling against his hold and yelling at him to let her go.

"Y'all have been lying to us! You know where Isaiah is and haven't said anything to anyone! I heard y'all whispering and sneaking around yesterday!" she shrieked.

People were starting to filter into the tunnel, heading towards the training room for drills.

As they walked by, they were staring towards the disruption, trying to figure out what was going on.

Big Man suddenly burst into the room and closed the door behind him, cutting off the onlookers' access.

"Whatever is going on in here...needs to calm down right now!"

Drea snatched away from Solo as he was letting go of her arm. Her face was balled up in sharp angry lines and she immediately reached up to her locket for comfort.

Solo frantically rambled out what the whole issue was to Big Man. It was the quickest I had ever heard him divulge critical information.

Solo basically told Big Man that if she would have successfully turned off his security system, the Syndicate would have been able to find us, with the greatest of ease, within minutes.

Everyone looked to Drea for an explanation.

She defended herself by saying that she was only looking for information about her husband's location and she didn't know that the button was so important.

"Take her to the community room. I'm gonna go get Elijah. Raya, you and Ryan go gather the people...meeting in thirty minutes," Juda ruled, before leaving the room.

After he left, I asked Solo, very bluntly, why he left his room unlocked in the first place.

"I didn't! Miss Detective Gadget over here picked it. I got an alarm on my phablet and got here just in time to stop her from telling the whole world where we are," he defensively answered.

I could tell he was still unsettled.

His voice was higher than normal and he was breathing like he had just jogged a mile.

Drea sneered at him.

Big Man and Solo escorted a reluctant Drea to the community room after Solo did his best to secure the room again.

Ryan and I broke off at the stairwell.

He went to the lower levels while I went to the third and then back up to the first.

We gathered as many people as we could and in thirty minutes' time, just about everyone was present in the community room.

Big Man stood next to a seated Drea at the head of the room.

Everyone was gawking and murmuring amongst themselves about the purpose of the meeting.

Elijah and Juda finally emerged and stood near Big Man.

Elijah looked very concerned and fatigued.

He was rubbing at his temples with the pads of his fingertips.

He looked out across the room and then began,

Many of you have been made aware of some of the shortcomings of our dear sister, Drea, seated before you. And although she has suffered much trauma at the hands of the so-called Syndicate, I believe it's safe to say that we all have. Whether it be missing family members or suffering through first-hand attacks, we have all been touched in some way by this nightmare group that hunts us down...like criminals...all because we believe in the truth of the gospel of Christ. Trauma does not condone the type of behavior she has continuously exhibited. If it did, we would all be acting out of order by now and that's not the case. The trauma that we have in common has done the opposite and should do the opposite. It has brought us together and allowed the love we should truly have for one another to flourish. Everyone has their place and everyone contributes. It's the only way the Sanctuary will function properly and keep us safe. So with that being said, please know that this sister has been addressed numerous times in private, and grace has been allowed time and time again. But there comes a time even for grace to run out and, unfortunately, that time is now.

Drea gnashed her teeth at him and held a scowl on her face. Her anger unpleasantly matured her and disfigured her beauty.

Elijah continued,

Because of selfish schemes, Drea put us all in harm's way this morning and that will not be tolerated. Period. She broke into our security room...a room that she did not belong in, based on information that she did not fully understand. Instead of asking for clarity, she took it upon herself to tamper with security systems set in place to keep us hidden and set apart...all so she could figure something out that wasn't meant for her to figure out. From this day forward, Drea will be confined to her room. Lillian, her family, and Ms. Deborah will be moved into the pod with her. This is for her own protection and companionship. Her son will remain with her unless one of her pod-mates takes him out for activities and meals. Drea will be allowed to sit at the far corner of the community room, removed from everyone else, during designated meal times and during Shabbat lessons. No one is to engage with her outside of her pod-mates. If anyone has any questions or concerns, please voice them now.

There was a general murmuring orbiting the room but no one voiced any questions.

Ms. Deborah was bouncing Little Isaiah on her knee and looked concerned but didn't articulate anything.

With no one speaking up, Elijah dismissed the assembly and escorted Drea to her pod.

I could tell that she was not only angry about the whole situation but embarrassed.

When everyone dispersed, I walked quietly back to the training room with Solo, Ryan, Juda, and Naomi. I didn't know how this Drea situation would play out but she wasn't exactly remorseful for the role she just played.

John told everyone that since training was interrupted, it might as well be canceled.

I wanted to continue my session with the speed bag and walked over to it, poised to begin.

Solo and Juda decided to stay and run laps around the room. Soon, James, who had stayed behind, as well, fell into rhythm with them on their second lap.

Naomi chose to stay and exercise with some resistance bands for strength training.

Ryan, looking out of place, came over to the sparring ring and watched my repetitions for a few minutes.

"Do you think you can teach me some self-defense moves?" he sheepishly asked, from a few feet away.

I stopped what I was doing and moved towards the middle of the mat.

"Sure, if you don't mind being hit by a girl," I chided.

He gave me a half smile and then replied, "I don't plan on being hit by a girl, so there's that."

I shook my head at him and then instructed him on the proper way to use the wrist wraps and gloves.

We then worked on his stance and footwork.

Each time Juda passed by, he cautiously glared at us.

I wasn't sure why, though. I had every intention of showing the boy-soldier what time it really was.

After a quick lesson on jabbing and crossing, we began. After thirty minutes of sparring with me, Ryan sported a split lip and tapped out.

Solo, Juda, and James were taking a water break near the ring when Solo's phablet thing went off in alarm.

It was that doorbell ring that we had all grown accustomed to.

Solo looked at it and was in the middle of turning it off when he did a double-take at something on the screen.

"Uh...guys! You might want to come see this," he said loudly.

Me, Ryan, and Naomi rushed over to where they were standing.

From my position, the feed on the phablet was portrayed upside down.

On the screen, I could make out shoes walking by one of the low-placed cameras.

"Can I see?" I asked Solo, and he handed me the device.

When I flipped it over and the image played again, I was able to confirm that it was, in fact, shoes that I saw.

Drea's shoes.

THIRTY-THREE

S OLO DROPPED HIS WATER bottle and took off for the Lookout. We all followed suit. He barely sat down before he typed in some sequence of digits.

It looked like calculus math to me and my eyes crossed a little, trying to focus on it.

A map, with a bird's eye view, quickly pulled up a rendering of our woods. There was a pinging dot moving slowly away from the exit.

My eyes widened when I realized what I was looking at. That dot was Drea, trudging through the woods, trying to run away.

Solo looked up at me and said, "It's her locket."

He admitted to us that when she went 'missing' the first time, he had an intuitive feeling that it wasn't gonna be the last time she tried to disappear.

I didn't know how to feel about that.

Gifting someone a tracking device was a little under-handed, if not brilliant, considering who we were dealing with.

Solo handed me the holographic sheet with my mole comms. He had been doing some enhancements on them for the past week but he never said if they were ready or not.

I slapped them on and headed for the door. Ryan, Juda, James, and Naomi didn't wait while I put on the comms. They were already several feet ahead of me.

We were sprinting for the exit.

Even though no one wanted Drea here, we had to get her back inside, if not just for the safety of others.

She knew too much and had too much hatred in her heart against us.

Drea had become a liability.

Once we got to the exit, Ryan swiveled the hatch open, shaking the Franklin tree violently. The fall leaves had started to turn a reddish-pink hue and some fell to the ground with the abruptness of movement.

We all bounced out of the opening, everyone rush-ing with adrenaline. James came out last and hurriedly swiveled the door close but I didn't hear the familiar *click* sound of its closure.

There was no time to worry about that.

Solo directed us northeast and told us that Drea had stopped about half a mile due east. We switched directions and ran through a mixture of deciduous and evergreen trees, making a noisy path on our way to Drea.

Juda and Ryan led the way, outpacing us considerably.

We heard Drea's screams echoing around the trees and everyone picked up the pace. Naomi and I flanked to the left of Juda and Ryan while James headed to the right of our semi-circle.

A clearing came into view and two young, bald men wearing the Syndicate blue camo colors took shape before us.

One was holding Drea's arms behind her back, putting a zip tie around her struggling wrists. She screamed again and the other soldier punched her viciously across her left temple with full force.

Her voice immediately died down to soft whimpers. The soldier that landed the blow was rearing back his right fist to hit her again when Juda socketed him in the gut.

He crumpled forward to the ground, coughing, and sputtering, trying to catch his wind.

The second bald soldier, still holding onto Drea's arms, had a slight mental delay while watching his buddy fold to the ground.

He got wide-eyed at the tall boy who came sprinting out unexpectedly through the woods, attacking them.

His brain eventually caught up with his extremities and he threw Drea to the ground next to him, preparing himself for a fight.

She hit the ground with a huff and didn't try getting back up again. She curled herself up in the fetal position, attempting to make herself smaller.

The second soldier was not ready for what came next.

He put his fists up, poised to lunge at Juda. Naomi, yelling out, ran up behind him and hit him across the back with a sizeable tree branch with all her might. The soldier's body lurched forward.

That was my cue.

I emerged into the clearing and gifted him a forceful front thrust kick to the chest, sending him flying back again.

Naomi pivoted out of his way and he landed on his back, sliding a few inches across some crunchy fall leaves.

He lay there motionless.

Since he was down, Naomi and I turned our attention to freeing Drea.

I could see Juda and Ryan taking on the first soldier in my peripheral view. The soldier was circling and taunting them, calling Juda a 'boy' and some other not-so-choice bywords. When he saw Ryan ready to defend Juda, he threw out some divisive names at him, too.

Ryan rushed the soldier and barely missed landing another gut punch. The soldier laughed at him and in a deeply southern drawl said, "You ain't got more sense than a Billy goat, do you, wigger?"

Juda rapidly approached the first soldier and clocked him in the mouth. He then aggressively pushed him down to the ground and Ryan began kicking at him forcefully.

Where is James?

I turned my attention back to Drea.

Naomi was trying to get the zip ties off her but we didn't bring any weapons or sharp objects in our hurry.

She began frantically searching the ground for anything with a sharp edge, like a pointy stick...anything.

I saw the fear in Drea's bleeding face.

"Hurry!" she pleaded.

She looked into my eyes and I could see the regret behind hers.

Her expression signaled to me that she finally understood why she shouldn't have left in the first place.

She had chosen to learn that lesson the hard way.

I was just grateful that we made it to her in time and that this was one of those moments she left her son behind.

I didn't even want to think about her blameless baby being a part of this ordeal.

Then I heard an extremely loud POW ricocheting behind me.

I knew it was gunshot but my body did not obey its fight-or-flight demands. I was frozen, on my knees, before Naomi and Drea.

I heard the clipped sound of Juda screaming 'no'.

I looked down in slow motion, knowing that I had just been shot...again.

I instinctively touched my stomach, waiting for the warm, red liquid to begin oozing out like a dam finally broken.

But there was nothing.

I was whole.

I turned my confused head just in time to see Ryan fall to the earth behind me, his face smacking the leaves as gravity overtook him.

His lengthy auburn hair shielded his eyes from view, but I knew he was either completely out or dead.

He had a gunshot wound, to the middle of his back, that was quickly soaking his yellow T-shirt with pools of red.

Ryan had stepped in between me and the trajectory of the second soldier's gun.

The bullet was intended for the girl that had humiliated him. The one that kicked him senseless.

That bullet was for me.

The first soldier proceeded to get up from the ground and while wiping blood from his lip, he aimed and discharged his weapon.

Juda was trying to get to us, to protect us, when the second loud BANG was heard from that soldier's high-powered gun.

I supposed he was finally realizing that he was armed and we were not.

I watched as his bullet struck Juda in the left temple, instantly yielding him limp and lifeless. Juda fell to his right side with a dehumanizingly loud thud onto the hard ground.

My brain was overloaded with the repetition of his name and wouldn't let me fully embrace what I had just witnessed.

Before my mouth could even formulate a full scream, a dull, unexpected pain entered the back of my head, as the second soldier struck me with the butt of his gun.

I locked focus on Juda's open eyes before the black stars dancing across my vision twirled me into a deep abyss of unconsciousness.

EPILOGUE

JAMES

A s I RAN TOWARDS the clearing, this overwhelming sixth sense to hide overtook my body.

I stopped short of the opening in the woods and ducked down behind a very thick oak tree, sweating and breathing heavily from all the exertion.

I tried to remain as quiet as possible but I could hear my own labored breath in my ears.

I could also hear the scuffling of leaves and blows delivered and it seemed Juda, Ryan, Raya, and Naomi had everything under control...until I heard the gunshots resonating through the air.

I peeked out from behind the tree, hoping no one was looking this way.

Two soldiers were tying Raya and Naomi's wrists with zip ties.

Raya was face down in the dirt, unmoving.

Naomi was crying uncontrollably while staring at Juda, lying there. Drea just looked complacently at the leaves and pine needles beneath her and made no noise at all.

Ryan was sprawled out on the ground motionless, but the soldiers ignored him and Juda, only focusing on the women who had been captured.

"Should we take the traitor?" the shorter one asked the taller.

"Naw. I'll radio this into headquarters and they can come dispose of these two. That stupid kid bust my lip," Taller responded and spat blood towards Juda's body.

He got on his two-way radio, called for backup, and gave his latitude and longitude coordinates.

Afterward, the taller soldier made the two conscious girls stand up and move west towards the break in the woods that bucked against the interstate.

The shorter one was left with the task of dragging Raya's body behind them.

He complained about her dead weight as he pulled her by her extended arms. She looked like an old ragdoll that was too bothersome to carry as he dragged her behind him.

After I couldn't see or hear them anymore, I darted out from behind the tree and made my way to Juda and Ryan.

I would have to move quickly if I was going to beat the soldiers who were on their way to collect the bodies.

There was no way I could drag both Juda and Ryan to safety.

I had to make a quick decision.

I figured Ryan had a better chance of surviving at the hands of his prior group, so I left him and carefully picked up Juda's limp body. As I was hauling him over my shoulder, I heard a faint gasping of air coming from his throat.

He's alive!

I turned, with great effort, and trekked back towards the exit hatch, going as quickly as my legs would carry me.

The adrenaline was still amped up in me so I half jogged back to the Franklin tree.

To my immense relief and gratitude, the hatch door wasn't all the way closed, so I was able to swivel it open again, after lightly setting Juda down nearby.

I climbed down the piped rungs and ran, yelling down through the tunnel for help.

Solo met me halfway, with Big Man in tow.

"It's Juda..." I barely got out.

We all took off running towards the exit and Big Man went up and out of the opening.

He came back cradling Juda in his arms like a sleeping child.

After he made it down the steps safely, I went back up and secured the hatch door.

Correctly...this time.

Solo took one look at Juda's head, with the entrance wound to his temple, then took off down the tunnel, screaming for Adina.

Me and Big Man swiftly followed behind him with the limp Juda in tow.

"Where are the others?" Big Man managed to ask me.

I shook my head and responded, "They're gone."

Acknowledgements

All scriptures read or mentioned were quoted from the King James Version of the Holy Bible.

A special acknowledgment to the pastor of The Free Church of Christ, based in Sugar Hill, GA. All sermons or biblical conversations were derivative from prior devotional excerpts, with expressed permission.

To our good friends, Iesha and Shamai, gratitude is given for your constructive feedback and for helping us think critically throughout the development of our plot.

And as always, the utmost gratitude to my mother, Margit Hutton, for her incredible support in editing and being our first beta reader. Without her keen eyes, we would be lost.

To our family and friends who endured through this journey with us, a million thanks.

About the Authors

Cheyenne Nikole is a first-time author from Tuscaloosa, AL. She currently resides with her family in Atlanta, GA. She is a high school graduate from Liberty University Online Academy. She loves all things Y/A dystopian and had the vision for this story based on her personal faith mixed with her love of post-apocalyptic literature.

Elisabeth Fowler is her co-author and mother. She is from Tuscaloosa, AL. Being of mixed descent, she is also a German citizen. She has a BS in Financial Planning, Human Environmental Sciences College, University of Alabama. She currently resides in Atlanta with her family.